SHE DID NOT HAVE ANY PERSONAL INTEREST IN VISCOUNT FULLERTON, GWEN ASSURED HERSELF

She did not miss him. She did not miss his slate-colored eyes and startling gray hair, his mischievous humor, his frequent flashes of warmth. She merely missed their conspiracy, and it was entirely natural for her to think of his lordship often, to speculate on the progress of his quest. For they did, in fact, agree that the outrageous affair between Mama and Lord Scarborough had to be stopped at all costs. That accomplished, Gwen could go back to resuming her calm, safe life.

Yes, it was entirely natural for her to be aware of Lord Fullerton. Even alone in the darkness, she felt her cheeks warm. . . .

FAMILY AFFAIRS

SIGNET Regency Romances You'll Enjoy

FAMILY AFFAIRS

by

Diana Campbell

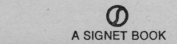

A SIGNET BOOK

NEW AMERICAN LIBRARY

NAL BOOKS ARE AVAILABLE AT QUANTITY DISCOUNTS
WHEN USED TO PROMOTE PRODUCTS OR SERVICES. FOR
INFORMATION PLEASE WRITE TO PREMIUM MARKETING
DIVISION, NEW AMERICAN LIBRARY, 1633 BROADWAY,
NEW YORK, NEW YORK 10019.

SIGNET TRADEMARK REG. U.S.PAT. OFF. AND FOREIGN COUNTRIES
REGISTERED TRADEMARK—MARCA REGISTRADA
HECHO EN CHICAGO, U.S.A.

SIGNET, SIGNET CLASSIC, MENTOR, PLUME, MERIDIAN and
NAL BOOKS are published by New American Library,
1633 Broadway, New York, New York 10019

First Printing, July 1984

1   2   3   4   5   6   7   8   9

PRINTED IN THE UNITED STATES OF AMERICA

—1—

"Guinevere? You really must hurry, dear, if you are to have breakfast before Sir Neville arrives."

Mrs. Marshman, as was her wont, had opened Gwen's bedchamber door without knocking, and she wagged an admonitory finger in the general direction of the dressing table.

"I *am* hurrying," Gwen snapped, "and I daresay I can finish without your supervision . . ."

But the elderly servant had already departed, clicking the door to behind her, and Gwen emitted a small sigh. To say the truth, she was glad Mrs. Marshman had failed to hear her ill-tempered remark; it was scarcely the hapless housekeeper's fault that Sir Neville Lynch was so dismally predictable. When he had undertaken his courtship, just above a year before, he had called on the widowed Mrs. Hathaway every afternoon promptly at two and had remained for precisely one hour. Now that Gwen had accepted his offer and they were engaged to be married, Neville had altered his habits: he rode into Cranbrook each morning, collected any mail at the post, reached Rosswood exactly at ten, and departed at three o'clock sharp to dine with his mother.

Gwen sighed again, rose, and went to the window, recognizing that this was a habit *she* had recently developed. Whenever she was inclined to be short with or about Neville, she visually reminded herself how very much her situation had improved.

To her left, just beyond Rosswood's modest grounds, Gwen could see the numerous chimneys of Viscount Brigham's home, where she had spent the most wretched year of her life. Peter Hathaway, Lord Brigham's eldest son, had not been in the least predictable, Gwen reflected; but his mercurial, occasionally cruel ways had merely served to fascinate an innocent girl of twenty. Nor had she been oblivious of Peter's good appearance, his wealth, his assurance of a title—all of which, Mrs. Marshman pointed out, recommended him most favorably as a husband.

"You should count yourself very fortunate, Guinevere," Mrs. Marshman added. "I had feared that your lack of fortune would render it excessively difficult for you to make a suitable match. As it is, or so I am given to understand, Lord Brigham is extremely eager to see Mr. Hathaway wed; I fancy his lordship hopes that marriage will settle the lad down. Were it not for that circumstance, I daresay Lord Brigham would direct his son to seek a far wealthier woman."

Mrs. Marshman had served as Mama's governess, then as nanny to Gwen and her younger sister, Portia; and she clearly felt that these historic ties entitled her to speak her mind with no discretion whatever.

Be that as it might, Gwen had needed no encouragement to accept Peter's suit, and they were married a few days after her twenty-first birthday. Following a brief wedding trip to Brighton, they settled in Lord Brigham's commodious house, and a few days after that, Peter left for London. And over the ensuing year, by actual count, he stayed eight-and-thirty nights under his father's roof.

Gwen initially believed her husband's claims that he must "remain in town to tend to business" or "go shooting in Scotland" or "see to Papa's property in Cheshire." However, since Peter's lengthy absences did not compel her to remain sequestered at Brigham Park, she soon caught snatches of several delicious *on-dits*. It was said, for example, that the Honorable Mr. Hathaway had run up the most astonishing gambling debts at White's; that he was frequently seen in Hyde Park with the Golden Vixen, a notorious cyprian; that, indeed, he had perpetrated a public scene upon the discovery of another admirer in the Vixen's opera box. Gwen attempted not to hear these scandalized whispers, but she could not pretend to be surprised when Viscount Brigham received word that his eldest son had been killed in a duel. The disagreement, his lordship's solicitor delicately explained, had apparently revolved around "the honor" of a young woman . . .

No, far from being surprised by the news of her husband's death, Gwen was—though she hardly dared own it even to herself—enormously relieved. While Peter Hathaway had not *physically* abused her (unless one counted his rough, loveless marital embraces), she judged herself far better off without him; and immediately before, during, and after his funeral, she was hard pressed to affect an appropriate degree of grief. To augment her difficulty, Lord Brigham had put it about that his heir had been killed in a carriage accident; and it required most of Gwen's limited thespian talents to maintain this fiction.

However, on the whole, she thought she acquitted herself quite well. She was consequently astonished when, a few days after the funeral, her father-in-law summoned her to his library and effectively evicted her from Brigham Park.

"I do not mean to suggest that you are not *welcome* to remain, of course," the viscount amended. Since his previous words had unmistakably implied that she was most unwelcome indeed, Gwen attached little importance to this disclaimer. "But as I indicated, we must both face the reality that Rodney is now my heir." Rodney was his lordship's second son. "And though I hesitate to suggest any criticism, you are no doubt aware that Caroline is somewhat inclined to jealousy." Caroline was Rodney's wife, and her "inclination" to jealousy had been (next to Peter himself) the principal bane of Gwen's existence from the moment of her marriage.

"In short . . ." Lord Brigham coughed. "As I indicated . . ." Another cough. The viscount never stated anything; he invariably "indicated" or "suggested." "In short, as I suggested," his lordship went on at last, "I daresay we should all be happier if you were to return to Rosswood. I am sure you will agree that Rodney and Caroline could better get the . . . the *feel* of Brigham Park were you not here." Gwen entertained an uncharitable notion that Lord Brigham was also rather relieved by the demise of his rackety son.

"I shall send a check from time to time, of course . . ." The viscount's voice expired in yet another cough, and he sprang out of his chair, patted Gwen's shoulder, and ushered her firmly, finally, out of the library.

Gwen realized that she could have issued an objection: though Lord Brigham had no *legal* obligation to support her, he was, surely, *morally* bound to do so. Particularly in view of his awareness that Peter's rakeshame conduct had quite obviated any bequest to his widow. But, truth to tell, Gwen was frantically eager to escape any reminder of her short, unhappy union, and—buoyed by the prospect of an occasional check—she speedily moved back to Rosswood. She had been home for nearly three years now, she calculated, frowning at the chimneys of Brigham Park, and she had yet to receive the first farthing from Viscount Brigham. Perhaps, she allowed, his lordship had been distracted by the three grandchildren Rodney and Caroline had subsequently produced: an insufferable set of two-year-old twin boys and an infant girl who betrayed every sign of emulating her siblings' dismaying behavior.

Gwen shook her head and transferred her gaze to the rooftop at her right. Smith House—as it had been unimaginatively christened by its previous owner—had been purchased by Sir Neville Lynch shortly before Peter's death. (Lady Olivia Lynch, Neville's widowed mother, had been attempting to rename the estate since the very day of their occupation, but as she conceived and discarded approximately half a dozen appellations every

week, Gwen doubted she would ever succeed.) At any
rate, after a rather more than suitable interval, Sir
Neville began to court Mrs. Hathaway; and it was,
again, Mrs. Marshman who urged a second marriage.

"You are no longer in the bloom of youth, Guinevere,"
the housekeeper said dolefully.

At five-and-twenty, Gwen could hardly judge herself
old, even middle-aged, but she nodded.

"And you must be aware that your dear mother can ill
afford to provide for you," Mrs. Marshman continued.

Gwen was, in fact, aware of this, for she well knew
that the late Sir Walter Ross had left his widow and
daughters most precariously fixed. Though Mrs. Marshman grandly styled herself Rosswood's "housekeeper,"
she was compelled to perform many of the domestic
chores herself: the additional staff comprised a rheumatic
cook, a man of all work, and a slovenly part-time maid.

"And while you are comely enough," Mrs. Marshman
concluded, "you cannot expect to be wed for your beauty
alone."

Gwen sighed once more, stepped back across the room,
and examined her reflection in the ancient cracked
cheval glass. She had always recognized that she was a
trifle too short and a bit too thin and that her chin was
decidedly too pointed. And, worst of all, her hair was a
vile shade of brown, truly the hue of a common field
mouse. On the other hand, except for the chin, the shape
of her face was excellent: the cheekbones were high, the
cheeks arrestingly hollow, the jaws firm but not too
prominent. And, *best* of all, her eyes were truly magnificent—large and thickly-lashed and a deep, astonishing green in color. She was, in short, precisely as Mrs.
Marshman had described her: "comely enough," but certainly lacking the sort of beauty a man would die for.

Or even marry for, Gwen acknowledged grimly, turning away from the mirror; and there was no question that
she had been right to accept Sir Neville. Well, *little*
question, she amended. She did not love Neville, but in
view of her experience with Peter, she did not hold "love"

in particularly high esteem. In retrospect, she realized that she had entertained only an adolescent infatuation for her husband (and that only briefly), but how was one to know the difference between infatuation and love? If, indeed, the latter existed outside the poems and novels Portia so assiduously read. Though Neville was utterly predictable and rather dull and excruciatingly proper, he was also kind and dependable and . . . and . . .

And, in any case, it didn't signify because she *had* accepted Neville's offer, and they were to be married on the twenty-ninth of August. Today, if Gwen recollected correctly, was the first of June, which meant that the wedding was under three months hence. She had already procured the bulk of her trousseau, the invitation list was long since finished, and it was far too late to reconsider. Even had she desired to do so, which, she hastily assured herself, she did not. She glanced into the cheval glass one final time, then left her bedroom and hurried down the stairs.

In lieu of the wages Mama was often unable to pay, Mrs. Marshman had evidently decided it her due to eat with the family; and Gwen found her and Portia at the small table in the breakfast parlor. The latter, as had become her custom, was merely picking at her food, and Gwen bit back a reprimand. Though reluctant to confess it, she feared she had been equally dreamy, equally irritating at sixteen; and besides, to say the truth, Portia was distinctly too plump. Gwen thus ignored her sister's vacant eyes and deep, sorrowful sighs and served herself from the sideboard. However, as she took her chair, Portia drew an especially melancholy breath, and Gwen felt obliged to react.

"Whatever is the matter, Portia?" she snapped.

"I was just thinking of the delightful time we might be having if Mama had permitted us to accompany her to London for the Season." Another tremulous breath.

"You know that was impossible," Mrs. Marshman said dourly. "Indeed, if I may be permitted to say so, Miss Fanny had no business going to town herself. Not when she can scarcely manage to operate her household."

Lady Frances Ross was six-and-forty, well of an age to have grandchildren, but to Mrs. Marshman she would forever be "Miss Fanny." The housekeeper glowered at her plate, and Gwen was forced to own that the scrambled eggs seemed a little more diluted than usual. She also suspected that Mrs. Marshman had failed to receive her salary for the month of May, and she could not but come to Mama's defense.

"Whatever our problems, they can scarcely be attributed to Mama," she said soothingly. "Mama's stay in London will cost her virtually nothing—nothing beyond the fare, that is. And she did not even hire a chaise; she took the stage. She is residing with Aunt Constance—"

"Which is all the more reason *we* should have gone too," Portia interjected.

"Guinevere neglected to mention the necessity of clothes." Mrs. Marshman pursed her lips with disapproval. "I shudder to contemplate the sum Miss Fanny expended on her wardrobe, and had you traveled with her, she would have been required to rig you out as well."

This was a valid observation: Mama *had* spent rather too much at the local mantua-maker's. Or, to be more accurate, Lady Ross had run up a shocking bill; on the occasion of Gwen's last visit, Miss Freeman had gently but firmly reminded her that the Rosses' account was well in arrears. But Gwen did not judge it the time to discuss their perennial poverty, and she quickly redirected the conversation.

"More to the point, Portia," she said, "*I* could not go to London because I am busy preparing for the wedding. At which, you may recall, you are to attend me." Portia appeared slightly mollified by the recollection of the splendid gown Miss Freeman had created for the event: her tragic demeanor brightened to one of mere unhappiness. "Furthermore," Gwen went on, "you are much too young for a Season in town; you will have a proper come-out when you are eighteen."

These were altogether the wrong words: Portia's

chubby face sagged again, and she viciously stabbed her fork into her scrambled eggs. Fortunately, Gwen was spared response by the arrival of Sir Neville Lynch.

"Good morning," the baronet said cheerfully, striding into the breakfast parlor. He stopped, studied the half-empty plates on the table, and frowned; Neville felt that the world would be a far better place if everyone revered punctuality as much as he did.

"Good morning, Neville," Gwen rejoined.

She had quite tired of the tasteless concoction on her plate, and she pushed the plate aside. Sir Neville, evidently interpreting this as a sign that they *had* finished eating after all, continued his morning ritual: he proceeded to the sideboard, laid the mail upon it, poured himself a cup of coffee, retrieved the mail, walked to the foot of the table, placed mail, cup, and saucer on the tattered lace tablecloth, drew out the chair, and sat down. It occurred to Gwen that though the phrase was not normally applied to men, the baronet might also be described as "comely enough." He was just below six feet in height, and while Gwen would have preferred him to lose a stone or so, he could by no means be termed fat. No, clad as he was in buckskin breeches and a riding coat of brown Bath, he could better be called "robust." Except that he was much too pale: his hair was the color of straw, his eyes a light, somewhat watery blue; and his complexion was so fair as to border on unhealthy. At the present moment, his cheeks flushed with exercise and summer sun, he looked as most men looked in the dead of winter. But he was not *un*handsome, Gwen reproached herself, and at any rate, appearances were not important. Portia had once, and for once correctly, judged Peter Hathaway as handsome as a Greek god.

"Well," Neville said brightly, "I have brought the mail."

He brought the mail *every* morning, Gwen thought irritably; must he always reiterate the obvious? She remembered his excessive kindness, his unblemished character, and dutifully extended her hand.

"There is a communication from Miss Freeman," the baronet announced.

He passed Gwen an envelope, and she reflected that this was also a part of the ritual: insofar as he could, Neville must *explain* each and every piece of mail he so faithfully delivered. However, this particular item required no further explanation—Gwen was quite sure it was an invoice—and she set it gingerly on the table.

"And a letter from London," Sir Neville continued, examining a second envelope.

"A letter from Mama," Portia said glumly. "Telling us, no doubt, how very amusing the Season is."

Gwen once more elected to ignore her sister's mopes; she accepted the proffered envelope and glanced idly at the direction.

"But it is *not* from Mama!" she said. "It is from Aunt Constance."

"From Mrs. Cunningham?" Mrs. Marshman gasped. "Oh, I do hope there is nothing amiss with Miss Fanny."

Gwen judged the housekeeper's concern altogether justified: Aunt Constance was an indifferent correspondent at best and *never* wrote to anyone but Mama. Gwen tore the envelope open with trembling fingers and hurriedly unfolded the letter inside.

"My dear Guinevere," the missive began. Apart from Mrs. Marshman, Aunt Constance was the only person in the world who called Gwen by her full name.

"I am sure I need not tell you that all London was horrified and saddened by the recent foul murder of Mr. Perceval in the very lobby of the House of Commons."

Despite this protestation, Aunt Constance went on to describe the assassination of the Prime Minister and the subsequent execution of his assailant in tedious detail, and Gwen's eyes raced impatiently down the paragraphs.

"I am sure I need not add," Aunt Constance continued at last, "that the whole terrible episode has greatly dimmed the normal gaiety of the Season, though I personally have noticed no difference."

Her name notwithstanding, Aunt Constance had never

been notably consistent in her discourse, and Gwen scanned a few paragraphs more.

"However"—the gist of the message started on page three—"I did nòt write to inform you of the murder and Mr. Bellingham's hanging, for I fancy the papers have already reported these events. The fact is, I am extremely alarmed about your dear mother. Much as I might wish to delay my intelligence"—Gwen felt that two pages was more than adequate postponement—"I am obliged to advise you that Fanny appears well in the way of contracting a most unsavory marriage. Naturally it was my hope, when I invited her to town, that Fanny would find a suitable second husband." Since Aunt Constance, Mama's elder sister, had never been entirely persuaded that Sir Walter Ross was a suitable *first* husband, Gwen continued to read with the proverbial grain of salt. "With that objective in mind, I attempted to present her only to those bachelors and widowers of flawless reputation, but to my unspeakable distress, she has conceived a decided *tendre* for the Earl of Scarborough."

The Earl of Scarborough! Gwen's eyes flew up, and she instinctively crumpled the letter between her fingers and her palm. Though she could not claim an intimate familiarity with the *ton*, Lord Scarborough was known throughout the length and breadth of England. Known, despite his advancing years, as an incorrigible rake, with numerous seductions to his so-called credit . . .

"There *is* something wrong with Miss Fanny," Mrs. Marshman wailed. "Is it . . . is it fatal?"

"That remains to be seen," Gwen replied grimly. "It appears that Mama has fallen in love with the Earl of Scarborough."

"Fallen in love?" Portia emitted an ecstatic sigh. "How very romantic."

"Fallen in love?" Sir Neville echoed incredulously. "With that . . . that libertine?"

"A libertine!" Portia squealed with delight and clapped her hands. "Oh, that is very romantic indeed."

"You are excused, Portia," Mrs. Marshman said severely.

"Excused? But my entire future may be at stake—"

"Excused!" Mrs. Marshman bellowed.

When the erstwhile governess/nanny chose to exercise her authority, she projected a most formidable impression, and Portia leaped up and hurried out of the breakfast parlor. As soon as she had disappeared (though Gwen suspected she might well be lurking just outside the archway), Mrs. Marshman began to wring her own hands.

"Where did I go wrong?" she lamented. Evidently she had heard of Lord Scarborough too, but, Gwen dismally reflected, who had not? "I tried to rear Miss Fanny with every regard for propriety, but apparently I failed."

"Apparently you did," Sir Neville unsympathetically agreed. "The Earl of Scarborough! The man has had two wives already."

"Come now, Neville," Gwen chided. There seemed no recourse but to make the best of an admittedly dreadful situation. "It is scarcely Lord Scarborough's fault that he has been widowed twice over; I am sure he did not *kill* either of his wives."

"Perhaps not directly," the baronet conceded, "but he may well have been *responsible*. He frolicked about with cyprians and actresses while his wives pined away in the country."

Much as Peter Hathaway had "frolicked about," Gwen thought, gazing at the tablecloth; and if she had truly loved him, would she also have "pined away"? She raised her eyes and found Neville's face quite scarlet—whether for her discomfiture or his own indiscreet remarks, she could not be sure.

"There is *one* factor in Scarborough's favor." Sir Neville smiled rather too bravely. "I was briefly acquainted with his elder son at Cambridge, and Viscount Blake appeared a most upstanding person."

"Well, you see," Gwen said brightly, "it *is* an ill wind that blows no good."

"On the other hand"—the baronet's countenance collapsed once more—"Scarborough has a *second* son. Viscount Fullerton was sent down from Oxford after—ah—compromising the daughter of a don." He flushed again. "Though he was subsequently readmitted . . ." He stopped and pursed his lips in disapproval, as though he himself felt that the circumstances warranted eternal damnation.

Sir Neville's *on-dit* was hardly comforting, but at this juncture, Lord Scarborough's progeny did not seem to signify, and Gwen voiced her earlier opinion aloud. "I fear we shall simply have to make the best of the situation."

"Perhaps *we* could make the best of it," Neville said heavily, "but have you paused to consider my mother's reaction?"

Gwen had not, but she now conjured up an image of her future mother-in-law. Lady Olivia Lynch stalked through life in a state of permanent, passionate disapproval: her perennial frown might equally address the weather, the latest fashions, or the conduct of the war. Gwen could, in short, well and miserably imagine Lady Lynch's reaction to the news of Mama's scandalous *tendre*, and she narrowly repressed a shudder.

"On the other hand"—this was one of Sir Neville's favorite phrases—"Mama might be even more shocked if Lady Ross were to dissolve her engagement." *Proper* people, his tone implied, did not change their minds about such matters. "Unless the engagement could be dissolved before Mama learned of it." He tugged at his neckcloth in an agony of indecision. "I presume they *are* engaged. Your mother and Lord Scarborough."

His words offered a slender ray of hope, for Gwen suddenly recollected that she had not finished Aunt Constance's letter. She hastily smoothed it out and located the point at which she'd stopped reading.

"At the risk of effecting an irreparable breach between Fanny and myself," Aunt Constance said, "I have stated my opposition to Scarborough in no uncertain terms." She went on to elucidate this opposition at maddening length, and Gwen flipped to the next page, searching for some suggestion of transition.

"However"—it did not come till page five—"Fanny has chosen to disregard my advice, and I am persuaded that without additional intervention, she will soon become engaged to him."

"They are *not* yet engaged," Gwen reported happily, beaming at Neville and Mrs. Marshman in turn.

"And?" the baronet pressed. "What else does your aunt say?"

To Gwen's astonishment and relief, there was only one more sentence, and she read it aloud: " 'I therefore implore you to come to London yourself so as to convince your dear mother of the tragic folly of the course upon which she is embarked.' "

"Well, you must go, of course," Mrs. Marshman said firmly, as Gwen looked up again.

"Indeed so," Neville concurred. "We shall leave without delay."

"We?" Gwen repeated.

"Surely you did not suppose I would permit you to travel to town alone," the baronet said indignantly. "That I would abandon you to the combined mercies of Scarborough and Fullerton." Though his phraseology left something to be desired, Gwen could not doubt his sincerity, for he visibly shivered with horror.

"I daresay you are right, Neville," she murmured. "Fortunately, we needn't be gone above a night or two, so packing will present no problem. Perhaps we could go this afternoon."

"This afternoon?" Mrs. Marshman echoed sharply. "A night or two? No, you have failed to reckon for Miss Fanny's stubbornness, Guinevere; I fear you might have to remain in London some weeks."

"Weeks!" Gwen protested. "But I've no clothes—"

"You have your lovely new trousseau," Mrs. Marshman corrected. "And I am sure that in the circumstances, Sir Neville would not object if you were to avail yourself of your wedding clothes somewhat prematurely."

"Certainly not," the baronet agreed. "Indeed, if Lady Ross cannot be brought to see the error of her ways, there may well *be* no wedding."

Gwen cast him a sharp glance; had he uttered a threat or merely a jesting—albeit thoughtless—comment? Neville never jested . . .

"It is settled then." Mrs. Marshman interrupted Gwen's speculation. "You will pack today and depart for town tomorrow." She shook her gray head and wrung her hands again. "I do wish I could accompany you, assist you, but I dare not leave Portia alone."

"No, you dare not," Gwen eagerly concurred, shuddering to contemplate the ancient housekeeper's "assistance." Mrs. Marshman's chin began to tremble, and Gwen groped for a credible sop. "And even were it *not* for Portia, I should want you here," she continued. "In the event we should require any aid at this end."

"What kind of aid?" Mrs. Marshman demanded suspiciously, her incipient tears forgotten.

But Gwen's imagination was exhausted, and she essayed a mysterious smile. "Who knows, Mrs. Marshman? Who knows what might happen when we reach London? I shall take enormous comfort in the awareness that you are here if we should need you."

The housekeeper seemed reasonably satisfied with this reply; at any rate, she lumbered out of her chair, and Gwen and Sir Neville rose as well. Gwen thought she detected a frantic rustling in the hall, but it was soon drowned by Mrs. Marshman's reminder that they must pack *immediately* and depart for town *tomorrow*. By the time they stepped into the corridor, it was empty; and Neville forgot himself sufficiently to leave Rosswood at once, four full hours in advance of his normal schedule.

2

"Thank *God* you have arrived!"

Aunt Constance's tone implied that weeks—possibly months—had elapsed since her frantic plea for "additional intervention." In fact, Gwen and Sir Neville had departed Kent, as planned, early that morning and had reached Mrs. Cunningham's house in Orchard Street a mere six hours later.

"And I am so grateful that you elected to come as well, Sir Nigel," Aunt Constance added.

"Sir *Neville*," the baronet corrected politely. "And I assure you, Mrs. Cunningham, that it is in my own interest to provide whatever assistance I can. I can scarcely bear to contemplate my mother's reaction if Lady Ross were to wed Lord Scarborough."

"Wed!" Aunt Constance wailed. "Oh, let us not even *think* of such a dreadful outcome."

Since Mrs. Cunningham had suggested this very outcome herself, Gwen swallowed a sharp retort. "There have been no further developments then?" she asked instead.

"No further developments?" Aunt Constance echoed bitterly. "Fanny has been with *him*"—apparently she could not bring herself to utter the awful name aloud—"every night, dancing till well past dawn. But if you refer to an engagement, none has occurred. At least," she amended ominously, "none has been *announced*."

"We are in time then." Neville expelled a great sigh of

relief. "And it would prove most helpful, Mrs. Cunningham, if you could explain the precise circumstances of the . . . er . . . the relationship."

"What is to explain?" Aunt Constance said dramatically. "As I recollect, Fanny arrived on the seventh of May. Or was it the eighth? Let me consider. It was the day of Mrs. Bennett's breakfast party, though well *after* the party, of course, and I do believe that was on a Thursday. However, it could have been a Friday—"

"It doesn't signify," Gwen snapped impatiently. "Please go on."

"Yes, I shall. On the day of Fanny's arrival—well, that evening actually—we attended Lady Chisholm's ball. Or was it the *next* evening?"

Aunt Constance was taking a monstrous long time to explain a situation that required no explanation, and Gwen shot her a quelling look.

"But I daresay that does not signify either." Mrs. Cunningham sighed. "Whatever the date, it was during Lady Chisholm's ball that Fanny was presented to . . . to him. Not by *me*, of course," she hastily elaborated. "No, as I advised you in my letter, *I* presented Fanny to only the most *suitable* gentlemen. To Lord Parkhurst and Mr. Grayson . . . Mr. Grayson is a *bishop*. Who could be more suitable than that?"

"Be that as it may, Lady Ross *was* introduced to Scarborough." Even the ever-courteous baronet sounded a trifle exasperated by Aunt Constance's interminable account. "What has happened since then?"

"To put it simply"—Gwen fervently prayed she would —"*he* has swept Fanny quite off her feet. We should none of us be surprised, of course, for he has had ample practice in that regard. *On dit* that he presently keeps *two* barques of frailty—one in an opera box and the other upon the stage."

Mrs. Cunningham set her mouth most grimly, as if to intimate that Lord Scarborough had frequently disported with his women in full view of the entire audience at the King's Theatre. Gwen was hard put to repress a giggle, but when she looked at Neville, she found him suffused in a furious blush.

"At any rate," Aunt Constance went on, "Fanny has spent nearly every waking hour in his company from that day to this, and if they are *not* engaged, it is only because he has not offered. I have spoken with Fanny till I am short of breath"—she panted a bit in confirmation— "but it has been to no avail. However, I am sure *you* can talk her round at once."

In light of Mrs. Cunningham's own failure, this seemed a formidable—indeed, an *unfair*—assignment. But before Gwen could state an objection, Aunt Constance began to wring her hands with relief.

"You are to stay with me, of course," she continued graciously. "Crenshaw? Crenshaw!" She tugged the bell rope in the vestibule.

Gwen irritably wondered just where else her aunt had fancied she would stay: Sir Walter Ross had been compelled to sell his town house long before his death. But there was, perhaps fortunately, no opportunity to comment on this either, for the postilion had already borne her and Neville's luggage into the entry hall.

"I cannot seem to locate my butler." Mrs. Cunningham stared balefully at the bell rope as Sir Neville paid and tipped the postboy. "Really, Guinevere, it is quite impossible to engage dependable help these days."

How times changed! Gwen reflected wryly. Though she had been but ten years old when Mama's elder sister *finally* found a husband (this had been Papa's phrase), she could well recall the shock the engagement had occasioned. Mama had wept for four full days, leading Mrs. Marshman to hint at the possibility of self-destruction. Such a course was by no means unlikely, the nanny added darkly, sniffing back tears of her own, for it was rumored that poor Grandmama Alford was at that very moment starving herself to death. However, it was left to Papa to explain *why* everyone was so distraught, and it turned out that Aunt Constance's fiancé was *in trade*.

"Which does not *necessarily* speak ill of Mr. Cunningham," Papa went on kindly, "though it *probably* does. In any case, it is the first such connection in the Alford family, so you can understand the general distress. I personally feel that Constance is lucky to get a husband at all"—this half to himself—"because she certainly isn't a *handsome* woman."

Gwen, with the faultless judgment of her whole ten years, smugly agreed with Papa in this respect. *Mama* was handsome: her hair was a lovely shade of brown, her eyes a sparkling green; and she was tiny and energetic and gay. Whereas Aunt Constance, while she shared Mama's coloring, was a tall, rawboned, coarse-featured woman who lumbered about much like the elephants Gwen had once seen at the Exeter Exchange.

"Aunt Constance *is* lucky," she said.

Evidently the rest of the family soon agreed, for neither Mama nor Grandmama Alford committed suicide after all; and at the wedding, the latter's sobs might almost have been interpreted as a sign of uncontrollable joy.

Several years had elapsed before it became apparent how *very* lucky Aunt Constance was, Gwen thought now. Sylvester Cunningham had proved an excellent husband, especially when he had had the grace to die at a relatively early age and leave his widow exceedingly well-fixed. At fifty, after ten years of widowhood, Aunt Constance was certainly no more handsome than she had been at five-and-thirty: her hair had faded to a dull gray-brown, her eyes to a pale gray-green; and she was still tall and strapping and awkward. But she owned a splendid London town house, estates in Surrey and Suffolk and Staffordshire, and her own carriage to whisk her amongst them. In short, Aunt Constance unmistakably had the advantage of her younger sister and was entitled to weep—if only figuratively—over the latter's choise of a *parti*.

"Crenshaw is obviously occupied," Mrs. Cunningham said peevishly, with a final glare at the bell rope.

"Perhaps, rather than wait for him, you should go up and speak to Fanny at once."

"She is here then?" Gwen asked with some surprise.

"Oh, yes, indeed. Yes, she and his lordship keep such very late hours that Fanny seldom rises before afternoon."

This report elicited a frown of intense disapproval from the baronet, who firmly subscribed to a theory that early retirement and early rising were the cornerstones of health.

"Yes," Aunt Constance continued, "I expect Fanny is in her sitting room making sheep's eyes at the miniature he gave her."

"I daresay he maintains a ready supply of such souvenirs," Neville sniffed.

"I daresay so," Mrs. Cunningham sniffed in agreement. "At any rate, if the two of you wish to proceed, I shall see to your baggage."

The baronet nodded his acquiescence to this plan, but Gwen hesitated. Though Mama had never voiced any criticism of Neville, she had equally failed to state any *praise*; and Gwen had long entertained a suspicion that Lady Ross did not find her future son-in-law entirely compatible. As she sought a tactful means by which to discourage his participation in the difficult discussion ahead, a maid and two footboys raced into the foyer.

"I am so sorry, ma'am," the maid panted, "but I figured you was ringing for Mr. Crenshaw. And Tom here just told me that Mr. Crenshaw is—"

"Never mind," Aunt Constance snapped. "I shall deal with Crenshaw later. For the moment, you may show Mrs. Hathaway and Sir Niles to their rooms."

Gwen glimpsed the perfect, tactful solution to her dilemma, and before the baronet could issue a correction (even to Mrs. Cunningham's latest distortion of his name), she seized upon it. "While you accompany the servants, Neville, I shall speak privately with Mama." It was impossible to miss the new crease between his pale brows, and she rushed on. "As I think on it, I fear Mama would be quite overwhelmed if we were both to confront her with her . . . her misdeeds at the same time."

Whether or not he concurred in this opinion, there was no opportunity to argue: the footboys were already bearing their luggage up the staircase, and the maid was eagerly poised at the bottom. With a stiff bow, Neville preceded the latter up the steps, and Gwen watched until they were well out of sight. When the party's footfalls had altogether died away, she realized that she was merely postponing an unpleasant task, and she sighed and looked back at Aunt Constance.

"Well, I shall go on up now," she said miserably. "If you like, I shall come to your bedchamber after we've finished and tell you what occurred."

"No, I shall be busy, dear. My hairdresser is due at any moment; he is to coif me for my trip to Surrey."

"You are going to Surrey?" Gwen protested. "At the very height of the Season?"

"Not to *stay*," Mrs. Cunningham replied. "Perhaps I neglected to mention that Percy died the day before yesterday. Or was it Saturday? In any event, the funeral is Thursday morning."

"You did neglect to mention it," Gwen confirmed. "Furthermore, I was under the impression that you and Percy were . . . were estranged." In fact, Gwen was under the impression that Aunt Constance had *loathed* her brother-in-law, Sylvester Cunningham's younger brother.

"Estranged?" Aunt Constance snorted. "I have not spoken to Percy these past ten years, and I shall not speak to him on Thursday either. And I shall wear black *only* to the funeral, not one minute more. Nor shall I linger in the country; I shall leave as soon as the service is over. But it wouldn't be proper not to *go*."

"I suppose not," Gwen agreed dubiously.

"And by the time I return, I am confident you will have set Fanny *quite* straight. Go on up now, dear; she is in the yellow room."

Her assignment was rapidly assuming herculean proportions, Gwen reflected grimly, trudging up the stairs to the first story. She sagged against the corridor wall, attempting to rehearse her conversation with Mama. But it was impossible to plan such a potentially emotional interchange, impossible to predict what Lady Ross might say in her own defense. Gwen wearily heaved herself upright and proceeded toward the next flight of stairs, but she was distracted by an odd series of noises emanating from the drawing room—a loud, discordant humming sound, puncuated with frequent thuds and grunts.

Overcome by curiosity (or perhaps, she admitted, grasping at a last straw of procrastination), Gwen crept to the door, peered inside, and recoiled in horror. She initially collected that Mama was situated quite brazenly in the middle of the saloon, locked in passionate embrace with Lord Scarborough. However, upon closer inspection Gwen perceived that Lady Ross's male companion was far too young to be his lordship, which rendered the shocking scene infinitely worse.

"Mama!" she gasped.

"Gwen?" Lady Ross glanced distractedly at the doorway. "Come in, dear; Crenshaw and I were just practicing the waltz. I believe we have nearly got it, Crenshaw," she continued, turning back to the young man, "if we can but follow the rhythm. Let us try again: one, two, three; one, two, three . . ."

Mama resumed her awful, off-key humming, and she and Crenshaw began whirling about the floor of the drawing room. Despite his youth, the butler appeared a most proper servingman, and he was flushed quite scarlet with the humiliation of this public display. However, his humiliation was soon tempered by grimaces of pain as Lady Ross trod on his left toes, crashed him into the onyx-veneered side table, kicked him vigorously in the right ankle.

This was the waltz? Gwen marveled. She had, of course, heard of the scandalous dance the Russian Countess Lieven had introduced to London, but Gwen

had somehow fancied it would be more . . . more . . .
Mama stumbled into the long-case clock, and Crenshaw
—in an agony of embarrassment by now—heroically
managed to keep them both erect.

"Gwen, dear," Mama trilled. "What—two, three—
brings you—two, three—to London? Two, three."

"Aunt Constance"—Gwen paused for two beats—
"invited me to come"—two beats more . . . "Stop it,
Mama!" she shrieked. "We cannot talk while you are
dancing!"

"No, I suppose not."

Lady Ross released her reluctant partner, and lest she
change her mind, he negotiated a clumsy bow and fairly
galloped out of the saloon. Mama gazed after him,
sorrowfully shaking her head.

"To say the truth, Gwen," she whispered, "Crenshaw
has no real talent for the waltz. I much prefer to practice
with Tilson, the first footman; he has a *splendid* sense of
rhythm. But Connie sent Tilson to Bond Street to get her
a pair of black gloves for Percy's funeral." She
sighed with regret. "But that is neither here nor there, is
it, for I doubt you came to London to learn the waltz."

Lady Ross indelicately swabbed her forehead with the
back of one hand, and Gwen distantly hoped she would
look half so well at six-and-forty. Like Aunt Constance's,
Mama's hair was generously laced with gray, but she remained—in weight as well as height—as tiny as she had
been at thirty. And unless one chanced to notice the little
lines around her emerald eyes, the small grooves at the
corners of her mouth, one might well judge her no older
than that.

"And if not to learn the waltz," Lady Ross went on,
"why *did* you come?" She walked across the room, sank
onto the gilded beechwood settee, and motioned her
daughter to sit beside her.

"Why did I come?" Gwen perched on the opposite end
of the settee, belatedly reflecting that she should at least
have rehearsed her opening remarks.

"Never mind." Mama drew a deep, tired breath. "I

daresay I can guess. Connie no doubt *implored* you to travel up from the country, warning of the most dire consequences if you did not."

This was so near the truth that Gwen felt her mouth drop open, and Lady Ross emitted a rather brittle burst of laughter.

"There is no magic in it, Gwen; Connie has been lecturing me above three weeks now. Reminding me, at every opportunity, that Charles's reputation leaves much to be desired."

Charles. Though Gwen was not entirely surprised by Mama's use of his Christian name, it was an ominous indication of their familiarity. However, Gwen elected to ignore it, for Lady Ross herself seemed to have provided an excellent opening.

"Which is precisely why Aunt Constance is so concerned," Gwen said soothingly. "Why *I* am so concerned. Why . . ." Mama had raised her pale brown brows, and Gwen judged it best not to add Neville and Mrs. Marshman to the list. "Lord Scarborough's reputation *does* leave much to be desired," she continued instead. "Indeed, *on dit* that he presently has two barques of frailty—"

"*Had,*" Lady Ross snapped. "As I have repeatedly told Connie, Charles severed those . . . those connections the very day after we met."

"So he *says,*" Gwen pointed out gently. "One finds it difficult to believe that a man of Lord Scarborough's habits could reform literally overnight—"

"*You* may find it difficult to believe," Mama interposed. "*I* do not find it so in the least. You and Constance refuse to recognize that Charles *loves* me. As"—Lady Ross squared her delicate shoulders—"as I love him."

"Love?" Gwen echoed kindly. "Come now, Mama; the two of you can't possibly be in love. You have been acquainted but a few weeks—"

"And we have loved from the first moment we saw one another." Lady Ross's eyes grew moist, distant; and she clasped her hands as if in prayer.

"From the first moment?" Gwen's tenuous patience was fast evaporating. "That is *certainly* impossible, Mama."

"You think it impossible because you have never experienced it." Lady Ross was quite alert again, her green eyes bright and probing. "Indeed, I wonder if you've experienced love at all. I *hope* you didn't love Peter: were one to compare his behavior and Charles's, I daresay Charles would qualify for sainthood. You have evidently decided to take Peter's pure opposite for your second husband, and I sincerely wish you happy. But I should be astonished to learn that you are genuinely attached to Neville either, so do not speak to me of love."

"Perhaps there isn't such a thing," Gwen said stiffly.

"If you believe that, I am truly sorry for you."

They had clearly reached an impasse, though not of the sort Gwen would have predicted, and she gazed sightlessly at her hands.

"Gwen, Gwen." Mama sighed once more. "Can you not give Charles a *chance?* Withhold your judgment till you have met him? I assure you you will find him most charming. Him and his family as well—Lord and Lady Blake and Viscount Fullerton."

Gwen had no doubt that Lords Scarborough and Fullerton were "charming": they must have *some* appeal if they had jointly seduced half the women in England. But she did not feel it the proper time to state this view, and she seized upon a curious circumstance she had previously overlooked.

"How is it that *both* of Lord Scarborough's sons are viscounts?" she inquired. "The second son as well as the heir?"

"That was Charles's doing," Lady Ross said proudly. "Well, not *entirely* Charles's doing; he did have some assistance from Lord Fullerton's maternal grandfather. They had different mothers, you see—Lord Blake and Lord Fullerton—and Lord Fullerton's mother was the only child of the Marquis of Lydney. After she died, leaving Lord Lydney but a single grandson, he and Charles prevailed on their mutual friend the late king to grant the boy a title. Well, he is not the *late* king, of course; merely the . . . the . . ."

"The *mad* king," Gwen suggested, her head whirling with confusion.

"Yes, the late, mad king, and his majesty graciously acceded to their request. Fortunately, Charles is also a great friend of the Regent . . ."

Lady Ross rattled on, and Gwen's temples began to throb.

"But I shall say no more about Charles," Mama concluded at last. "No, I shall let you form your own opinions of him and his *sweet* sons when you meet them this evening."

"This evening?" Gwen repeated sharply.

"Yes, this evening. I am sure Lady Bascomb will not object to an extra person at her ball. In fact, as Connie will be resting in anticipation of her trip to Surrey, there will *be* no extra person."

"But there would be, Mama." Gwen tried to sound regretful. "I failed to mention that Neville accompanied me to town."

"Did he?" Lady Ross's face and tone were equally impassive. "I am certain Lady Bascomb would not object to his presence either."

"Maybe not," Gwen mumbled. She cast about for another excuse. "However, I am too . . . too tired to attend a ball."

"Tired?" Mama lifted her brows again. "It is not yet three in the afternoon." Gwen elected not to point out the decided difference in their schedules. "No, Gwen, I do not believe for a moment that you are tired; I fancy you are *afraid* to go to Lady Bascomb's."

Gwen started to protest, then realized that Lady Ross was half-right. Though, Gwen assured herself, she had no *innate* fear of Lord Scarborough and his rackety son, she desperately desired more time in which to prepare for their introduction.

"And I know *why* you are afraid," Mama added triumphantly. "You are afraid because *you do not know how to waltz*. Fortunately, that problem can be easily resolved, for I daresay Tilson is back by now. I shall ring for him—"

"No!" Gwen yelped. "No, I was merely tired, and I already feel much better, and I fancy I shall feel much, *much* better by this evening."

"Well, if you are sure, dear," Lady Ross murmured.

Gwen bobbed her head, leapt off the settee, and raced to the drawing-room door. She did not look back, but she thought she detected the soft rustle of muslin behind her; and she dismally suspected that Mama was preening a bit with satisfaction.

—3—

To Gwen's relief, she *did* feel much better after a brief nap and a long bath, and by eight o'clock she was able to view Lady Bascomb's ball with considerable aplomb. However, her confidence was shattered anew when Maggie, the lady's maid Aunt Constance had appointed to attend her, opened the wardrobe doors, peered inside, and shook her head.

"Just what did you plan to wear this evening, Mrs. Hathaway?" Maggie's courteous tone failed to mask her dismay at the scanty contents of the wardrobe.

Gwen crossed the Aubusson carpet and gazed over the abigail's shoulder. She had included only three evening dresses in her trousseau, suspecting—in light of Neville's habits—that this might well be two too many. And because Neville despised "gaudiness," she had kept even these few selections as simple as possible. Now, as she contemplated the glittering throng she would no doubt encounter at Lady Bascomb's, she, too, felt a tremor of dismay.

"The yellow one, I suppose," she muttered.

Maggie withdrew the specified garment and shook her head again. But apparently Gwen's dejection was written on her face, for the maid gave her a kind smile.

"Do not tease yourself about it, ma'am," she counseled. "Actually it's quite an interesting gown, being as old-fashioned as it is."

On this cheering note, Gwen began to dress, but as she

31

examined her reflection in the cheval glass some forty-five minutes later, she was not unduly displeased. Perhaps the gown *was* old-fashioned by city standards, but the square lace-trimmed neckline, the elbow-length sleeves, the long bow trailing from just beneath the bust, perfectly suited her slight frame. Maggie adjusted the bandeau in Gwen's short curly hair, fastened a string of pearls around her throat and matching earrings in her ears, tugged on her long kid gloves, and stood back with a look of triumph. I have succeeded against *overwhelming* odds, Maggie's expression seemed to say; and when Gwen inspected her mirrored image one final time, she immodestly judged that she looked very handsome indeed. The mantel clock was chiming nine, the hour at which they were to leave, and with a nod of appreciation to the maid, Gwen hurried out of her bedchamber and down the stairs to the entry hall.

Neville was pacing impatiently about the foyer, and Gwen could not but observe that his smallclothes appeared a bit *too* small and his wasp-waisted coat rather *too* nipped in. She surmised that the baronet had gained half a stone or so since the fitting of his ensemble and resolved to put him on a stringent diet as soon as they were married. She was at the point of announcing this intention when (and no doubt fortunately) Mama raced down the stairs and ushered them breathlessly out to Aunt Constance's landau, which was waiting in the street.

"Well, Neville . . ." Lady Ross said at length. They had traveled some distance before she regained her wind sufficiently to speak: punctuality was *not* one of Mama's virtues. "I must say that you are looking quite . . . quite . . ." Her voice trailed off, and she frowned at the unmistakable paunch above the waistband of his breeches.

"Quite so," the baronet agreed stiffly. "I daresay my alarm has rendered me physically ill."

He sounded astonishingly like his mother, Gwen

reflected: Lady Lynch was generally recognized as the foremost hypochondriac in Kent.

"And how is your dear mother?" Apparently Mama had noted the similarity as well.

"When I left, she was in reasonably good force." Sir Neville's phraseology implied that Lady Lynch might well have suffered a precipitous decline since morning. "However, her *continued* health depends largely on you, does it not?"

"On *me?*"

Mama's new frown was one of great puzzlement, and Gwen recollected that she had not cited Lady Lynch as one of those most avidly "concerned" by Lady Ross's choice of a *parti*. Nor had she advised Sir Neville of the inauspicious outcome of her conversation with Mama; she had merely, cravenly, dispatched Tom, the footboy, to inform the baronet that they were to attend an assembly at nine o'clock that evening.

"But let us not talk of ill health," Gwen said hastily. "Let us talk of Lady Bascomb's ball."

"Let's." Lady Ross eagerly bobbed her head, and her ostrich plume seemed to nod its own independent concurrence. "As I told Gwen this afteroon, Neville, I am certain you will find Charles altogether charming—"

"On second thought," Gwen interposed shrilly, "let us talk of the weather. Though I judge it pleasantly cool this evening, I fear, with the crowd, it may be excessively *warm* at Lady Bascomb's."

Sir Neville agreed, Mama did not, and Gwen somehow kept the debate going till they reached the Countess of Bascomb's stately home in Berkeley Square.

Whatever the ultimate temperature of the assembly might prove to be, it immediately became clear that their hostess could not, in fact, object to an extra person, for her "ball" could more accurately be termed a "rout." It took Gwen and her companions a full fifteen minutes to toil up the stairs to the third-floor ballroom, at which point it became additionally clear that Lady Bascomb would never know they were there. Indeed, Gwen thought it quite possible that her ladyship had elected to avoid the crush altogether—an opinion strengthened when Mama glanced desultorily around and announced that she could not seem to find the countess anywhere.

"So let us look for *Charles,*" Lady Ross proposed.

Sir Neville visibly winced at this familiarity, but Mama was already peering round the room again. Evidently her eyesight had improved most remarkably since her first inspection, for she soon yanked Gwen's sleeve, nearly tearing off the lace border.

"There he is!" Lady Ross squealed. "There, just there —the one with the *wonderful* gray hair."

Gwen had no chance to search for a "wonderful" gray head in the crowd; Mama was tugging her frantically forward, and—lest he become quite lost in the throng— Gwen drew the baronet in their wake. Clasped hands notwithstanding, their pilgrimage was not an easy one: at one juncture, Gwen lost, then narrowly retrieved her left shoe; and at another, her skirt twined round a passing ankle and was hiked to an indecent point just below her knees. At last, however, they achieved their objective, and Mama abruptly dropped Gwen's hand.

"Charles," she said tremulously.

"Fanny." He heaved a great sigh.

Lord Scarborough *feigned* love extremely well, Gwen conceded: he was gazing at Mama with an expression of evident adoration. And "charming" or no, he was undeniably a handsome man. From the ages of his sons, Gwen had deduced that the earl must be close to sixty, but he looked perhaps a decade younger—tall and straight and sturdy, though not in the least plump. Indeed, his lordship's appearance could be faulted in only one respect: he was a rather colorless man, with pale gray hair and matching eyes and a complexion nearly as fair as Neville's.

"And this"—the earl tore his eyes from his supposed beloved and transferred them to Gwen—"this is no doubt your elder daughter. She bears a keen resemblance to you, Fanny, though, if she will forgive me for saying so, she is not *quite* so lovely."

"Oh, Charles." Mama emitted a pretty titter, and Gwen willed herself not to raise her own eyes to heaven. "Yes, this is my daughter, Gwen Hathaway, and her fiancé, Sir Neville Lynch. Whom I should like to present to *your* splendid family—"

"Lynch?" The interjection came from the man at Lord Scarborough's right. "Were we not acquainted at Cambridge?"

"Indeed we were"—the baronet beamed—"and I am flattered that you remember me, Lord Blake."

Gwen had calculated, following Neville's previous mention of their acquaintance, that Viscount Blake was in his middle to late thirties; but *he* looked to be rather older than his years. Nor did he bear any other resemblance to his father: he was somewhat below the average in height, almost painfully thin; and his eyes were an exceedingly dark brown. Well, there was one similarity, Gwen amended. Lord Blake's hair was already almost entirely gray; only a few brown strands remained to mingle with the silver.

"May I introduce my wife, Amanda?" the viscount said.

He drew her forward, and the three of them exchanged courteous nods. Gwen had no way of reckoning Lady Blake's age, but she looked even older than her husband —a tiny, wasted woman with a face pinched to the verge of emaciation. However, Gwen noted charitably, Lady Blake did have astonishingly thick blond hair and truly beautiful blue eyes.

"What a remarkable coincidence," the viscount said heartily. "Who could have dreamed, Lynch, that after our brief acquaintance, after all the ensuing years, we might be in the way of becoming *related?*"

The baronet's countenance, which had been quite cheerful since the moment of Lord Blake's recognition, abruptly collapsed, and there was a moment of awkward silence.

"But you have not yet met Viscount Fullerton," Mama chirped. Sir Neville's face fell a bit further. "Come now, Lord Fullerton, do not lurk in the shadows."

The man at Lord Scarborough's left had, in fact, been somewhat shadowed inasmuch as he had been gazing most rudely round the ballroom throughout the preceding introductions. He now turned his head toward Mama and stepped forward a bit, and Gwen sucked in her breath.

Viscount Fullerton might not be the most attractive man she had ever encountered, but he was certainly the most arresting. He was tall, almost exactly his father's height, and probably shared the earl's weight within half a stone. However, Lord Fullerton was differently *constructed:* he had excessively broad shoulders, a narrow waist, slender hips; and long shapely legs, disconcertingly revealed by his immaculately tailored breeches and clinging silk stockings. Gwen felt her cheeks warm most oddly, and her eyes flew back to his face. None of his weight was there, she thought; indeed, his chin and cheekbones were a trifle too sharp, his cheeks and jaw a bit too lean. She glanced on up at his hair, observed that it was predominantly gray, and glanced quickly down again. But he could not be above five-and-thirty, she decided; evidently premature graying ran in the Lovell family. She risked an inspection of his eyes and suppressed another gasp, for they were of a hue she had never seen before—a deep, nearly opaque gray. The color of slate or of ashes in a winter fireplace . . . Gwen suddenly became aware that the viscount's remarkable eyes were inspecting *her*, and she flushed again and looked hastily away.

"My daughter Gwen Hathaway and her fiancé, Sir Neville Lynch," Mama repeated.

"Mrs. Hathaway. Sir Neville." Lord Fullerton's bow and tone were equally noncommittal.

"And now we have all met," Lady Ross said brightly.

Another silence followed her gratuitous remark, but just as it threatened to grow strained, the orchestra struck up a song. It was one Gwen had not heard before, and she thought the rhythm rather odd, but Mama clapped her hands with joy.

"A waltz!" she cried. "I have been practicing *all* afternoon, Charles, and you must stand up with me."

Gwen did not suppose there could possibly be any room for dancing, but as she gazed over Lord Scarborough's shoulder, she observed a small clear space in the middle of the floor. The earl nodded his consent to Mama's proposal and propelled her toward the clearing, and, with nods of their own, the Blakes trailed after them. Viscount Fullerton looked at Gwen and Sir Neville.

"I daresay you would like to stand up as well," he said politely. "So if you will excuse me—"

"In point of fact," the baronet interposed, "I do not dance."

This was not entirely true: while Neville did not much *care* for dancing, he could normally be enticed into half a dozen sets or so during the course of a given evening. Gwen therefore collected that he was reluctant to try this scandalous new step, and in view of her own lack of expertise, she welcomed his little falsehood.

"No?" Lord Fullerton said. "Then perhaps you would not object if *I* were to stand up with Mrs. Hathaway."

"But . . . but . . ."

Gwen attempted to voice *her* horrified objection to this plan, but before further words could emerge, the viscount had taken her elbow and was steering her toward the floor. The cleared space, limited to begin with, had rapidly filled up, but eventually his lordship located a tiny hole and turned Gwen to face him. He placed one arm about her waist and clasped her opposite hand, and Gwen recoiled with shock. She had, of course, witnessed the daring posture of the waltz, but she had not expected it to be so . . . so *intimate.* Lord Fullerton pushed her backward, then pulled her forward, and she stumbled into him, increasing their already unnerving proximity.

"I do not know how to waltz!" she hissed, in an agony of embarrassment.

"I fancied as much," he said dryly. "I assure you it is really very simple. Just watch my feet."

"But . . . but . . ."

"No one *else* will be watching; I promise you that."

Gwen stole a mortified glance in either direction and concluded that he was right: all the surrounding couples were intently studying their *own* feet.

"It is merely a step, slide, step," the viscount said. "One, two, three; step, slide, step; just follow my lead."

Gwen frowned with concentration, and after a few false starts, she decided that the waltz *was* rather easy after all. She was even becoming accustomed to his lordship's arm around her, to the hard muscles of his back beneath her hand, to the touch of his fingers, strangely warm despite the fact that both of them wore gloves. At length she felt sufficiently confident to look up, and she noticed that Lord Fullerton's complexion—unlike his father's—was quite dark. Though perhaps that was partially in contrast to his thick graying hair and unsettling charcoal eyes . . .

"Gwen."

The viscount abruptly interrupted her scrutiny, and Gwen thought for one awful moment that he had so far presumed upon their potential relationship as to use her Christian name. However, she soon perceived that his peculiar eyes had narrowed, as if he were only musing.

"Gwen," he repeated. "Gwendolyn then? I had not realized your family was Welsh."

"It is not." She shook her head. "No, my family is *romantic.*" All except for me, she silently added. "My full name is . . . is Guinevere." She had always hated her name, and it was with some difficulty that she confessed it.

"I see."

A grin tickled the corners of his lordship's mouth, and Gwen irrationally felt that he had betrayed her small display of trust.

"You obviously find that very amusing," she said stiffly. "*I* ceased to find it amusing at approximately the age of ten."

"I *do* find it amusing," he admitted, "but not for the reasons you might suppose. I, too, have a perfectly terrible name. Chadwick."

He made a moue of great distress, and, somewhat to her surprise, Gwen giggled aloud.

"And in my case, there was no romance involved," he went on. "Chadwick was my mother's family name, and, or so I am told, Grandpapa Lydney fairly insisted on it." He affected a great sigh. "Fortunately, I also have an acceptable sobriquet; my friends call me Chad."

He *was* hinting at their future connection now, and Gwen felt her smile fade as quickly as it had come. She had no wish to be his "friend," much less his relative, and she judged it best to set him straight at once.

"Let us be clear upon one point, Lord Fullerton," she said coolly. She hoped she had laid sufficient stress on the final pair of words. "Your family may welcome the prospect of a marriage between Lord Scarborough and my mother, but I am unalterably opposed to such a union."

"I am delighted to hear you say that, Mrs. Hathaway, for I quite agree with you."

"I anticipated your protest," Gwen continued doggedly, "and at the risk of offending you . . ." She belatedly registered his words. "You *agree?*" she gasped. "But Lord Blake seemed immensely pleased."

"It would not be the first difference of opinion between Harold and myself," the viscount said wryly.

"But why?" Gwen demanded. "Why do you not approve of Mama?"

"I do not disapprove of Lady Ross *personally*; indeed, I find her rather charming. But I object most strenuously to my father's entrapment by a fortune hunter."

"A fortune hunter?" Gwen echoed indignantly. "That is absurd. We may be . . ." She decided that "poor" was altogether the wrong word. "We may not be *rich*, but Papa left us reasonably comfortable."

"Did he really?" the viscount drawled. "I wonder, then, why Lady Ross has subsequently taken out three mortgages against her estate."

Gwen was only aware of *two* mortgages, and she covered her surprise with further indignation. "It appears," she said frigidly, "that you have undertaken a thorough investigation of Mama's circumstances. And *I* wonder if you put yourself to such trouble over every . . . every demirep who captures Lord Scarborough's fancy. I wonder, for instance, if you investigated the cyprian and the opera singer currently under his protection."

"It appears that you have conducted an investigation as well," Lord Fullerton said mildly.

"Any investigation of your father's character would be quite unnecessary," Gwen snapped. "Lord Scarborough's behavior has been the *on-dit* of England for nearly forty years. And I am given to understand that you show every indication of following in his footsteps."

She regretted her latter comment at once and braced herself for a sharp retort, but, again to her surprise, the viscount merely flashed a grin.

"You do me too much credit, Mrs. Hathaway," he said. "I was involved in a rather serious scrape as a youth, but apart from that . . . Well, I make no claim to sainthood, but I fear I shall never have Papa's way with women."

It was an odious remark, but probably deserved, Gwen conceded; and she seized the slight advantage he had seemingly provided.

"You do not deny it then," she said triumphantly. "You do not deny that Lord Scarborough presently has two barques of frailty—"

"Actually, I do deny it," he interjected. "Papa *had* two . . . er . . . friends prior to his first enounter with Lady Ross, but he has since terminated those liaisons. Indeed, it is that very factor which renders the situation so alarming: I believe that, for the first time in his life, Papa is genuinely in love."

"He *pretends* to be in love," Gwen sniffed. "And—I must own—most credibly."

"As does Lady Ross," his lordship said coolly.

This line of discussion was clearly fruitless, but Gwen glimpsed another apparent chink in his defenses. "Even if Lord Scarborough *did* love Mama, which I do not credit for a moment, it could hardly be his first attachment. He has been married twice before—"

"And he was not *attached*, as you put it, to either of his wives. Yes, I know I imply an insult to my own mother, but it is true nevertheless. Both of Papa's marriages were arranged, and I collect that both were dismally unsuccessful."

"They could scarcely have been anything *but* unsuccessful in view of your father's conduct. I am told he was a wretched husband."

"I am sure you were told right," the viscount said, "and I daresay Papa would be the first to confess his shortcomings in that regard. In fact, I suspect that is why he has not remarried since my mother's death. She died when I was but nine months old, and he has been alone for the ensuing three-and-thirty years."

"He has been *unwed*," Gwen corrected. "He has hardly been *alone*."

"You need not belabor your point," the viscount snapped. "Papa, at least, has reformed; your mother remains a fortune hunter."

"Mama is not a fortune hunter!" But there was nothing to be gained by belaboring this point either, and Gwen gritted her teeth. "Do not tease yourself about it, Lord Fullerton," she said icily, "for I came to London *specifically* to talk Mama round. I must admit that our first conversation was not . . . not encouraging, but, having met you and Lord Scarborough, I shall redouble my efforts." His lean jaws tightened a bit, and she rushed on. "It may require some days, but I am confident that I can ultimately persuade Mama to dismiss your father and accompany me back to Kent—"

"No, you will not," his lordship interrupted. His slate-colored eyes had narrowed most dangerously. "I will not allow Papa to be humiliated, and if Lady Ross attempts to 'dismiss' him, I shall advise him what you are at. No, if there is any jilting to be done, Papa will do it."

"You reveal yourself for the scoundrel you are," Gwen said warmly. "You are well aware that any *true* gentleman would permit the lady to cry off."

"Perhaps so," he agreed. "However, as you yourself have persistently reminded me, Papa is not a gentleman. Therefore, to repeat, *he* will be the one to cry off, and I shall urge him to do so at once."

"You may urge all you like," Gwen hissed, "but I will not allow Mama to be humiliated either. No, if Lord Scarborough tries to dissolve their relationship, I shall tell her what *you* are at."

"It seems we are at an impasse then."

The music ended, and Lord Fullerton dipped her precipitously toward the floor; Gwen thought for a dreadful instant that he was deliberately going to drop her. But, mere inches from disaster, he tugged her upright—none too gently—and smiled sardonically down at her.

"It seems we are at an impasse," he said again. "Would you prefer me to call you 'Sister Guinevere' or 'Sister Gwen'?"

He took her elbow to escort her off the floor, but Gwen jerked it furiously out of his grasp and stalked away without a backward glance.

—4—

Gwen was awakened by the peal of the mantel clock, and she sleepily counted the strokes. Eleven! Her eyes flew open, and she bolted upright in the four-poster bed. If, as she assumed, the first chime had jarred her awake, it must be noon, and she could not remember the last time she had slept so late. On the other hand, she could not recall when she had last been *up* so late: it had been nearing four when Aunt Constance's carriage rolled to a stop in Orchard Street.

Four o'clock, and, Gwen guiltily recollected, Sir Neville had been most annoyed. The baronet had begun to yawn shortly after eleven, and by midnight he was broadly hinting that it was well past the hour to leave. But Mama would have none of that—she and Lord Scarborough must stand up for *every* set—and eventually Neville crept to Lady Bascomb's drawing room and dozed off in one of the chairs. Or so Gwen presumed, for he had been soundly asleep when Lord Fullerton located him at half-past three.

Lord Fullerton. Gwen pursed her lips with irritation. He had not—thank God—asked her to dance again, but she had been unable to escape the sight of his arresting hair bobbing about the ballroom. He had condescended to rejoin their party at precisely the wrong moment, prompting Mama to send *him* in search of Neville. And the viscount, of course, could not resist reporting exactly what he had found: had he arrived a second later, he

43

joked, he feared Sir Neville would have "slid entirely out of the chair and been prone upon the carpet."

Gwen had been so very vexed that she had almost forgotten their earlier conversation, but she now reconstructed it in vivid detail. However, in this regard, she discovered she was not quite as angry as she had been the night before. She could understand how Lord Fullerton might conclude that Mama was a fortune hunter: the Rosses were undeniably poor, and the Lovells were magnificently rich. In view of Lord Scarborough's shameless past, it was harder to understand the viscount's refusal to have his father "humiliated" by Mama's dismissal; perhaps, Gwen decided, that was merely male conceit. But whatever Lord Fullerton's motives, what was she to do next? Meekly submit to becoming his "sister"? The notion was so appalling that she could not repress a shudder, and she hastily summoned Maggie to help her dress.

It was well after one when Gwen reached the breakfast parlor, steeling herself for a confrontation with Neville. However, to her relief, the room was empty except for Crenshaw, who noisily filled a plate from the dishes on the sideboard, fairly crashed it down in front of her, and stood stonily at her side as she began to eat. It was clear that the butler was in exceedingly poor humor, and at length Gwen ventured an upward peep.

"Where . . . where are the others?" she asked.

"Mrs. Cunningham departed for Surrey early this morning," he replied stiffly. "Sir Neville left about an hour since to take a walk, and I have not yet seen Lady Ross."

"Umm," Gwen muttered.

"More to the point," Crenshaw continued frigidly, "I have not yet seen *Tilson*, whose responsibility it is to serve at meals. I cannot imagine where he is, but when I locate him . . ." The butler's voice trailed ominously off.

Gwen could *well* imagine the first footman's whereabouts: he was no doubt waltzing in the saloon with Mama. She was debating whether to share this surmise with Crenshaw when she was rescued by the peal of the doorbell. The butler bowed and stalked away to answer the summons, and Gwen wolfed down her eggs and bacon, half a muffin, and half a kidney. With any luck, she would be finished by the time Crenshaw returned—

"It is a caller for you, Mrs. Hathaway," he announced, striding back into the breakfast parlor.

"For me?"

Would he describe Sir Neville as a "caller"? And if not the baronet, who . . . Crenshaw was frowning with impatience, and Gwen nodded, rose, and trailed him to the entry hall.

"Lord Fullerton!" she gasped. Had she speculated all that day and half the next, she would never have guessed it to be he.

"Good afternoon, Mrs. Hathaway," the viscount said pleasantly.

"But what . . . what . . ."

"That will be all, thank you."

His lordship graciously but firmly waved Crenshaw off, and the butler bowed his way into the dining room. Their backgrounds were, indeed, very different, Gwen reflected: Lord Fullerton was quite accustomed to ordering about a horde of servants. Crenshaw disappeared, and she turned back to the viscount.

"I was at the point of asking why you have come," she said coolly.

"I have come because the weather is so fine." He seemed to be speaking rather too loudly, and Gwen wondered if he might be a trifle hard of hearing. "I remembered your mentioning last night that you would like to drive in Hyde Park before you left London. As your stay is to be a brief one, I fancied we should avail ourselves of the *very* fine weather while we have the chance."

Gwen had mentioned no such thing, of course, and she studied him suspiciously. But it was impossible to judge from his attire whether he had planned a drive before he dressed or acted from some sort of impulse. His black pantaloons, his ivory waistcoat, his dove-gray tailcoat would have been equally suitable in the park, at the gaming tables of his club, or in London's finest drawing rooms. However, Gwen collected that he had planned his *ensemble* very carefully indeed: the subdued colors complemented his graying hair and peculiar charcoal eyes . . .

"Do you fear to be seen publicly with a reprobate such as myself?" His voice had dropped so low that she could scarcely hear him, but she thought she detected a wry undertone. "If so, permit me to assure you that it is not the fashionable hour to visit the park."

"Perhaps not, but—"

"And a drive would afford us some privacy," he hissed.

He tilted his brows toward the dining-room archway, and Gwen perceived a shadow just beyond the threshold. She nodded with comprehension, then gazed down at her own ensemble. She was wearing a simple white muslin gown—hardly a proper carriage dress—but maybe if she added a bonnet . . . She raced upstairs and plucked her leghorn hat off the wardrobe shelf, rushed back down, and allowed Lord Fullerton to escort her outside.

"Spying!" she marveled indignantly. "Crenshaw was *spying.*"

"Servants always spy," he said. "And butlers in particular: they regard omniscience as a premier qualification of their lofty calling."

Gwen found herself giggling again, and it occurred to her that when he was not being infuriating, Lord Fullerton was most amusing.

"And," he added, "it is critically important that our discussion not be overheard."

Gwen sobered at once. Apparently the drive *had* been an impulse, but his lordship's call clearly was not, and she had no wish to pursue the "discussion" they had conducted at Lady Bascomb's ball. She stopped, preparing to tell him so, but realized they had already reached the street, where a carriage and team were drawn up next to the footpath.

Gwen eyed the equipage with considerable misgiving.

The vehicle was a dangerous-looking high-sprung curricle, and the horses—a splendid pair of matched bays —were tossing their elegant heads and enthusiastically pawing the paving stones. Though she had grown up in the country, Gwen had always had an irrational terror of horses, and she started to shake her own head. But it was, again, too late; the viscount was already assisting her up to the seat. She watched apprehensively as he untied the team, clambered into the driver's position, and clucked the horses to a start.

Gwen tried to relax, but the early stages of the drive proved even worse than she had feared. Insofar as the shafts would allow, the horses danced from side to side; and they alternately shied away from or lunged at every passing carriage. Indeed, she soon began to wonder if they had ever been properly broken, and eventually— literally trembling with fright—she closed her eyes. Shortly thereafter, she sensed that the animals had calmed, and she silently owned Lord Fullerton an exceedingly accomplished driver.

"I do apologize, Mrs. Hathaway," he said at last. He sounded a bit breathless. "I can offer but one excuse: these are not my horses. One of my pair has injured his foot, and I borrowed Papa's team and carriage. I fancy one might term that a *lame* excuse, eh?" Gwen emitted a weak chuckle. "Papa warned me that his horses were skittish, but I did not realize *how* skittish till after I'd set out."

"It's . . . it's quite all right," Gwen assured him bravely, her eyes still tightly closed.

"Then please do open your eyes," he said dryly. "I promise to alert you well ahead of time if I anticipate imminent death."

Gwen cracked her right eye, then her left, and peered cautiously about. They seemed dreadfully far above the ground, but the team was trotting along very nicely, and she heaved a tremulous sigh of relief.

"Allow *me* to apologize, Lord Fullerton," she murmured. "I . . . I am rather afraid of horses."

"So I collected, and I cannot but wonder why. Were you thrown as a girl?"

Gwen opened her mouth, intending to confess that her terror was merely an abberation, but she suddenly recalled the perfect explanation. "No," she replied. "No, my husband was killed in a carriage accident."

There was a long pause, and Gwen feared the viscount was going to demand the mythical details, which she had long since forgotten. But at length he shook his gray head.

"No, he was not, Mrs. Hathaway," he said levelly. "Your husband was killed in a duel."

Gwen stiffened with shock and whirled to face him, but his eyes were fixed on the horses.

"You must not suppose that the manner of Hathaway's death is common knowledge," he went on. His voice remained remarkably casual, almost toneless. "It is not. As it happens, he and I belonged to the same club—White's—and I was well acquainted with Hathaway's second. He—Baron Denham—babbled the truth to perhaps half a dozen members, and we urged him to silence. I believe he maintained that silence till his own death; ironically enough, he *was* killed in a carriage accident."

"I see." Gwen cast about for something further to say and ultimately took refuge in his lordship's own brittle form of humor. "If you knew Peter at White's, he must have owed you a great deal of money when he died."

"He owed *everyone* a great deal of money, but that is hardly your concern, is it?"

"No, I fancy not." It was a splendid opportunity to terminate this unexpected, unsettling conversation, but there was a matter about which Gwen had always entertained a perverse curiosity. "Did you know the Golden Vixen, too?" she blurted out.

"Yes, I knew her. *Know* her, I should say; she is still quite alive and maintains her box at the King's Theatre."

"I daresay she is very beautiful," Gwen said harshly.

"Beautiful?"

Lord Fullerton looked away from the horses, looked at her; and Gwen observed that he was frowning, as if mulling over the proper answer. Eventually his face cleared, and he nodded.

"Yes, I daresay she *is* beautiful, but she is too garish to suit my taste. No, if the choice were mine, Mrs. Hathaway, I should infinitely prefer you to the Golden Vixen."

Gwen searched his slate-colored eyes for a hint of sarcasm but found something far more distressing: sympathy. She felt her cheeks begin to color and gazed hastily down at her hands. She belatedly realized she was wearing no gloves, and she transferred her scrutiny to the street below.

"Did you love him?" the viscount asked abruptly.

"No, I did not." Gwen was astonished at how easily the answer came.

"I suspected as much; Hathaway merely wounded your pride. And you must recognize, in fairness, that all men are not alike."

But Gwen had had quite enough of his philosophy. "You are wasting your breath, Lord Fullerton," she snapped. "If you initiated our 'discussion' so as to persuade me of your father's good character, you are altogether wasting your breath."

She raised her eyes to stare haughtily ahead and saw that they had entered Hyde Park. She remembered it as it had been seven years before, when she had first arrived in London for her come-out; but now, some weeks later in the Season, the chestnut and lilac blooms had largely faded. However, it was still one of the loveliest spots in England and, as the viscount had promised, virtually deserted at this early hour of the day.

Unfortunately, the latter circumstance seemed to excite rather than soothe Lord Scarborough's skittish horses, and they began to prance about again. The curricle lurched alarmingly along the path for a time, but at length Lord Fullerton, with a muffled curse of annoyance, guided the team into the grass and stopped beneath a copper beech. The reins slackened, and Gwen braced herself for a headlong gallop, but after a moment of apparent puzzlement, the horses began placidly to graze. She drew another great breath of relief and perceived, from the corner of her eye, that his lordship had turned in the seat to face her.

"No, Mrs. Hathaway," he said. He spoke as if there had been no lapse in their conversation. "No, I shall not attempt to persuade you of Papa's good character, for I suspect I *should* be wasting my breath. I shall instead attempt to persuade you that we should work together to achieve our mutual objective."

"Mutual objective?" Gwen echoed suspiciously. She decided she could not continue to talk to the horses' bay rumps, and she reluctantly shifted her own position to look at him.

"Have you altered your view since last night?" He countered question with question. "I assumed you remained opposed to a marriage between our parents; maybe you have changed your mind."

"To the contrary," Gwen said warmly. "I grow more firmly opposed with every passing minute."

This was not precisely true, and she wondered why she had said it; perhaps she couldn't bear the thought that he knew the circumstances of Peter's death. His lean jaws tightened a bit, and his eyes briefly darkened, but when he went on, his voice was once more expressionless.

"Very well," he said. "As I indicated, I propose we work together to dissolve their relationship before any such unhappy outcome can occur. Before they reach the point of marriage, that is. If I may, I should like to begin by outlining my plan in a general way."

Gwen could not quell her suspicion that he was at some sort of mischief, but she granted him a cautious nod.

"The first step must be to separate them," the viscount said. "To entice one of them to leave London. Let us suppose, for the sake of illustration, that your mother will be the one to depart."

Gwen studied his face for some sign of devious cunning, but, finding none, she nodded again.

"Once Lady Ross is out of town," he continued, "she will write a letter to Papa. The letter will regretfully, but firmly, terminate their friendship—"

"No." Gwen shook her head. She vaguely recollected that last night, in a fit of pique, she had confidently spoken of talking Mama round in "some days," but it seemed the time to admit the truth on this head. "No, Mama could not be persuaded to write such a letter."

"Mrs. Hathaway." Lord Fullerton shook his own head. "I fear you are an exceedingly poor conspirator. Lady Ross will *not* write the letter, of course. *You* will."

"I?" Gwen gasped. "But Lord Scarborough would recognize at once that it was not in Mama's handwriting."

"No, he would not," the viscount said smugly. "I investigated that very point last evening as we were driving home from Lady Bascomb's. I joked Papa about his love letters from Lady Ross, and he joked back that —because they see each other every day—there has been no need for an exchange of correspondence."

"But if I am to . . . to . . ." Gwen groped for an acceptable euphemism to describe his scheme, but nothing came to mind. "If I am to forge a letter from Mama, I fail to understand why she must leave London. I must further own myself astonished that you have so rapidly altered *your* view. You insisted most adamantly that you would not permit Mama to dismiss Lord Scarborough—"

"Nor shall I," he interjected testily. "Pray allow me to finish, Mrs. Hathaway." Gwen bit her lip and once more bobbed her head. "As soon as Lady Ross has quit town, Papa will also write *her* a letter. That is to say, *I* shall do so." Gwen had already surmised this. "Papa's letter will state—with equal regret but equal firmness—his desire to dissolve their relationship too. Since, for all practical intent, the letters will be delivered at the same time, Papa and Lady Ross will be *simultaneously* jilted. That is why one of them must be out of the city: they must be given no opportunity to compare notes. So to speak."

"It appears to me," Gwen protested, "that they will be simultaneously humiliated as well."

"I'm afraid that is unavoidable." Lord Fullerton's sigh sounded genuinely remorseful. "But I have devised a means of ensuring that neither will be *publicly* humiliated. After a few days, each of us will report to his or her parent the *on-dit* that he or she jilted the other."

Gwen's head was spinning with confusion, and she frowned.

"You will tell Lady Ross that everyone presumes *she* dismissed Papa," he explained. "I shall tell Papa that it is generally supposed *he* jilted Lady Ross. The pride of both will be salvaged, but as both will believe the opposite, neither will dare to capitalize on his advantage. Is that clear?"

If not exactly clear, his plan was roughly comprehensible, and, more important, it seemed fair to all parties.

"Yes." Gwen nodded again, this time with growing enthusiasm. "Yes, I fancy your idea is excellent, but how are we to implement it?"

"How are we to implement it?"

Gwen thought he laid slight stress upon the "we," as if relieved by her approval, and he did look relieved: he extended his long legs as far as he could and laced his fingers over his ribs.

"As you have no doubt inferred, I began to formulate my plan before we left Lady Bascomb's. However, as you may also collect, I perceived no way to entice Papa to quit town. Not immediately, at least, and I am sure you will agree tht time is of the essence. I therefore started to consider what I knew of Lady Ross and recalled that you have a younger sister still at home. It occurred to me that we could utilize her—your sister—to lure your mother back to Kent."

"No." Gwen shook her head once more. "No, Portia would never cooperate; she judges it very romantic that Mama is involved with a libertine . . ." His eyes had narrowed in the forbidding fashion she remembered from the ball, and her voice trailed off.

"Let us agree upon another point, Mrs. Hathaway," he said coolly. "We both have our reasons for wishing to separate our parents; let us not continue to enumerate their faults. If you will cease calling Papa a 'libertine,' I shall not remind you that Lady Ross is a fortune hunter."

"But Mama is not . . ." His eyes flickered a warning, and she stopped. "Very well," she said stiffly. "But inasmuch as Portia is concerned—"

"Inasmuch as your sister is concerned, I do not intend to solicit her *active* assistance. My notion is to use . . . Portia, is it? . . . as bait. To advise Lady Ross that her younger daughter is gravely ill and requires her prompt attention."

"That is a *wonderful* notion!" Gwen clapped her hands. "And as it happens, it will be very easy to execute because Mrs. Marshman, our housekeeper, *will* cooperate. Indeed, she will be delighted to do so; she was *horrified* to learn that Mama had taken up with Lord Scarborough . . ." The viscount raised his brows, and Gwen coughed and hurried on. "I shall write to Mrs. Marshman at once and ask *her* to write Mama with the news of Portia's illness. Yes, it will work perfectly; the situation will be entirely resolved within a week or two."

"A week or two?" Lord Fullerton repeated.

"Well, there is a small problem with the post. Neville has been getting the mail in Cranbrook, and he didn't have time to advise the postal authorities of his departure. And Mrs. Marshman may not think to send *our* man to town for some time."

"Then that approach will not do at all," his lordship said. "As I indicated, time is critical; we cannot risk the loss of a single day. No, you will have to forge a letter from your housekeeper as well."

"But I can't," Gwen wailed. "I daresay Mama knows Mrs. Marshman's handwriting better than mine. Mrs. Marshman is forever composing little reminders and strewing them about—"

"Then you will have to forge a letter from someone

else," the viscount snapped. "I fancy a neighbor would be best. What neighbors do you have?"

"The Hathaways," Gwen replied grimly, "but they wouldn't come to Rosswood if the house was burning down. Neville is our next-closest neighbor, and he is here."

"Does Sir Neville live alone?"

"No, he lives with his mother. Lady Olivia Lynch."

"Would your mother recognize Lady Lynch's hand?"

Gwen pondered his question a moment and decided not. Insofar as she was aware, Lady Lynch had written to the Rosses only once, inviting them to an excessively dull ball at Smith House. A housewarming, so it must have been above three years since.

"No," she said aloud, "but Lady Lynch would not bestir herself to call at Rosswood while I am away. Indeed, she rarely visits while I am *there.*"

"Mrs. Hathaway." Lord Fullerton shook his head with exasperation. "If we are to have any hope of success, you must learn to distinguish the *probable* from the *possible.* Is it not *possible* that your future mother-in-law would call at Rosswood in your absence? Perhaps she would be eager to learn the precise circumstances that impelled you to come to London."

That *was* possible, Gwen conceded.

"She calls at Rosswood," the viscount went on, "and discovers that Portia is desperately ill. Can she be so callous as to ignore the situation? To drive away without another thought, without a word to your mother?"

Gwen suspected Lady Lynch might well be just that callous.

"No!" his lordship said dramatically. "No, Christian charity, if nothing else, inspires her to write to Lady Ross. Her message is brief but poignant—"

"Pray save your imagination, milord," Gwen interrupted dryly. "We may have need of it later. Very well, I shall forge a letter from Lady Lynch to Mama and 'deliver' it in tomorrow's post."

"Is there no other means of delivery?" Lord Fullerton

fretted, half to himself. "That seems the only conceivable flaw in my plan: the absence of postal markings."

Gwen elected to overlook his typical male immodesty, for he had, if inadvertently, suggested another excellent idea.

"There *is* another means," she said eagerly, "and it will lend credence to Lady Lynch's letter. We shall say that the letter was delivered by her coachman, whom she sent to town to bring something Neville forgot. His . . . his favorite neckcloth, for example. Lady Lynch's message to Mama will thus appear to be an afterthought, which would be much more in character than an act of 'Christian charity.' "

"Sir Neville's neckcloth?" The viscount laughed. "Come now, Mrs. Hathaway; I calculate that Sir Neville is several years older than I. His mother would hardly dispatch a servant all the way from Kent to bring him a neckcloth."

"Yes, she would." Though she could not have said why, Gwen realized that her cheeks were warm with embarrassment. "She would, and in the circumstances, we should be grateful for her . . . her consideration."

"But what will you do for a neckcloth?" A maddening grin still teased the corners of his lordship's mouth. "If someone should demand to see it?"

Gwen had not considered this complication, and she intently examined her fingernails.

"Never mind; take mine."

Gwen's eyes flew up, and she watched as Lord Fullerton untied his intricate Oriental. His shirt-points sagged a bit, but his shirt was buttoned to the throat, and she wondered if the hair on his chest was dark or gray. It was a shocking speculation, and as she quelled another blush, he tossed his neckcloth in her lap.

"There. It may not resemble Sir Neville's *favorite*, but I daresay it is plain enough that his mother would never know the difference."

"I daresay not," Gwen concurred, her mouth oddly dry.

"That leaves only the timing, does it not?" the viscount said cheerfully. "Lady Lynch would surely send her coachman off early in the morning, and he would arrive in midafternoon. Which"—he consulted his watch—"it is already. Consequently, it is too late for him to come today, so let us deliver our letter tomorrow. Our letter and, if necessary, my neckcloth. Though, to say the truth, the neckcloth *is* one of *my* favorites, and I hope you will not give it to Sir Neville unless you absolutely must."

Lord Fullerton pulled the horses up and steered them onto the path, and they exhibited their displeasure by dancing all the way back to Orchard Street. But Gwen was too distracted to be frightened: she was busily composing Lady Lynch's note to Mama.

—5—

" 'I do not wish to imply that Portia is at the point of death,' " Lady Ross read aloud.

Though Gwen feared Lord Fullerton might not have approved, she had felt it necessary to include this disclaimer: she could not bring herself to drive Mama fairly wild with alarm. Furthermore, she believed it enhanced the following lines:

" 'Indeed,' " Lady Ross continued, " 'I should not have written were it not for the circumstance that I was compelled to send my coachman to town anyway.' "

Unfortunately, Gwen had been unable to recollect the name of the Lynches' coachman, but apparently Mama had not remarked the omission.

"Well, that certainly *sounds* like Lady Lynch," Aunt Constance sniffed from her perch on the edge of Mama's bed. "Why *did* she send her coachman to London?"

"To deliver one of Sir Neville's neckcloths," Lady Ross replied. "Was that not it, Gwen? You were the one who spoke to him."

"Yes, that was it," Gwen mumbled. She had thus far managed to preserve the viscount's neckcloth, and she did not want to dwell on it now. "Pray go on, Mama," she added hastily.

"Very well." Lady Ross looked back at the sheet of paper in her hand. " 'However, I believe that Portia is suffering a very severe melancholia, which will surely damage her physical health if not soon remedied. I therefore urge you to come back to Kent at once.' But here, Connie, I shall let you read the letter for yourself."

This seemed a trifle gratuitous inasmuch as Mama had already recited the entire message, but she passed the paper to her sister nevertheless. Aunt Constance scanned it and frowned.

"It certainly *sounds* like Lady Lynch," she sniffed again.

Gwen repressed a grin of triumph, for she immodestly judged that she had executed the first phase of her and his lordship's plan to absolute perfection. Well, Lady Ross and Lord Scarborough had helped a bit, she conceded: they had departed for a drive in Hyde Park at three o'clock the previous afternoon. When Mama returned, just after six, Gwen presented her with "Lady Lynch's" letter and waited till Mama was reading to murmur a vague explanation about Sir Neville's neckcloth.

"It seems I must go back to Kent." Lady Ross sighed and extended the message. "Do you not concur, dear?"

Gwen took the proffered paper and pretended to peruse it most intently. "It seems you must," she eventually agreed. "What a shame; I know you dread the prospect of separation from Lord Scarborough."

"Separation," Mama repeated mournfully.

Gwen thought for one awful moment that she had gone too far, but Lady Ross soon lifted her chin and drew another deep breath.

"No, I cannot shirk my maternal responsibilities; I shall leave for Kent tomorrow. In the meantime, I trust you will not take it amiss if I go to Mrs. Baxter's ball this evening. So as to bid Charles . . . to bid Charles farewell." Mama's mouth briefly quivered, and she bravely bit her lip.

As it happened, Lady Ross bid the earl a rather *extended* farewell, for they danced every set together. Gwen and the viscount stood up only once—so as to avoid suspicion, he said—and used the time to whisper of their initial success and plot their future strategy. Gwen had taken it upon herself to resolve one problem he had not even considered: she had composed a note to Mrs. Marshman roughly outlining their scheme and soliciting the housekeeper's cooperation. Gwen intended to send the note with Mama, with the explanation that it concerned some minor household task. Lord Fullerton congratulated her for her brilliance.

"And best of all," Gwen hissed, "Neville knows nothing about it." She nodded toward the perimeter of the ballroom, where the baronet was dozing in a delicate gilt chair. "I think it quite possible that Mama will depart before he learns about his neckcloth. *Your* neckcloth, that is."

"Excellent," his lordship hissed back. "After Lady Ross has left, I shall call in Orchard Street. It occurs to me that it might be best if we were to write our letters of dismissal together."

Gwen bobbed her head, the music ended, and the viscount escorted her off the floor.

"However"—Aunt Constance interrupted Gwen's smug review—"it does not look like Lady Lynch's handwriting at all."

Gwen cast her a quelling glare, but Aunt Constance was frowning at the letter. To say the truth, Gwen had forgotten that her aunt was due back from Surrey last night. Mrs. Cunningham had arrived late—after their departure for the assembly—and evidently Crenshaw had mentioned her sister's imminent journey to Kent. In any event, Aunt Constance had come to Mama's bedchamber at the veritable crack of dawn to demand an explanation.

"How would you know Lady Lynch's hand?" Gwen asked warily.

"I was at Rosswood when we were invited to that *terrible* ball," Aunt Constance responded. "I read the invitation, and I have a splendid memory for script. Lady Lynch writes very straight—up and down—and this script is slanted backward."

Gwen had fancied herself quite clever in this regard—her own hand slanted decidedly *forward*—and she swallowed a threat of panic. "Well, I daresay Lady Lynch was somewhat handicapped by her . . . her injury," she said.

"Injury?" Mama ceased her packing. "What injury is that?"

"The injury to her hand," Gwen gulped. "Yes, to her right hand, her *writing* hand. When she was gardening last week, she pricked her forefinger on a thorn"—it sounded like the fairy tale it was—"and it has since grown infected. Indeed, I am surprised she could manage a pen at all."

"Olivia was *gardening?*" Lady Ross's eyes widened with astonishment.

"She made no mention of such a wound," Aunt Constance protested. She scanned the letter again and shook her head in puzzlement. "And I was under the impression that Lady Lynch delights in suffering. Particularly her own."

"Perhaps, on this occasion, she was more concerned with *Portia's* suffering," Gwen suggested desperately. Mama and Aunt Constance exchanged moues of disbelief, and Gwen rushed on. "Be that as it may, we have no time to speculate, do we? No, if Mama is to take the early stage, she must leave for the Swan without delay—"

"But I am not taking the stage, dear," Lady Ross interposed. "Charles is driving me to Kent. Or, to be more accurate, his coachman is driving the both of us."

"*Charles?*" Gwen gasped. "Lord Scarborough?"

"Wasn't it sweet of him to offer?" Mama clasped her hands and assumed a tender smile. "When I explained the situation, he agreed that I must go to Portia's side at once, and in the very next breath he insisted on accompanying me. He felt it was a splendid opportunity to meet my other daughter, and I daresay his presence will cheer Portia enormously."

"But . . . but . . ." Gwen's wonderful plan was falling apart, and as she frantically groped for a solution, she heard the rattle of a carriage in the street.

"Charles," Mama said. "Is he early or am I late? Never mind; go down and chat with him while I finish packing, dear."

Gwen nodded and raced out of the room, along the corridor, and down the steps, her mind churning far faster than her feet. Mama and Lord Scarborough could *not* be permitted to go to Kent together; that much was clear. It was less clear just how the trip could be aborted, but Gwen fancied the first step was to send his lordship away. Yes, she would tell him that Lady Ross had decided the journey was unnecessary after all. Then, when he had left, she would concoct some sort of story for Mama . . .

Gwen threw the front door open before the earl could ring the bell and found Lord Fullerton standing on the porch.

"Lord Fullerton!" She sagged against the jamb and panted a moment to regain her breath. "Thank God you are here," she wheezed at last.

"I am deeply flattered by the warmth of your welcome, Mrs. Hathaway," he said dryly. He stepped into the foyer, tugged Gwen in behind him, and closed the front door. "However, do you not recollect that we discussed my call last night? I presumed your mother would take an early stage—"

"Mama is not taking *any* stage. Your father is driving her to Kent."

"Papa?" To Gwen's perverse satisfaction, the viscount paled a bit. "Now that I think on it, one of the grooms was hitching his barouche as I drove out of the coach yard, but it did not occur to me—"

"It doesn't signify!" Gwen snapped. "We must somehow prevent them from going."

"Yes; yes, we must."

Lord Fullerton wrinkled his brows, and Gwen distantly noted that they were entirely black. As black as his hair must once have been . . .

"I believe I have it," he said at last. "I shall leave immediately so as to intercept Papa before he reaches

Orchard Street. I shall tell him that Lady Ross has received encouraging news of Portia and has elected to cancel her trip. Meanwhile . . . Did your mother hear my carriage?"

"Yes, she did. She thought it was Lord Scarborough, of course—"

"It does not matter who she *thought* it was," he interjected impatiently. "She does not *know* it was I. Consequently, you will tell her that it was some other neighbor of yours, delivering a message about Portia."

"But I haven't the time to forge another letter," Gwen protested.

"A *verbal* message, Mrs. Hathaway. You need only say that the neighbor saw Portia yesterday and found her to be in excellent health. Lady Ross *will* cancel her trip . . ." His voice trailed off, and he frowned again. "Indeed, upon consideration, I daresay it would be more realistic if I allowed Papa to come ahead. Your mother can then be the one to tell him that she has decided not to go to Kent."

In view of the fact that it was a desperate improvisation, Gwen judged his plan remarkably good. And in any event, she reflected grimly, they hadn't the time to scheme at leisure either; they must act at once.

"Very well," she agreed. "But you must still leave immediately so Mama will not realize the carriage was yours—"

"Lord Fullerton?"

Gwen whirled around and, to her inexpressible horror, saw Mama and Aunt Constance descending the stairs to the entry hall.

"Good . . . good morning, Lady Ross," the viscount choked.

"Good morning," Mama trilled back. "But whatever brings you to visit at such an early hour? Unless"—she clapped her hands with delight—"unless you are going to Kent as well." She peered over his shoulder. "Where is Charles?" she demanded.

His lordship hesitated so fractionally that Gwen did not believe anyone else had noticed, for he soon flashed a sheepish grin.

"Papa is on his way," he said, "and I must own myself most embarrassed in that regard. Had I come an hour since, I could have spared you both a good deal of trouble." He heaved an apologetic sigh. "A *great* deal of trouble because I came to report a most welcome development. After you left Mrs. Baxter's last night, I chanced to encounter one of your neighbors. A . . . a . . ." He stopped and shot Gwen a penetrating stare.

"Lady Falk," Gwen blurted out. It was the first name that came to mind.

"The Falks are in *London?*" Mama gasped. "I was under the impression that Sir Guy is mortally ill."

"Apparently he has improved substantially," Lord Fullerton said. "Though I did not actually meet *him*, you understand," he added quickly. "No, I met only *Lady* Falk, and as we were discussing our mutual acquaintances, she happened to mention that she had seen Portia in . . . in Cranbrook yesterday morning. And according to Lady Falk, Portia seemed in the very bloom of health."

"Portia went from 'severe melancholia' to the 'bloom of health' in four-and-twenty hours?" Mama wrinkled her own brows.

"Is that truly so surprising?" the viscount said gently. "We all know that adolescents suffer torments of dejection the rest of us are spared."

"I suppose so," Mama agreed dubiously. "However, since I am packed and Charles is already on his way, I fancy we should go to Kent anyway."

"Go . . . to . . . Kent . . . anyway." His lordship strung the words endlessly out, but there was nevertheless a lengthy pause before he went on. "I do hope you will reconsider, Lady Ross," he said at last, "for, to say the truth, Papa is most reluctant to leave London just now."

"Reluctant?" Mama echoed. "To the contrary, Charles told me he was *eager* to meet Portia."

"And he is!" The viscount vigorously bobbed his gray head. "Yes, he is *very* eager to meet Portia, but not at the present moment. Papa quite adores the Season, you see; he anticipates these few months in town with almost childlike enthusiasm from one year to the next."

Lady Ross's eyes grew a trifle moist.

"He would never admit it to you, of course." Lord Fullerton issued another great sigh. "And I fear he would count me a terrible tattle-box if he knew I had betrayed his little secret. You *will* respect my confidence, will you not, Lady Ross?" he asked anxiously.

"Of course I shall." Mama dabbed her eyes with one sleeve of her spencer. "And I shall naturally *insist* that we remain in London until the Season is over."

"Excellent." His lordship sounded somewhat tremulous, as though he were at the point of tears himself. "Then when Papa arrives . . ."

He stopped and tilted one ear toward the street, and Gwen heard the clatter of another carriage.

"But I believe he is here already," the viscount continued. "And I shall leave it to you, Lady Ross, to explain your change of plans."

Mama nodded and, with a final swipe at her eyes, bounded toward the door. She waited—somewhat coquettishly, Gwen thought—till the bell had sounded, then flung the door open and hurtled across the threshold.

"Olivia?"

Mama stumbled back into the foyer, and Gwen, for her part, felt the threat of an incipient faint. She shook her head, hoping to overcome her dizziness, and looked wildly about for some instrument of support. Since Lord Fullerton was closer than the staircase banister or the marble-topped side table, she grasped his arm and watched—literally stricken dumb—as Lady Lynch sailed into the entry hall.

"Olivia?" Mama repeated. "Is Portia worse then?"

"Portia?" Gwen thought Lady Lynch's perennial frown had deepened a bit though it was difficult to tell.

"Worse than what? I encountered Portia in Cranbrook yesterday morning, and she seemed in *splendid* force to me." Her tone was one of keen vexation, as if she judged it wretchedly unfair that the rest of the world should enjoy good health while she lingeringly, painfully disintegrated.

"That is exactly what Lady Falk reported," Mama said happily. "At Mrs. Baxter's ball last night. But I do appreciate your coming all the way to London to set my mind at ease."

"Winifred Falk is *here?*" Lady Lynch scowled with more than her normal disapproval. "Well, I must own myself shocked if not surprised. How she could travel to town with Sir Guy literally on his deathbed—"

"Let us not dwell upon Sir Guy," Gwen hastily interposed. Though she had found her voice, it was not nearly so steady as she might have wished. "Aunt Constance will show you to your bedchamber, Lady Lynch, for I am sure you must be exhausted. I collect you set out in the small hours of the morning."

"Actually we set out last evening," Lady Lynch said, "and spent the night at Sevenoaks. I cannot find words to describe how *miserable* the inn was. But I do not resent my discomfort for a moment." She drew a martyred breath. "No, I should do *anything* for Neville, and when I chanced to notice—as I was going through his wardrobe yesterday afternoon—that he had left his *favorite* neckcloth behind, I immediately decided to bring it to London."

Lady Lynch opened her reticule and withdrew a hopelessly crumpled length of fabric, and Gwen detected an odd, strangling sound beside her. She examined the viscount from the corner of her eye and saw that he was valiantly, if not altogether successfully striving to quell a laugh. It was hardly the time for levity, she reflected furiously, and with a glare she dropped his arm.

"*Another* neckcloth?" Mama said. "In addition to the one Higgins brought yesterday?"

"Yesterday?" Lady Lynch's small blue eyes blazed with

indignation. "Higgins drove to town yesterday without my permission? Well, I assure you it will be his *last* such trip . . ." She stopped and frowned. "But he could not have." She sounded almost disappointed. "We did not return from Cranbrook till after noon, and we left for London at six. He could barely have traveled one way in that interval; certainly not both."

"Then you did not write the letter either!" Aunt Constance said triumphantly. "You see, I told you it was not in her script. And I knew the discrepancy could not be due to a simple injury."

"What letter? What injury?" Lady Lynch spun her head so rapidly amongst them that she nearly dislodged her French bonnet.

"The injury to your hand." Mama elected to address the latter question first. "Gwen explained that you pricked your finger on a thorn while you were gardening."

"Gardening?" Lady Lynch repeated. "I *never* garden."

Lord Fullerton succumbed to a sudden fit of coughing, and had Gwen had a weapon at hand, she thought she might quite cheerfully have killed him. How he could be amused when they were being drawn ever deeper into this awful morass . . .

"I . . . I daresay I misunderstand," she stammered. "Neville must have said that you pricked your finger while *sewing.*" This excuse was not as random as it sounded, for though Lady Lynch loved needlework, she was a sorely unaccomplished seamstress.

"Perhaps I did," her ladyship conceded. Her eyes darted round the foyer again. "Where *is* Neville?" she demanded.

"He . . . he is out for a walk," Gwen replied. This seemed a fairly safe assumption as well: had the baronet been in the house, he would surely have appeared before now.

"Humph," Lady Lynch snorted. "That is most unfortunate because I am sure *he* could explain the situation at once." Her tone implied that her son was the repository of all human knowledge. "At any rate, if I collect aright, *someone* forged a letter, purporting to be from me, to *someone* here." She glowered around, as though the recipient of said letter was quite as guilty as the forger. "What was the substance of the message?"

"It dealt with Portia's health . . ." Mama began.

Lady Ross chattered on, and Gwen's mind began to churn once more. By some stroke of fortune, both Mama and Aunt Constance had failed to introduce Lord Fullerton, and Lady Lynch must be dispatched upstairs before either could recall this oversight. And of course it was *unthinkable* that her ladyship should be presented to Lord Scarborough . . . As if on cue, Gwen heard the sound of still another carriage in the street.

"Enough of the letter!" she said shrilly. She suspected she had interrupted Mama in mid-word. "Aunt Constance must show Lady Lynch to her bedchamber *immediately.*"

"Now?" her ladyship protested. "But I believe I have some notion as to who might have forged the letter." She peered about the entry hall again and lowered her voice. "Miss Freeman!" she whispered dramatically. "Who would have better reason to lure Fanny back to Kent? I saw Miss Freeman just yesterday morning, and she was complaining about your bill."

Good God; the situation grew worse and worse. The rattle of the carriage had, ominously, stopped, and Gwen decided that desperate measures were required.

"That may be so, Lady Lynch"—she was speaking so fast that her words ran all together—"but you really must rest awhile. If you will pardon me for saying so, you look most unwell."

"Unwell?" Her ladyship hastily felt her forehead and, just as hastily, withdrew her hand, as though she had discovered it aflame with fever. "Well, perhaps I should at least remove my hat."

"You certainly should," Gwen concurred fervently. "And Aunt Constance will take you to your room at once, will you not, Aunt Constance?"

"Now?" Mrs. Cunningham also seemed reluctant to miss a single moment of the delicious unfolding mystery, but Gwen cast her another pregnant stare, and she relented. "Very well. This way, Lady Lynch."

Aunt Constance beckoned their uninvited guest up the staircase, but at the landing, her ladyship turned back.

"However, once I have removed my hat and rested a moment, I shall return. I have never much cared for Miss Freeman, and I shall not stand idly by while she uses *my* name to dun her customers. I—"

Mrs. Cunningham propelled her, none too gently, on up the stairs, and to Gwen's unutterable relief, the two women disappeared. And not an instant too soon, for the doorbell immediately pealed. Mama, who chanced to be nearest the door, pulled it open, and Lord Scarborough stepped across the threshold.

"Good morning, Fanny." His lordship swept Mama a deep bow. "Good morning, Mrs. Hathaway." Another bow. "Good morning, Chad. Chad?" The earl briefly frowned, but apparently, fortunately, he was too preoccupied to dwell on his son's presence in Orchard Street at such an uncivilized hour. "Are you ready, Fanny?" he asked, turning back to Mama.

"Yes, I am ready. That is to say, I am *not* ready. What I mean is that I *was* ready, but we are not going to Kent."

Lord Scarborough, not surprisingly, looked a bit confused, and Lady Ross shook her head as if to clear it.

"The most astonishing thing has happened, Charles. To begin with, Lord Fullerton encountered Lady Winifred Falk at Mrs. Baxter's last night—"

"That *is* astonishing," his lordship interjected. "I am well acquainted with Lady Falk, and *I* did not see her at the assembly. Furthermore, I was given to understand that her husband recently died."

"He is *dying*," Gwen corrected.

"However, he is slightly *improved*." The viscount corrected her correction.

"In any event," Mama continued, "Lady Falk told Lord Fullerton that she met Portia in Cranbrook yesterday morning and found her in the very bloom of health."

"How astonishing." The earl shook his own gray head.

"No, that is not the astonishing part," Lady Ross said. "The astonishing part is that Lady *Lynch*, the one who advised me of Portia's illness in the first place, has come to London. She arrived not fifteen minutes since."

"Why is that so astonishing?" Lord Scarborough's thick white brows knit in puzzlement.

"It is astonishing because Olivia insists she did not write to me of Portia's illness. She—Lady Lynch, that is —suspects my mantua-maker forged the letter so I should return to Kent and pay my bill—"

"Pay your bill!" The earl stomped one of his highly polished Hessians on the foyer floor. "I told you weeks ago that I wished to satisfy your debts."

"And I told you I should not permit you to do so," Mama retorted. "Even if I *had* any debts," she added quickly, "which I do not."

Lord Fullerton was in Gwen's direct line of vision now, and she observed that his slate-colored eyes had narrowed.

"No," Lady Ross went on, "there is merely a . . . a small dispute between Miss Freeman and myself. And no matter what the circumstances, I do not believe she would go to such lengths to entice me back to Kent."

There was a brief bewildered silence, interrupted when a man puffed through the front door, which Lord Scarborough had left ajar. Gwen recognized the Lynches' coachman at once, and Mama did as well.

"It is Lady Lynch's coachman!" Mama proclaimed brightly. "Good morning, Higgins."

"Good morning, Lady Ross."

He crashed a portmanteau and a dressing case upon the marble floor, bowed, and retreated through the door again.

"Well, we can confirm one point immediately," the earl said. "Is that the man you spoke to yesterday afternoon, Mrs. Hathaway?"

"No," Gwen muttered. "No, it is not."

"But how could you have failed to detect the imposture?" Mama protested. "You have known Higgins for *years.*"

"Yes," Gwen gulped. She groped for a straw of salvation and, miraculously, found one. "However, the man who came yesterday stated that he was Lady Lynch's *new* coachman, and as you know, she is forever discharging and replacing servants. Discharging, replacing . . ." But she could not conjure up any suitable synonyms, and she stopped.

"So you simply took the word of the . . . the impostor" —Lady Ross couldn't seem to think of any synonyms either—"and accepted the letter at face value. The letter and the neckcloth . . ." She stopped as well. "I wonder whose neckcloth it was?" she mused.

The viscount emitted another strangled cough, and Gwen repressed an inclination to kick him soundly in one of his splendid gray-pantalooned shins.

"I . . . I can't imagine," she replied.

"Nor does it signify," Lord Scarborough said sternly. "If Fanny is persuaded that her mantua-maker was not responsible, we must attempt to determine who *did* perpetrate this nasty hoax. And, more important, why."

There was another silence, but Gwen's imagination was quite exhausted. She fixed Lord Fullerton with a paralyzing stare, and he eventually cleared his throat.

"At the risk of sounding indelicate," he said, "I fancy I have an idea. It occurs to me that one of Papa's former . . . ah . . . friends might have forged the letter. Perhaps she hoped to separate Papa and Lady Ross, and she would no doubt have had a supply of neckcloths readily at hand."

"It could just as easily have been one of Mama's former *partis,*" Gwen snapped. She would not allow him to twist their mutual failure to his and his father's advantage.

"One of my *partis?*" Lady Ross frowned, evidently recollecting that she had *had* no suitors in the five years since Sir Walter's death.

"It doesn't signify," Gwen said hastily, paraphrasing the earl. "The important thing is that no real harm was done. I propose we put the entire episode out of our minds."

"The entire *sordid* episode," the viscount concurred gravely. "An excellent notion, Mrs. Hathaway, for I daresay the perpetrator will not be so bold as to try a similar prank in the future."

He sounded altogether too innocent, and Gwen felt her own eyes narrow with suspicion. But his lordship's face was blank—vacuously pleasant—and Mama was already nodding her agreement.

"We *will* put it out of our minds," she vowed. "I should not wish to ruin the Season for you, Charles"— she patted the earl's arm—"and no real harm *was* done. To the contrary, you will be able to meet Gwen's future mother-in-law without delay. Olivia has gone upstairs to remove her hat, but I'm sure she'll be back at any moment—"

"No!" Gwen screeched. "No. Lord Scarborough and Lord Fullerton have an *imperative* errand to attend to."

She stared again at the latter, and his charcoal eyes momentarily flickered with confusion. But apparently he read the desperation on her face, for he bobbed his gray head.

"Indeed we do," he said. "I mentioned to Mrs. Hathaway earlier, Papa, that I am most alarmed about your horses. Your curricle team. I believe they're deuced *dangerous*, and I want you to replace them at once. I suggest—as I also mentioned to Mrs. Hathaway—that we go to Tattersall's before they've auctioned off the best of the day's lot."

"But there will be another lot *tomorrow . . .*"

The earl was still objecting as his son steered him firmly out the front door, and Lady Ross gazed after them, shaking her head again. Gwen slammed the door resoundingly in their lordships' wakes and collapsed against it, desperately attempting to compose herself before Lady Lynch reappeared.

—6—

As it happened, Gwen's respite was monstrous short: the rattle of their lordships' carriages had scarcely died away when Lady Lynch and Aunt Constance loomed up on the landing again. Evidently, Gwen noted, her ladyship had not even taken the time to comb her hair, and the mass of wild gray curls sprouting round her face lent her a more ferocious aspect than normal. She and Mrs. Cunningham began to descend the final flight of stairs, and Gwen wearily squared her shoulders, trying to marshal her thoughts. But only one thought was clear: Lady Lynch must *not* be allowed to learn of Mama's relationship with Lord Scarborough.

"Well, it was good you suggested I remove my hat, Gwen," Lady Lynch said as she reached the vestibule.

This was the highest compliment she had ever paid her future daughter-in-law, and in other circumstances, Gwen might have been gratified.

"Yes," her ladyship went on, "I daresay I was merely overheated, for I feel *much* better." She peered around the entry hall. "But where is the young man who was here earlier? And, for that matter, *who* was he?"

"Did I fail to introduce him?" Mama sighed with regret. "It was—"

"Mr. Lovell," Gwen hastily interposed. "His name is Mr. Lovell."

"Would that be his legal name?" Lady Ross wrinkled her forehead. "Maybe so."

73

Mama occasionally displayed a remarkable lack of sense, and for perhaps the first time in her life, Gwen welcomed one of these lapses.

"Unfortunately," Mama continued, "you also missed the chance to meet another dear friend of mine. The—"

"The father of Mr. Lovell," Gwen supplied.

"Well, it doesn't signify, does it?" Lady Lynch snapped. "I should not suppose the Lovells have any connection with Miss Freeman's letter. Lovell." She frowned. "Have I not heard that name before?"

"I should certainly hope so," Lady Ross said. "It is the family name of—"

"It doesn't signify, Mama!" Gwen interjected. "Lady Lynch is right on that head: the Lovells have nothing to do with Miss Freeman."

"But Miss Freeman didn't write the letter," Lady Ross protested. "Indeed, the more I think on it, the more I am inclined to lend credence to the theory proposed by—"

"Mr. Lovell's theory *could* be correct," Gwen interrupted desperately. "However, we all agreed to put the letter entirely out of our minds."

"So we did," Lady Ross acknowledged, "and so I shall. I shall not give the letter another thought."

"No?" Lady Lynch scowled at Gwen and Mama in turn and, for good measure, at Aunt Constance, though the latter had yet to speak a single word. "You may be prepared to forget the letter, but I most definitely am not. Someone is using my name to create mischief, and I will not rest until I know who the guilty party is. No, I shall remain in London till the mystery is unraveled."

Gwen gazed frantically about the foyer, but this time she glimpsed no prospect of salvation. Lord Fullerton, who had got them into this bumblebath, was no longer here to extricate them, and she fervently wished she *had* killed him. Perhaps it would be best, safest, to persuade Lady Ross that Miss Freeman had forged the letter after all . . .

"Mama?"

Sir Neville had yanked the door open, and Gwen—

still leaning against it—literally fell into his arms. He pushed her unceremoniously back into the entry hall, thrust her aside, and bounded across the floor.

"Mama!" he repeated joyfully. "I thought I recognized our carriage in the street, but I scarcely dared believe it was really you."

He seized his mother in a passionate embrace, and as Gwen struggled to regain her balance, Lady Lynch buried her face in his shoulder. Had the baronet's arrival not been so very opportune, Gwen might have been annoyed. As it was, she brushed off the spot where he had trod on her skirt, hoping the sole of his boot had not left a permanent mark.

"Neville," her ladyship sighed. She stood him away and examined him with growing alarm. "Have you not lost weight?" she asked anxiously. In fact, Sir Neville had *gained* a pound or two since his arrival in London, but Lady Lynch selflessly extended her hypochondria to the world at large.

"Lady Ross posed that very question." Sir Neville heaved a sigh of his own. "And as I explained to her, I fear my mental distress may have affected my health."

"Mental distress?" Lady Lynch echoed sharply. "What distress?"

"I am sure Neville is referring to our excessively busy schedule," Gwen said. "As you can well imagine, Lady Lynch, we have been invited to one ball upon another, and neither of us is accustomed to such a hectic pace. That is it, is it not, Neville?"

She attempted to look him a signal, but he was gazing down at his waistcoat, as if to confirm that he had not shrunk altogether away.

"You are not distressed about anything else, are you, Neville?" she reiterated. "Certainly nothing you would *want to trouble your mother about.*"

The baronet raised his head and started to frown, but his pale blue eyes suddenly widened with mingled comprehension and horror.

"No!" he concurred. "No, there is nothing whatever

wrong with my health except our busy schedule, which, as Gwen pointed out, has necessitated our attendance at one assembly after another . . ." He ran out of breath, and his voice expired in a wheeze. "But what brings you to London, Mama?" he panted, partially regaining his wind.

"I chanced to discover that you had left your *favorite* neckcloth behind. The blue one, the one that matches your eyes. The one you always wear with this coat . . ."

Lady Lynch stopped and glowered at Sir Neville's ecru neckcloth, and Gwen bristled a bit. Amidst all the confusion, she had forgotten that she herself had counseled the baronet to discard the ancient blue rag in his mother's reticule.

"At any rate," Lady Lynch sniffed, "it is fortunate I did come or I should not have learned that someone is forging letters from me to Fanny."

"Someone is forging letters from *you?*" Sir Neville gasped. "Who would perpetrate such a dastardly deed?" He sounded like a character from one of Portia's insipid romances.

"That is precisely what I intend to discover," her ladyship said grimly.

"Actually there was only one letter," Gwen corrected, "and Mama has generously agreed to forget it. I do pray you can convince your mother to forget it as well, Neville. Otherwise she will be compelled to *remain in town* for an *extended period of time.*"

"But of course Mama must stay!" The baronet beamed from Gwen to Lady Lynch. "That is, if Mrs. Cunningham has no objection."

"Certainly not," Aunt Constance assured him.

"It is settled then," Lady Ross said brightly. "And I daresay you *will* forget the letter, Olivia, once you are exposed to the delights of the Season. Tonight, for instance, we are invited to Lady Heathcote's ball, and I am sure she will not mind if you go with us. I think it very likely that we shall meet Lord Byron there. To say

nothing of the two gentlemen you so unfortunately
missed this morning."

"I would not so lower myself as to *look* at a man of
Byron's character." Lady Lynch shuddered with disapproval. "However, perhaps I shall find your friends
agreeable: Mr. Lovell and . . . er . . . Mr. Lovell. Be that
as it may, I really must rest before the assembly; I believe
I mentioned that my journey was grueling in the
extreme."

Her ladyship drew a martyred breath. It was, Gwen
calculated, her first in over half an hour—a most unusual
oversight.

"Yes, you must rest," Aunt Constance agreed kindly.
"If you will escort Lady Lynch back to her room, Fanny,
I shall have her bags sent up. At least I shall *try* to do so; I
find it increasingly difficult to locate my male servants
when they are needed."

Mama flushed a bit and, apparently eager to terminate
this line of conversation, hastily beckoned Lady Lynch
toward the staircase. Gwen watched as they ascended the
landing, rounded it, disappeared; then whirled furiously
on Sir Neville and her aunt.

"How can you be so *obtuse?*" she hissed. "Do you not
perceive our peril? We can't let Lady Lynch learn of
Mama's liaison with Lord Scarborough."

"Obtuse?" the baronet echoed indignantly. "Surely
you did not suppose *I* should tell her."

"Nor shall I." Mrs. Cunningham sounded equally
wounded.

"But *Mama* will tell her," Gwen snapped. "And if not
Mama, half the population of London."

Sir Neville and Aunt Constance exchanged glances of
appalled enlightenment, and Gwen rushed on.

"There is no time to discuss it," she said breathlessly.
"You, Aunt Constance, must go upstairs at once. You
must not allow Mama to be alone with Lady Lynch a
moment; I pray it is not already too late."

Mrs. Cunningham nodded and sped toward the staircase, and Gwen had the glimmer of a further idea.

"Mention to Lady Lynch that she is still looking very unwell," she called.

Aunt Constance bobbed her head once more and fairly galloped up the steps, and Gwen turned back to the baronet.

"I thought Mama seemed in quite good force," he protested. "Especially in light of her long drive—"

"For God's sake, Neville!" Gwen stamped her foot. "Do you not see what I am at? Your mother *can't* go to Lady Heathcote's ball. Indeed, she cannot set foot outside this house; if she does, someone will surely mention Mama's *tendre.*"

"Yes, I do see." He slowly inclined his own blond head. "So I daresay it will be left to me to ferret out the truth about the letter."

"*I* forged the letter, Neville." Gwen suspected she was hissing again, but he had driven her quite wild with impatience.

"You?" Every faint vestige of color drained from his face. "But why should you wish to embarrass Mama?"

"I *didn't* wish to embarrass your mother; it was only by chance that I used her name. Lord Fullerton felt she was the logical candidate—"

"Fullerton! I might have guessed he was behind it." Sir Neville glared about the vestibule, as if expecting to find the viscount crouched under the side table, but his anger soon gave way to puzzlement. "Why should *he* wish to embarrass Mama?"

"Lady Lynch had nothing to do with it!" Gwen belatedly recollected that the baronet knew nothing of their plot, that her impatience was most unfair, and she lowered her voice. "We were merely seeking to lure Mama back to Kent . . ."

She explained the initial phase of her and Lord Fullerton's plan, but when she had finished, Sir Neville looked nearly as puzzled as he had before she started.

"What was to happen when Lady Ross discovered for

herself that Portia wasn't ill?" he asked. "Did you fancy she would remain in Kent anyway?"

"Of course not," Gwen replied. "We . . ." It suddenly occurred to her that the rest of their scheme might yet prove useful, and she impulsively decided not to disclose it. "We . . . we intended to devise some means by which to separate Mama and Lord Scarborough permanently," she muttered.

"You and Fullerton."

"Yes, Lord Fullerton and I."

"Then I am pleased that your efforts failed," the baronet said frostily.

"Pleased!"

"Yes, *pleased*, for I thoroughly disapprove your association with Fullerton. I disapprove very strongly indeed, and I trust you will discontinue your unseemly behavior at once."

"Our conduct was in no way unseemly," Gwen said warmly. "Lord Fullerton and I were . . . were *conspiring*, nothing more." On second thought, this seemed quite unseemly enough, and she took another tack. "What of your mother, Neville?" she demanded. "Is it not imperative to drive Mama and Lord Scarborough apart before she learns of their connection?"

"I daresay it is," he mumbled.

"There you are, then. I cannot accomplish the task alone; I must have Lord Fullerton's assistance."

The baronet fumbled with his neckcloth—an unmistakable indication of uncertainty—and Gwen sought a final, telling argument.

"If it will put your mind at ease," she said gently, "I promise that Lord Fullerton and I shall be much more cautious in future. We shall not implement another plan until we are certain of success."

"Well . . ."

Sir Neville's hand left his neckcloth, and before he could waver again, Gwen rushed on.

"Meanwhile, we must confine your mother to the

house," she reminded him. "And since she so often fancies herself ill, you should find it easy to persuade her that she is far too unwell to attend the ball. If necessary, you must even offer to stay behind and nurse her."

"And leave you alone with Fullerton?" he protested.

"We shall hardly be alone, Neville; I daresay there will be several hundred people at Lady Heathcote's."

"Well . . ."

Gwen propelled him firmly toward the stairs, casting a sideward glance at the table as they passed. But the viscount wasn't beneath it after all, and she ushered Sir Neville on up the steps.

Gwen did not encounter the baronet again that day, and by eight o'clock she herself felt quite ill with apprehension. Her worst fears were confirmed when Maggie arrived to help her dress and greeted her with a sorrowful shake of the head.

"I'm afraid I have bad news, ma'am," the abigail said dolefully.

"Oh, no," Gwen moaned.

"Yes. Lady Lynch has decided she is much too unwell to go to the assembly, and Sir Neville has elected to remain behind with his mother. He desired me to tell you so."

Gwen had forgotten that her notion of "bad news" would be entirely different from Maggie's, and she quelled a great breath of relief.

"How unfortunate," she said. "But I fancy there is nothing to be done about it, and I believe I should proceed without them. So as to keep Mama company," she added hastily.

Maggie nodded and assisted Gwen into the last of her evening ensembles, at the end of which procedure Gwen studied her reflection with dismay. The gown was undeniably old-fashioned—a rather high-necked bodice of satin with transparent sleeves extending to the wrists and an overlong skirt. Its various shades of green, which had seemed so fetching in Miss Freeman's shop, now appeared to clash most hideously, and the Mameluke cap (which matched none of the *other* greens) looked positively matronly. But there was nothing to be done about this either: the gown was, in fact, her last, and it was too late to remove the headdress and repair her hair. Far too late; the mantel clock was already striking nine, and Lord Fullerton would be eagerly awaiting her arrival at the ball. She snatched up her gloves and reticule and, with a brief good-night to Maggie, hurried out of the room.

Gwen sped down the steps, and she had reached the final landing before she paused to reconsider her supposition. She had assumed the viscount would wish to devise another scheme, but in view of their near-disastrous failure, she could well be wrong. Indeed, she wondered why *she* was so anxious to pursue their dubious endeavor. Could it be that she was enjoying the conspiracy? No, more accurately, was she enjoying the association with Lord Fullerton which the conspiracy entailed? The thought was so appalling that she almost turned back, but at that moment Mama materialized beside her and tugged her on down the staircase.

"Well, Gwen." Lady Ross was, as usual, a trifle breathless, and the carriage was well under way before she spoke. "Though I hate to say it, dear, you are looking a bit . . . a bit dowdy tonight."

"Thank you, Mama," Gwen said dryly.

"Forgive me." Lady Ross sighed. "I fear I am somewhat out of spirits. When I took Olivia to her bedchamber this morning, I intended to tell her *all* about Charles. But before I could utter the first word, Connie appeared, and she did not allow me even to mention his *name*. She kept *interrupting*, chattering about the weather and such, matters in which Olivia could have no possible interest. It's a most annoying habit, don't you agree, Gwen? Connie's incessant interruptions?"

"Most annoying," Gwen concurred gravely. "But Aunt Constance has always talked rather too much—"

"And then Neville came," Mama interrupted, "and

began making over Olivia. One might have collected that she was *dying*. Well, in point of fact, he has persuaded her she *is dying*. Yes, I judge it quite possible she will quit London without ever leaving Connie's house. Without ever meeting *Charles*."

"Umm." Gwen repressed another breath of relief and permitted Mama to chatter of her love the rest of the way to Lady Heathcote's.

This assembly was considerably less crowded than Lady Bascomb's: Gwen and Lady Ross were properly met by a footman, escorted up three flights of steps to the ballroom, and greeted personally by their hostess. However, there was no time for an extended chat with Lady Heathcote—other parties were treading on their heels—and Mama drew Gwen aside and began peering about the room.

"There is Byron," she whispered, tilting her head to the left.

Gwen gazed at the poet and felt a stab of disappointment. But perhaps, she owned charitably, a genius could be excused that unruly mop of hair, that aloof, almost disdainful countenance.

"And if Byron is here," Mama whispered on, "Lady Caroline Lamb cannot be far distant."

"No?" Gwen murmured distractedly. She had lost any desultory interest she might have had in Lord Byron; her eyes were combing the ballroom for Viscount Fullerton.

"No," Lady Ross said. "No, she will not leave him alone a *moment*. She has even disguised herself as a pageboy and hunted him down in his rooms. Byron tries to avoid her, of course, and one can only shudder to imagine her *husband's* opinion of her shocking behavior. But there is Charles!" Mama cried. "If you will pardon me, dear . . ."

Lady Ross raced away, and Gwen continued to look about with what she hoped was perfect nonchalance. However, as the new arrivals swirled around her, it became clear that Lord Fullerton had *not* been awaiting her, at least not eagerly. At length she realized that her presence so near the entry posed a decided obstacle, but as she prepared to slink to the refreshment parlor, she was caught up by a familiar voice.

"Mrs. Hathaway!" Lord Blake raised one gloved hand in greeting and threaded his way through the crowd between them, dragging Lady Blake in his wake. "Mrs. Hathaway," he repeated when they had reached Gwen's side. "How delighted I am to see you. I must admit to some doubt as to whether you would come; I feared you might be unduly distressed by the events of the day."

"The events of the day?" Gwen echoed warily.

"Yes. Papa told us of the letter Lady Ross received, and I'm afraid I must agree with Chad about the source. I daresay one of Papa's odious female acquaintances was seeking to torment your dear mother."

Lord Fullerton had certainly wasted no time putting his "theory" about, Gwen reflected furiously. "Please do not care for it, Lord Blake," she said aloud. "Mama has determined to forget the letter, and I fancy we should all do well to follow her lead."

"Your mother is a remarkable woman." The viscount shook his head with admiration. "And I fancy we *should* forget the incident, for I do not suppose it will be repeated. No, once Papa's former . . . ah . . . friends learn that Lady Ross has *quite* reformed him, they will realize that any such machinations are entirely in vain."

"I do pray so," Gwen murmured. She could not but contemplate the great disparity between Lord Blake and his half brother: the former was a veritable model of upright conduct, the latter a self-described reprobate . . . "Where *is* Viscount Fullerton?" she asked.

"Umm." Lord Blake glanced around. "He went immediately to the refreshment parlor when we came, but I should think he would have had a glass or two by now. Yes, there he is."

He raised his hand again, and Gwen watched, tapping one foot with annoyance, as Viscount Fullerton sauntered toward them.

"Here he comes," Lord Blake announced gratuitously,

"so perhaps you will excuse us, Mrs. Hathaway. We have not yet had an opportunity to speak with Lady Heathcote, and I should like to do so without delay."

He bowed away, once more tugging Lady Blake behind him, and Gwen returned her full attention to Lord Fullerton. It was altogether like him, she thought angrily, to flash a winsome smile of greeting, as though nothing whatever were amiss.

"Good evening, Mrs. Hathaway," he said cheerfully. "I see you survived our trying day."

"With no thanks to you," Gwen snapped. "Lord Blake and I were just discussing Mama's letter. According to him, you are busily circulating the tale that it was written by one of your father's *chères amies.*"

His smile abruptly faded, and his slate-colored eyes narrowed. "I am not *circulating* any tale at all," he said coolly. "Harold and Amanda were frantically attempting to guess the author of the letter, and it would have looked exceedingly odd had I declined to venture an opinion. Would you have preferred me to speculate that your mother's mantua-maker wrote the letter? To explain that Lady Ross is unable to pay her bills?"

"Of course not, but—"

"I found that portion of the conversation most interesting," the viscount interposed. "I believe you once claimed that your mother is financially . . . Was 'comfortable' not the word you used? How is it, then, that she cannot afford to pay her seamstress?"

"I trust you also found it *interesting* that she refused Lord Scarborough's offer of assistance," Gwen retorted warmly. "That should prove beyond any doubt that Mama is not a fortune hunter."

"To the contrary, Mrs. Hathaway, it proves to me that Lady Ross is a *clever* fortune hunter. She would insist till the very eve of their marriage that she had no debts, and then, the morning after the honeymoon, she would present Papa with an enormous pile of bills."

"Well, I am sure he is familiar with such bills," Gwen

said acidly. "He would no doubt judge it a blessing to pay only *one* woman's dressmaker rather than two or three. Though I daresay his relief would be short-lived because he would soon revert to his normal habits."

The orchestra struck up a waltz, and several enthusiastic couples bounded past them to secure positions on the floor. Lord Fullerton glared at Gwen a moment more, his charcoal eyes narrowed to the merest slits, but at last he shook his head.

"I apologize, Mrs. Hathaway," he said. "I abrogated our agreement, and I shall try to guard my tongue in future."

"I . . . I am sorry too," Gwen muttered.

"Then as we are definitely standing in the way of progress, I suggest we avail ourselves of Lady Heathcote's excellent musicians."

He guided her to the floor and took her in his arms, and Gwen felt an odd inward tremor. Although she was accustomed to the waltz by now, waltzing with Lord Fullerton was somehow different, and she hastened to dispel the unnerving sense of intimacy engendered by his touch.

"You will be happy to learn," she said briskly, "that Lady Lynch has been confined to Aunt Constance's house. Temporarily, at any rate: Neville and my aunt and I have convinced her she is mortally ill."

"Now that I think on it, that is another interesting circumstance," his lordship said. "It was clear this morning that you desperately wanted to prevent Lady Lynch's introduction to Papa, and I couldn't fathom why. Did you think the two of them together might unravel our plot?"

"No, that wasn't it at all. No, Lady Lynch would be *horrified* if she learned of Mama's relationship with Lord Scarborough." His eyes flickered, and Gwen shook her own head. "I am not . . . not abrogating our agreement, Lord Fullerton; I am simply stating the truth. Lady Lynch is monstrous proper, and she would fly quite into the boughs if Mama married your father. Indeed, Neville has implied that *our* marriage might be jeopardized in that eventuality."

"Then if you will pardon me for saying so, I must question the depth of Sir Neville's devotion to you."

Gwen had questioned this very thing herself, but his forthright words nevertheless came as a shock. She cast about for a suitable rejoiner and—as often seemed to happen—took refuge in sarcasm.

"You are speaking from experience, of course," she snapped. "You have been in love countless times, and your undying *devotion* qualifies you as an expert on the subject."

"In point of fact, I have never been in love," he said mildly. "Though I was rather attached to an opera dancer when I was one-and-twenty."

"Lord Fullerton!" But she belatedly perceived that he was only jesting.

"No, I have never been in love," he repeated. "But if I were, I should not allow anything to come between me and the object of my . . . my *devotion*."

"That is easy enough for you to say," Gwen said stiffly.

She gazed studiedly over his shoulder and glimpsed Mama and Lord Scarborough on the far side of the floor. Lady Ross's ostrich plume was gaily waving, and the earl was whispering in her ear, and they were laughing. Gwen felt a stab of something very close to envy and looked hurriedly back at Lord Fullerton.

"If I may be permitted another observation," he said, "I do not believe you and your fiancé are in the least compatible. Sir Neville tends to doze off well before midnight, while you go on dancing for hours."

"We shall not be compelled to attend any balls in Kent," Gwen said. "We shall be in bed well before midnight."

"And are you looking forward to that?"

Gwen quelled a furious blush and peered down at his shoes.

"And what of Lady Lynch?" he continued. "I presume

you will reside with her, and I infer from your remarks that Sir Neville is very much under her thumb. I wonder the effect of her constant intrusion in your life."

"Do you know what *I* wonder?" Gwen angrily raised her eyes. "I wonder why you have any right to interfere in my affairs."

"I have no right at all," he replied calmly. "However, I discover that I have grown rather . . . rather fond of you during our brief acquaintance, and I should hate to see you make a second unfortunate marriage. I suspect—and now *I* but state the truth, Mrs. Hathaway—that your own financial circumstances impel you to wed again and that Sir Neville chanced to be a convenient candidate. He possesses an additional advantage, of course, one beyond mere proximity: he is as different from your late husband as a man could conceivably be."

He had divined her situation with astonishing accuracy, and Gwen once more felt her cheeks begin to color.

"The tragic aspect is that your sacrifice is entirely unnecessary," he went on. "As I attempted to tell you once before, you cannot presume that all men are more or less like Hathaway. He was utterly without principles, without scruples, without a shred of character; and you needn't marry a saint to protect yourself from another like him. And in any event, you needn't marry the first *parti* who happens along. You are very charming, very clever, very handsome . . ." To Gwen's further astonishment, he seemed a bit discomfited, and his voice trailed off.

"Handsome?" she echoed wryly, to hide her own embarrassment. "It is kind of you to say so, Lord Fullerton, but Mama has advised me that I look a bit dowdy this evening."

"Indeed?"

It had been altogether the wrong ploy: he studied her most intently, and Gwen's face positively flamed with mortification.

"Well, not *dowdy*," he said at length, "though I must own that your greens are somewhat ill-assorted, and none of them matches your eyes. And why should you wish to cover your hair with that ridiculous turban?"

"I . . ." Gwen started to reveal that she had always detested her hair as much as her name, but the conversation had already become far too personal. Dangerously personal, and she must end it at once. "Never mind," she said lightly. "Did you and Lord Scarborough purchase new horses today?"

"No, we did not. That was a stroke of desperation on *my* part, and when we were halfway to Tattersall's, Papa decided to keep his wild bays after all. At that juncture, I sincerely tried to talk him round, for I do feel they're dangerous. But, as usual, Papa proved most stubborn; he invariably refuses to take advice. Which brings us back to our plan, does it not?"

"Back?" Gwen repeated dubiously. "It did occur to me earlier in the day that we might be able to utilize a portion of the original plan—the simultaneous jilting. But I am no longer confident on that head, for Mama would never believe another forged letter. And if she cannot be enticed to quit town . . ."

"If Lady Ross cannot be enticed to quit town," the viscount finished, "Papa must be made to do so."

"But you said that was impossible," Gwen protested.

"I said it was impossible to lure him away *immediately,*" his lordship corrected. "I was also stating the truth this morning when I mentioned Papa's great enjoyment of the Season. However, time is no longer a factor. Well, it is a factor," he amended, "but we shall simply have to hope for the best."

"But *how?*" Gwen asked impatiently. "How are we to drive your father out of London?"

"We shall dangle a seaside estate before his nose," Lord Fullerton responded. "Papa has been seeking such a property for years; I daresay he is entranced by the Regent's Pavilion at Brighton."

"He has been looking for years?" Gwen said. "And you have suddenly found one?"

"I have not *yet* found one, Mrs. Hathaway, but I shall

leave tomorrow to conduct a search of my own. It may
well require a week or more, but I assure you I shall not
return empty-handed. I shall then tell Papa that the
owner is extremely anxious to sell and Papa must view the
estate without delay. Once he is gone, we shall compose
our letters of dismissal, and the plan will unfold as we
projected it to do before."

"A week or more?" Though Gwen could not imagine
why, she could scarcely bear the prospect of his absence.
"But anything could happen in such a lengthy interval."

"I recognize that, Mrs. Hathaway, but I perceive no
other way to separate our parents. While I am gone, you
must try to keep them apart as much as possible."

"But what if Lord Scarborough invites Mama to
accompany him?" Gwen objected. "As he invited himself
to escort her to Kent?"

"I have considered that contingency," the viscount said
smugly. "I shall insist that our man of business travel
with Papa so as to analyze the property from a financial
standpoint. Papa will have no wish to include Lady Ross
in an awkward threesome."

"And if you succeed?" Gwen pressed. "If Lord Scarborough *does* leave town without Mama, will our letters
of dismissal not be suspect? Both of them are now alerted
to the possibility of forgery."

"I have considered that as well. When the time comes,
we shall deliver our letters *personally*. You will take
yours—your mother's, that is—to our home, and I shall
bring Papa's message to Orchard Street. We shall make it
a point to chat with the respective butlers, and they will
subsequently report our visits. No one will suspect *us* of
forgery."

"No, I suppose not," Gwen agreed dully.

"What is wrong, Mrs. Hathaway?" His tone was surprisingly gentle. "If you have lost the will to proceed—"

"No," she said quickly, "no, I was merely concerned
about the details. But as you seem to have allowed for
every eventuality, we must certainly go on."

"Excellent." The music stopped, and his lordship

swept her a deep bow. "Then, as I stated, I shall depart early tomorrow morning."

He started to guide her off the floor, but they had negotiated only a step or two when Gwen heard a great gasp behind them. Lord Fullerton whirled around, and his grip on her elbow tightened.

"Good God!" he hissed.

Gwen entertained an awful notion that Mama and Lord Scarborough were announcing their engagement to the entire assembly. "What is it?" she asked frantically.

"Lady Caroline Lamb," he whispered. "Apparently she has slit her wrists. Yes, she has a broken glass in one hand, and there is blood all over her skirt. She intended to spite Byron, of course, but he is merely *smiling.*"

As often occurred, Gwen cursed her lack of height, but she decided it would be most unseemly to jump about in an attempt to view the sordid scene for herself. And on second thought, she was not at all sure she *wanted* to see Lady Lamb bleeding "all over her skirt."

"Her husband is now leading her away," the viscount reported. "Her husband and her mother-in-law, Lady Melbourne. I daresay they will pack her off to the country, as they should have done long since."

He propelled her ahead again, as though nothing terribly unusual had happened after all, and the uproar in the background began to subside. It was just another London scandal, Gwen reflected with amazement: it would be an *on-dit* for a few days and would then be forgotten. The incident strengthened her conviction that she would be quite happy married to Neville, for nothing so lurid could ever occur in their peaceful, rural community. Yes, she had surely been right to accept his offer, and she was glad neither he nor Lady Lynch had been present to witness Lady Lamb's horrifying conduct.

—7—

It was nearly two the following afternoon when Gwen
finished breakfast and judged herself obliged to pay her
respects to Lady Lynch. As she trudged back up the steps,
she detected a familiar chorus of thuds and grunts issuing
from the saloon, and—welcoming the opportunity to
postpone her call—she crept down the corridor. She had
intended merely to observe Mama's progress a moment,
but at the drawing-room entry she literally collided with
Tilson. The first footman, visibly perspiring and
obviously limping, was clearly in a monstrous hurry; and
after a breathless mumble of apology, he hobbled on
along the hall and fairly hurled himself down the staircase.

"Come in, Gwen." Lady Ross's face was also damp,
and she was vigorously fanning herself with a copy of
Ackermann's Repository. "I fear I can no longer practice
with Tilson; he has grown most impertinently critical of
late. He claims I have trod on his feet so often as to render
him lame. That is absurd, of course; I suspect he has been
stepped on by a horse or some such thing."

Gwen elected not to question how a first footman
could conceivably be injured by a horse. "I suspect so,
Mama," she concurred gravely.

"Fortunately, it doesn't signify," Lady Ross said. "I
doubt additional practice could in any way enhance my
mastery of the waltz." Gwen doubted this as well. "And
at any rate, we shall not be waltzing tonight; we are

going to the opera. Indeed, I am glad to see you, for I wished to mention that there is an extra seat in Charles's box. Lord Fullerton has quit town for a few days."

"Oh?" Gwen said casually.

"Yes, he has gone to the shore, claiming to require some rest from the Season. Really, Gwen, you young people put Charles and myself to shame."

Gwen thought Mama had entirely reversed her comment, but she chose not to remark on this either.

"In any event," Lady Ross continued, "as I stated, there is now an empty seat, and I thought to ask Olivia to go in Lord Fullerton's stead—"

"No!" Gwen protested. "No, Lady Lynch is far too ill to attend the opera."

"Still?" Mama frowned. "You have seen her today?"

"Yes," Gwen lied, "and she is even *worse* than yesterday." She belatedly recollected the viscount's admonition that she must attempt to keep Lady Ross and the earl apart. "In fact, Mama, now that I think on it, I fancy we should *all* forgo the opera in order to . . . to comfort her."

Lady Ross frowned a moment more, then nodded. "I fancy you are right, Gwen. I am sure Charles would not object to a quiet evening at home, and it would afford him an opportunity to meet Olivia—"

"No!" Gwen yelped again. "Now that I reconsider, I believe Lady Lynch would be most overset to have so many visitors milling about. Neville and I shall stay behind, but you and Lord Scarborough must go on to the opera."

"Well, if you are certain, dear . . ."

Gwen bobbed her head and raced away before Mama could change her mind.

As it happened, Gwen's call was postponed after all: when she tapped at Lady Lynch's bedchamber door, Maggie cracked it open and whispered that her ladyship was asleep.

"Mrs. Cunningham has desired me to watch after her," the abigail whispered on, "and to admit no one but herself and you and Sir Neville. Naturally I shall follow her instructions, but Lady Lynch doesn't seem all that sick to me."

"She is *very* sick," Gwen corrected sternly, "and you must certainly heed Aunt Constance's directive." She had a sudden brilliant notion; she thought Lord Fullerton would be proud. "You must be especially careful not to admit my mother. Though I'm sure Aunt Constance was too . . . too discreet to explain, you should know that Mama and Lady Lynch do not get on at all. No, I'm afraid a visit from Mama could well prove fatal."

"Fatal to whom, ma'am? To Lady Ross or Lady Lynch?"

"To Lady Lynch, of course," Gwen snapped. "When she wakes, tell her that Sir Neville and I shall join her for dinner in her room."

Gwen's latter statement had been altogether one of impulse, but on the whole, she thought, dinner went quite well. She was initially dismayed to observe that Lady Lynch appeared in high force—gray curls bouncing round the edges of her nightcap, cheeks healthily aglow —and that she consumed her meal with splendid appetite. However, after her ladyship had devoured a second lemon tart, Gwen sprang up, felt her forehead, and regretfully announced that her fever had returned.

"Perhaps you ate too much," Gwen suggested.

"Perhaps I was poisoned," Lady Lynch retorted. "Your aunt's cook would not remain in *my* employ above a day."

Gwen did not doubt this for an instant. "I shall speak to the cook," she said aloud. "Meanwhile, if you are ever to regain your strength, you must rest."

"Only if you and Neville promise to have breakfast with me." Her ladyship emitted one of her martyred sighs.

"We do promise," Gwen said soothingly, "and Neville will stay with you till you fall asleep. Will you not, Neville?"

The baronet nodded, seized and patted his mother's hand, and Gwen slipped out of the room.

To say the truth, Aunt Constance's cook *did* leave something to be desired, and to atone for the dubious quality of Lady Lynch's breakfast, Gwen personally helped Tilson deliver it. She was alarmed to find her ladyship out of bed and studying her reflection in the mirror above the rosewood dressing table.

"I have decided to go to church this morning," Lady Lynch announced as Tilson bowed out of the room. "When one suffers from ill health as I do, one cannot afford to neglect one's religious duties. One never knows just what might occur," she added darkly. "Furthermore, I shall not leave London without attending services at St. George's."

This was the worst of all possible threats, and Gwen pondered the situation a moment. If they drove directly to Hanover Square, permitted Lady Lynch to speak to no one, drove directly home, perhaps there would be no harm in it.

"Very well," she said. "While you and Neville start breakfast, I shall order out your carriage."

"That will not be possible. Higgins experienced some difficulty with one of the wheels during our journey to town, and he has taken the carriage to Hatchett's to be repaired. But I daresay Mrs. Cunningham will not object if we share her carriage."

Gwen judged it best not to reveal that the Alford/Ross/Cunningham clan had never been notably devout; she nodded noncommittally and sped out of the room and down the stairs. To her considerable surprise, she encountered Lady Ross in the vestibule.

"You are up early this morning, dear." Mama fairly snatched the words from Gwen's mouth. "And where are you headed in such a rush?"

"Lady Lynch wishes to attend church," Gwen replied, "and I need to order out Aunt Constance's carriage."

"But you need not!" Lady Ross said happily. "What a wonderful coincidence! As it happens, Charles is taking me to St. George's, and I am certain he would be delighted to include Olivia."

"St. George's?" Gwen gasped. "You and Lord Scarborough? Then Lady Lynch cannot go."

"Does she prefer some other church?" Mama frowned.

"Yes." Gwen eagerly bobbed her head. "Yes, that is it exactly; she prefers another church."

"How peculiar." Lady Ross's frown deepened. "I should have supposed Olivia would know that St. George's is the premier church in London. However, I'm sure Charles will agree to take her anywhere she chooses. He is *most* anxious to meet her."

"I'm sure he would."—Gwen gulped—"but there is another problem. The . . . the weather."

"The weather?" Mama's brows were now so creased that her eyes had begun to squint. "The weather is beautiful." She gestured vaguely round the foyer, but it had no windows, and she waved to either side. "You see? There in the library, there in the dining room? Sunlight all over the carpets. Indeed, Connie really should close her drapes; otherwise the sun will fade her rugs."

"It is sunny now," Gwen agreed desperately, "but I fear it will rain very shortly. I . . . I feel it in my bones."

"Do you have a touch of rheumatism, dear?" Lady Ross asked anxiously. "I do pray not; you are only five-and-twenty."

"Perhaps I do." Gwen drew a martyred breath of her own. "In any case, I must advise Lady Lynch not to go out today, so you and Lord Scarborough should proceed without her." She turned and toiled back up the steps, as though every movement aggravated her painful condition.

Lady Lynch was not so easily persuaded of the imminent inclemency as Mama. She, too, had rheumatism, she snapped (as well as a host of *other* maladies), and *her* bones were telling her nothing. Sir Neville had joined his mother by now, and eventually—after half a dozen frantic signals—he chimed in and cajoled her ladyship back to bed. To Gwen's great gratification, it did start to rain late in the afternoon, and Lady Lynch grudgingly conceded that her future daughter-in-law had been right. Although, of course, her *timing* had been substantially in error . . .

The rain continued into Monday, and Lady Lynch grew increasingly restive: despite the dampness, she insisted, she was sufficiently recovered to venture downstairs. But Gwen could not permit such an excursion— with Mama's waltzing practices abandoned, there was no way to predict when Lord Scarborough might call— and she tentatively proposed a game of cards. Her ladyship proved unexpectedly receptive to this suggestion; however, she added, casino was the only game she knew. Gwen hastily recruited Aunt Constance as a fourth, and they played from breakfast to dinner, from dinner to supper, and for an hour or more after supper, till Neville began to nod. At some juncture, Gwen realized that the interminable day was an excellent sample of her married life. Aunt Constance would not be with them in Kent, of course, but there were any number of lonely widows in the neighborhood. Indeed, if her and Lord Fullerton's plot succeeded, Mama might well play Aunt Constance's hand in the months and years to come.

After Lady Lynch had safely retired, Gwen retreated to her bedchamber, undressed, and crawled into bed, but she could not sleep. The long, dull day had reminded her of the viscount's questions about her marriage, and she was now forced to own that he had scored several telling points. She further recollected his supplementary remarks, his insistence that she need not wed the first suitor who chanced along. She wondered what would happen if she *did* terminate her engagement to Neville. She could not remain in London, of course—it would be all too obvious that she was on the catch for a replacement—but she could come back for the Little Season in the fall. And when she did, might Lord Fullerton initiate a courtship of his own?

Gwen could not conceive what had prompted such a shocking notion, and, even alone in the darkness, she felt her cheeks warm. She had no intention of dissolving her engagement; she was genuinely fond of Neville, and they would be exceedingly happy together. Nor did she have any personal interest in Viscount Fullerton. She did not miss *him*, she assured herself; did not miss his slate-colored eyes and startling gray hair, his mischievous humor, his frequent flashes of warmth. She merely missed their conspiracy, and it was entirely natural for her to think of his lordship often, to speculate on the progress of his quest. Entirely natural, for shortly after he returned from the shore, they would permanently separate Mama and Lord Scarborough, and she could go back to Kent and resume her calm, safe life with Neville.

But that prospect rendered her inexplicably desolate, and she put Lord Fullerton altogether out of her mind. The moon had risen, and she began to count the roses on the canopy above the bed and eventually tumbled into an uneasy sleep.

It was not until the next morning that Gwen recognized the significance of the moon: the rain had passed, and the day was absolutely clear. Following Sunday's near-disaster, Gwen had drawn Lady Lynch's bedchamber curtains against just this eventuality, but she had not really expected her ploy to work, and it did not. Immediately after breakfast, her ladyship strode to the window (looking frightfully robust), peered out, and declared that she was well enough for a drive in Hyde Park.

"Which is not to say that I am *well*," she speedily amended. "However, I fancy a drive in the park would provide just the restorative I need."

It was apparent that she would not again be diverted by Gwen's "rheumatic" bones; and Gwen, murmuring that she would check on the availability of the carriage, hastened downstairs to investigate the whereabouts of Mama and the earl. Crenshaw informed her that Lady Ross and Lord Scarborough had left for a shopping excursion not ten minutes since, and Gwen counted it most unlikely that they would venture to the park within the

ensuing hour or so. She consequently ordered out the
carriage, raced back up the stairs, and instructed Lady
Lynch to prepare for their outing at once.

In the event, "at once" took forever. Her ladyship had
worn her only proper carriage dress to London, she
fretted, and as it had not been pressed, she would have to
wear her primrose muslin, and she had no suitable hat to
match . . . The corridor clock was striking one when she
at last pronounced herself ready, and Gwen hurriedly
escorted her down the staircase and out to Aunt
Constance's waiting landau. Sir Neville, already en-
sconced in the rear-facing seat, frowned severely at their
tardiness.

"I am sorry, dear," Lady Lynch cooed, "but you know
how women are. Gwen and I had to debate interminably
upon our bonnets."

Gwen, who had selected her bonnet nearly an hour
before, bit back a sharp rejoinder, and the carriage
clattered to a start.

Aunt Constance's horses were well-behaved in the
extreme (indeed, they would have made splendid plow
horses, Gwen thought), and they reached Hyde Park
without incident. As had been the case during her and
Lord Fullerton's fateful drive, the park was virtually
empty, but her ladyship exclaimed over every tree, every
flower, every blade of grass. At length, the landau turned
back toward Park Lane, and it occurred to Gwen that
this might well be the solution to their problem. Yes, if
Lady Lynch were permitted a daily excursion while
Mama and Lord Scarborough were otherwise occupied . . .

Gwen heard the rattle of another carriage behind
them, and Jenkins, Aunt Constance's coachman, pulled
the landau well to the left to facilitate its passage. Gwen
glanced desultorily to her right and, to her horror, beheld
a familiar team of bays galloping beside them. Lord Scarborough was struggling to keep his curricle under some
semblance of control, and on the opposite side of the seat,
Mama was frantically clutching her leghorn hat.

"Good God!" Lady Lynch gripped the brim of her own bonnet. "Is that not—"

"Look!" Gwen shrieked, pointing wildly toward the left. "Look there!"

"What?"

Lady Lynch spun her head, and the curricule careened on by, swayed alarmingly for a moment, lurched back to the left, hurtled ahead.

"That . . . that tree," Gwen said. "The copper beech. I fancied there was some sort of animal in the branches, but it must have been a reflection."

"Animal indeed." Lady Lynch sniffed with annoyance and shifted her eyes back to the road, but the earl's carriage had rounded a bend and disappeared. "I wish you had not distracted me, Gwen, for I believe Fanny was in that curricule."

"Fanny . . . Fanny who?"

"Your mother Fanny," her ladyship snapped. "I nearly bought that hat from Miss Freeman, but I decided the style did not become me."

"No, it could not have been Mama." Gwen's mouth was dust-dry, and she vainly tried to moisten her lips. "Mama has gone shopping."

"Gone shopping how? We have your aunt's carriage."

"True." Gwen's throat was parched as well, and her voice emerged a very squeak. "True, but it is only a short walk to Oxford Street."

"Humph."

Lady Lynch, who never walked anywhere, was patently unconvinced, but they had emerged from the park by now, and Gwen hastily directed her ladyship's attention to a particularly colorful group of pedestrians on the footpath. Lady Lynch pronounced their stylish attire altogether "vulgar"—an observation which inspired her to deliver an impassioned lecture on the general decay of modern mores. Gwen nodded at appropriate intervals and nervously watched for the earl's rampaging curricule, fully expecting to find it overturned in the street, an eager crowd gathered round to view the mangled corpses of Mama and Lord Scarborough.

However, there was no sign of his lordship's carriage between Hyde Park and Orchard Street, and to Gwen's immense relief, the curricle was not drawn up in front of Aunt Constance's house. Lest her luck should expire at the last instant, she fairly dragged Lady Lynch out of the landau and into the foyer, advised her that she looked excessively "flushed," and counseled a long afternoon nap. Lady Lynch admitted that the drive *had* been rather exhausting for a person in her precarious state of health and allowed Maggie to assist her up the stairs. When they had vanished around the landing, Gwen sagged against the front door, fearing her own state of health was growing more precarious by the hour.

"*Was* it Lady Ross in the curricle?"

Gwen had quite forgotten Neville's presence, and she started, then bobbed her head. "Yes," she said wearily. "Mama and Lord Scarborough, of course."

She drew herself upright with some effort and peered warily about the vestibule. She did not detect Crenshaw's telltale shadow on either side, but a week of constant plotting had rendered her extremely cautious.

"Your mother must leave London," she hissed. "We have been exceedingly fortunate thus far, but sooner or later she is sure to meet Lord Scarborough. When will her carriage be finished?"

"Hatchett's promised for Friday at the latest."

"Friday." Could she possibly survive three more days of racing up and down the steps, manufacturing one tale upon another? "Friday," she repeated grimly. "She must then go back to Kent, even if you have to go with her."

"Go with her?" The baronet's pale eyes glittered with suspicion. "And what of you?"

"I shall not be far behind," Gwen said. "I have reason to believe that Lord Scarborough will soon be quitting town himself, and Mama will follow shortly thereafter—"

"You have been scheming with Fullerton again!" Sir Neville rarely angered, but when he did, the symptoms were characteristically predictable: he developed little spots of color high on either cheek, and his mouth literally quivered with indignation.

"We agreed that it was necessary," Gwen reminded him. "And Lord Fullerton and I have been very careful this time; indeed, I do not scruple to tell you that our plan is foolproof. Within four-and-twenty hours of his return to London, Mama and Lord Scarborough will be separated forever."

"What *is* your plan?" the baronet demanded.

"We . . ." But she did not want to disclose it; it was her and the viscount's secret, the only thing they would ever share. "I fancy it would be best if you didn't know," she said lightly. "If you don't know, you can be surprised at the proper times."

"Very well," he agreed stiffly, "but I shall grant you no more than a week beyond my own departure."

Another threat? Gwen wondered what he would do if she remained in London for *two* weeks, a month. But there was no chance to ask, even had she dared to do so, for at that moment the front door opened and Mama stepped into the entry hall.

"Gwen! Neville!" She glanced at her daughter's French bonnet, at the baronet's beaver hat, and clapped her hands. "It *was* you in the park! I told Charles so, and you must not take it amiss that we didn't stop to greet you. To say the truth, we tried to stop, but Charles's horses are quite . . . quite unruly at times. At any rate, I was thrilled to see that Olivia is up and about, and I elicited Charles's promise that he would obtain a voucher to admit her to Almack's tomorrow evening. At long last they will be able to meet—"

"If only they could." Gwen managed a deep, sorrowful sigh. "Unfortunately, the drive proved too much for Lady Lynch; she has suffered a relapse."

"A relapse." Lady Ross's bright countenance collapsed.

"Yes. Neville was just on his way upstairs to make her as comfortable as possible. I'm sure he'll agree it would be best not to mention the voucher; Lady Lynch would

only tease herself about it. She might even insist—
bravely *insist*—she is strong enough to go. Might she not,
Neville?"

"No," the baronet said. "That is, yes. Yes, she might
insist, I mean. So, no, I shan't mention the voucher."

Perhaps he found his words as confusing as Gwen did;
in any case, he negotiated a rather clumsy bow and
scurried up the stairs. Mama gazed after him and eventually shook her head.

"Is it my imagination," Lady Ross asked, "or is
Neville's behavior a trifle peculiar today?"

"I . . . I daresay he is concerned about his mother,"
Gwen said. "In fact, I should venture to guess that he
won't go to Almack's either."

"What a shame." Mama shook her head again. "But
you'll go, won't you, Gwen? Charles put himself to a
great deal of trouble to secure vouchers for you and
Neville, and I fear he would be most wounded if you both
declined to attend."

Gwen did not care a deuce for Lord Scarborough's
jaded sensibilities, but when she considered the alternative—another endless game of casino with Neville and
Lady Lynch and Aunt Constance—she nodded. "Yes, I
shall go."

"Then I shall make excuses for Neville and Olivia.
Charles will understand; he is a firm believer in family
loyalty."

Lady Ross walked toward the staircase, and Gwen recollected one final hitch in her latest plot.

"I hope you will not wear that hat again, Mama," she
said. "It is most unbecoming."

"Unbecoming?" Lady Ross whirled incredulously
around. "Charles adores this hat."

"Does he?" Gwen assumed a kind smile. "I must be
mistaken then; I thought it made you look somewhat . . .
somewhat old."

"Old!"

Mama ripped the hat off and studied it with keen distaste, as though it were some loathsome insect. She sped on up the stairs, gingerly dangling the bonnet from one gloved fingertip, and Gwen collapsed once more against the door.

8

Even as Maggie helped her dress, Gwen regretted her promise to go to Almack's, and an inspection of her image in the cheval glass did nothing to put her back in spirits. Having exhausted her limited supply of evening gowns, she had been compelled to wear the yellow again, and it no longer looked the least becoming. No, by contrast to London's glittering *ton*, she fancied she rather resembled a milkmaid rigged out for a country party. Everyone at Lady Bascomb's rout had no doubt noted this similarity as well, she thought darkly, and would recognize the dress at once. And everyone at Almack's this evening had no doubt been to Lady Bascomb's. But there was no help for it; she *had* promised; and as the mantel clock struck nine, she comforted herself with the reminder that Lord Fullerton would not be present to witness her humiliation.

Lord Scarborough was awaiting Gwen and Lady Ross at Almack's entry, and he ushered them proprietarily inside and began to introduce them to the formidable patronesses of the establishment. Gwen had met most of them before, during the Season of her come-out, but they did not seem to recollect the daughter of an obscure Kentish baronet. Not until Lady Jersey gripped her hands, stood her back, and beamed with recognition.

"Mrs. Hathaway, of course; you were Miss Ross when last I met you. I was puzzling over your identity when I glimpsed you at Lady Bascomb's. How clever of you to have worn the same dress tonight you had on then; I remarked throughout the evening that it is *most* unusual."

Gwen managed a polite mutter of thanks and fled on into the ballroom, but the countess had destroyed her last vestiges of confidence. She gazed about a moment, watching as Mama and Lord Scarborough greeted the Blakes, then crept to the refreshment parlor. To her surprise and relief, it was almost empty, but when she glanced at the table, she recalled why this had ever been the case: the patronesses' notion of "refreshment" was bread, butter, stale cake, lemonade, and tea.

Gwen sighed, served herself from these meager offerings, and perched on a delicate gilt chair in one corner of the room. The other inhabitants—two very elderly women seated diagonally across the parlor—did not appear to notice her, and Gwen soon surmised that they might, in fact, be asleep. She wolfed down the contents of her plate, gulped her glass of lemonade, and started to ponder a feasible means of escape. If she desired Jenkins to take her home at once, he could drive to Orchard Street and back before Mama or Lord Scarborough missed her—

"Mrs. Hathaway!"

The voice was little more than a whisper, but Gwen recognized it nevertheless. As her eyes flew to the doorway, she sprang to her feet, and her plate slipped off her lap. Fortunately, it broke into three neat pieces, and, as it was empty, only a few crumbs scattered over the floor. Lord Fullerton rushed forward, knelt, gathered up the debris; and Gwen stared down at him. She was utterly at a loss to explain why her heart was drumming against her ribs, why she should be so monstrous glad to see him.

"I believe that does it." The viscount rose and deposited plate and crumbs alike on one corner of the table. "I must own myself disappointed, Mrs. Hathaway; I can scarcely conceive that you actually ate this appalling fare."

"I . . . I had no supper," Gwen said.

"No? Well, we must have no more of that; you are quite sufficiently thin as it is."

He brushed his gloved fingers together, dislodging the last of the crumbs, crossed to her side, and gazed down at her. He was not so immaculate as was his custom, she observed: his neckcloth was a trifle untidy, and his gray hair flopped about his forehead a bit. Gwen repressed an inclination to reach up and rearrange the neckcloth, to smooth the hair away from his brows; stifled an inexplicable urge merely to touch him.

"I am exceedingly happy to find you here, Mrs. Hathaway," he said.

"You . . . you are?" Gwen felt her cheeks begin to color, and she hastily turned away and reclaimed her chair.

"Indeed I am." He took the chair next to hers and peered cautiously about the room. The ancient dowagers on the other side were visibly nodding now, but he nonetheless lowered his voice. "I feared I should be unable to see you until tomorrow, but I then recollected Papa's intention of securing you a voucher for Almack's this evening. I can consequently inform you of my success at once, and we can proceed without delay."

Gwen's heart abruptly slowed, and she chided herself for her momentary foolishness. Lord Fullerton had no personal interest in her whatever, nor—she sternly reminded herself—did she have any such interest in him. She eased her chair away a bit and essayed a bright smile.

"That is wonderful!" She thought her voice sounded a trifle hollow, but he didn't seem to notice. "You located a suitable property then? And in only five days' time?"

"Yes," he confirmed, "I was most fortunate in that regard. It occurred to me, following our conversation at Lady Heathcote's, that it would not do at all to select an estate on the southeastern shore; Papa and Lady Ross might well have met up again in future. However, since time was of the essence, I did not wish to venture to the *western* coast, and I consequently traveled northeast from London. By a great stroke of luck, I found a splendid property on Monday, in Essex, near Harwich. I negotiated a tentative agreement with the present owner yesterday and drove back to town today. As I fear you can see for yourself, I arrived under an hour ago; I had time only to change my coat and pantaloons." He tugged at his neckcloth, pushed his hair off his forehead, flashed his mischievous grin. "I do pray Brummell is not about to criticize my lamentable appearance."

Gwen wondered what the sharp-tongued Beau would say of *her* appearance, and she cast a mortified glance at her old-fashioned, familiar dress. When she looked up again, she found, to her further embarrassment, that the viscount was studying her most intently; but if he recognized the gown, he evidently elected not to say so.

"The most significant advantage of the property," he said instead, "is that the sale includes four tenant farms." His voice seemed rather empty as well, oddly flat, but Gwen surmised he was merely tired. "Four farms, and they are conveniently scattered about the southern portions of Suffolk. East and West Suffolk alike."

"Farms?" Gwen echoed. "I did not realize Lord Scarborough also wished to acquire farms. And if he does, I should think he would find their scattered locations an *in*convenience—"

"Mrs. Hathaway." Lord Fullerton sorrowfully shook his gray head. "What am I to do with you? I was not considering Papa's convenience; I was thinking of ours. Without the farms, he could journey to Essex in one day, view the property the next, and return on the third. It is entirely possible that Lady Ross would still be in London, still packing her things; women invariably tend to fall apart in an emotional crisis."

He gave her a kind, condescending smile, and Gwen bit back a sharp rejoinder.

"As it is," he continued, "it will take Papa one day to drive to Essex; one to view the primary estate; and two, perhaps three, to visit the farms. I shall, of course, advise our man of business that he and Papa must inspect *all* the farms. They—Papa and Mr. Colfax, that is—will then require another day to strike a final bargain with the owner and still another to return to town. In short, I can confidently predict that Papa will be away six days, possibly seven, and surely, in that interval, you can dry your mother's tears and persuade her to quit London."

"I'm sure I can," Gwen snapped. She did not care for his superior attitude at all. "In the meantime, *I* should like to be assured that Lord Scarborough will actually go to Essex. I daresay you have already secured his consent."

"Mrs. Hathaway." The viscount emitted a pained sigh. "Of course I have not yet secured Papa's consent; we cannot give him an opportunity to speak with Lady Ross prior to his departure. Fortunately, he had left the house before I arrived to change my clothes, and, now I've conferred with you, I shall slip away before Papa and I are forced to talk in your mother's presence. I shall mention the estate only after Papa has returned from Almack's. I shall add that, as the owner is extremely eager to sell, Papa must leave for Essex without delay. That was another stroke of fortune, by the by: Mr. Fowler plans to immigrate to Canada, and he *is* extremely anxious to sell."

Hard though she tried, Gwen could not find a flaw in his latest scheme, and she stared down at her hands. "And then?" she asked.

"Then matters will proceed as we have planned. I shall not retire tonight until I have composed Papa's letter of dismissal to Lady Ross." His implication was clear: he expected her to write all night as well. "Once Papa has quit town, I shall deliver the message to Orchard Street, and you must be certain Mrs. Cunningham's butler is aware of my errand."

"Yes, I shall," Gwen muttered.

"I believe I previously mentioned that you should personally deliver your mother's letter to Berkeley Square as well." Gwen distantly reflected that she had not known, until that moment, where he lived. "However, I have since reconsidered; I fancy you can put Lady Ross's message in my hands. In fact, I daresay such a maneuver will serve to emphasize the simultaneous nature of the jilting: you can point out in the butler's presence that your mother's letter was already written before Papa's arrived. You will have to be subtle about it, of course—"

"I shall attempt to be as devious as you are, Lord Fullerton," Gwen interposed wryly.

"Excellent!" It seemed impossible to set him down. "Then I shall see you tomorrow; if all goes well, I shall come at ten o'clock." He stopped and frowned. "Though that poses a difficulty, does it not? In normal circumstances, I should request to see Lady Ross."

"Do not tease yourself about it," Gwen said. "I shall await you in the library and admit you to the house, and we shall involve Crenshaw later."

"Excellent," the viscount repeated. He rose, and Gwen stood up beside him. "I really should creep off now, before Papa spots me . . ." He stopped again, frowned again. "But I fear I've been unpardonably rude, Mrs. Hathaway; I have not inquired how it goes with Lady Lynch. Have you succeeded in keeping her and Papa apart?"

"Yes," Gwen replied, "so I fancy we need worry about that complication no longer. Lady Lynch will be leaving London Saturday at the latest, long before Lord Scarborough's return from the north. Since Mama will scarcely be inclined to circulate the news of her jilting, there is no reason for Lady Lynch ever to learn of the connection."

"I am delighted to hear it; I should never forgive myself if my family caused a breach between you and Sir Neville. Well, until tomorrow then."

He bowed and walked to the door of the refreshment parlor, looked quickly to either side, sped on out. Gwen sank back in her chair, but at least he had given her something to do. She closed her eyes and visualized the opening lines of Mama's regretful missive: "Dear Charles. Much as it pains me to own it . . ."

" . . . In conclusion, while I shall always regard you

with the most sincere affection, I have recognized that the depth of my attachment is insufficient to permit a permanent connection. I have consequently decided to return to Kent, and I pray you will not attempt to see me again. Yours truly, Frances Ross."

Gwen blotted the paper, reviewed the message, and sighed. It did not sound precisely like Mama, she conceded, but Lord Scarborough couldn't possibly discern that, and Gwen was far too tired to make further changes. She had not stayed up all night after all; she had, instead, risen at five this morning, and some dozen discarded drafts littered the rug beneath the writing table in her bedchamber. Nor did she have the time to compose still another version: the mantel clock read ten minutes before ten.

Gwen sighed once more and folded the letter, shoved it in an envelope and scrawled the earl's name upon the front. She rose, stepped on one of the drafts, and frowned, wondering how best to dispose of them. It wouldn't do at all for the chambermaid to find her abortive efforts, and Gwen quickly knelt, scooped them up, and tore them into tiny pieces. She then went to the wardrobe and stuffed the scraps into the toes of her white satin evening slippers. If everything proceeded according to plan, she would not wear the shoes again until she— and Mama—were safely back in Kent.

It lacked but eight minutes to ten now, and Gwen left her bedchamber, descended the stairs, and hurried across the vestibule toward the library. As she passed the side table, she glimpsed a heavy ivory envelope on the top, and she stopped and idly picked it up. It had clearly not come in the post: the direction consisted of nothing but Mama's name.

"Ah, Mrs. Hathaway."

Gwen started and guiltily replaced the envelope on the table, and Crenshaw bounded to her side.

"I trust you will not judge me remiss in my duties, ma'am," the butler said, "but I hesitated to awaken Lady Ross so early this morning. It was only a few minutes past six when Lord Scarborough's coachman came, and he assured me his lordship's communication was not in the way of an emergency."

"Lord Scarborough's *coachman?*" Gwen echoed sharply. "*He* brought the letter? You are certain?"

"Quite certain, ma'am. Even had he not identified himself, I recognized the coat of arms on the carriage door. It was the same as this." Crenshaw snatched up the envelope, flipped it over, and pointed to the seal on the flap.

"I see," Gwen murmured. "You were right not to disturb Mama, Crenshaw, and I daresay we needn't wake her now either. No, I shall take full responsibility for the letter; do not tease yourself about it any longer."

"The letter and—" He was interrupted by the distant sound of a bell, and he drew himself up. "That is Mrs. Cunningham," he whispered, "and I fancy I should respond at once. If you will excuse me . . ."

He bowed away without awaiting a response, and Gwen stared at the envelope again. She was initially inclined to allow Lord Fullerton the benefit of doubt, to assume he had somehow been compelled to alter their plan. However, it soon occurred to her that he had utterly destroyed the myth of a simultaneous jilting: Crenshaw was well aware that Lord Scarborough's coachman had delivered a communication to Lady Ross hours before her ladyship arose. In short, the viscount had betrayed her, and even as Gwen ground her teeth in fury, she wondered if there was any way to counter his treacherous move. Perhaps the letter itself might offer a clue, and she once more plucked up the envelope, turned it over, and observed that it was very poorly sealed. No one would ever know if she opened it, read the message, sealed the envelope again . . .

She glanced around the foyer, but there was no sign of any servant, and with trembling fingers, she loosened the flimsy seal, extracted the letter from the envelope, and unfolded it.

"My dearest Fanny," she read. She could not repress a disdainful sniff; she judged this an exceedingly inappropriate salutation for a letter of farewell.

"I am sorry to advise you that I must be away from London for the next seven days." Gwen scanned Lord Fullerton's explanation of the precipitate journey to Essex and found it accurate, if not particularly articulate. "Naturally it is my hope"—he ended the first paragraph —"that the estate will soon be our mutual home."

Good God! Gwen thought; had the viscount taken utter leave of his senses? She plunged into the second paragraph.

"I hope you will accept the accompanying small token of my affection." Token? What token? Gwen peered about the table and spotted a small flat box situated on the far edge; it would have fallen to the floor had it not come to rest against the wall. Her eyes flew back to the letter. "I fear you might consider such a gift somewhat improper, but no one need know its source except you and me. Wear it while I am gone so you will not forget me."

There was one final, brief paragraph. "As I've another small errand to attend in the north, I shall plan to return next Thursday, in time to celebrate the occasion with you." Celebrate *what* occasion? Gwen wondered wildly. "In my absence, I remain your devoted Charles."

Lord Fullerton had *not* betrayed her, Gwen realized; the letter truly was from Lord Scarborough. The letter and the "token," which, based on the size of the box, could only be a piece of jewelry. And though the message might be torn to bits and jammed into her shoes with the rest of the scraps, the earl would certainly discover the disappearance of an expensive necklace or bracelet. She gazed at the letter, studied the box, and as her mouth began to quiver with frustration, the doorbell pealed. She raced across the entry hall, but at this juncture she fancied the devil himself might well be calling, and she cautiously cracked the door.

"Lord Fullerton!" She threw the door on open, seized

his arm, and literally dragged him across the threshold.

"I find your hysteria a trifle unwarranted, Mrs. Hathaway," the viscount said wryly as Gwen slammed the door behind them. "I cannot be above five minutes late, and I assure you that matters have proceeded exactly as we planned. Papa left for Essex at half-past six this morning, and"—he patted a pocket of his cutaway coat —"I have his letter here—"

"No, you do not!" Gwen hissed. "I have Lord Scarborough's letter, the one *he* wrote." She waved it under his nose. "I daresay he sent his coachman over just prior to his departure . . ."

Her voice expired in a moan, and Lord Fullerton snatched the paper from her hand. He frowned a bit as he began to read, but—to Gwen's perverse satisfaction—he grew increasingly pale as he continued.

"I daresay the token is a necklace," he muttered, when, evidently, he reached the second paragraph. "Papa fairly showers his *chères amies* with necklaces; he maintains a ready supply so he will not have to knock up a jeweler when the impulse strikes."

"Mama is *not* a . . . a . . ." But it was hardly the time for dissension, and Gwen bit her lip.

"And this quite confirms the validity of the letter." His lordship stabbed one long finger at the last paragraph. "Did you notice the reference to a celebration next Thursday? Even I had forgotten that next Thursday is Papa's sixtieth birthday. I fancied at first that the handwriting is a trifle larger than his normal script, but I daresay he was merely in a hurry. No, there can be no doubt about it: the letter is genuine."

He passed it gingerly back to Gwen, as if it had begun to burn his fingers, and she refolded it, replaced it in the envelope, and carefully refastened the seal. "What are we to do?" she asked. She was still moaning a bit.

"I am frankly at a loss to say." The viscount seemed uncharacteristically subdued. "We could easily destroy the letter, substituting my message in its place, but I perceive no way to dispose of the necklace. I cannot suppose that Lady Ross, fortune hunter though she is, would keep it without a word of comment."

Gwen swallowed another angry retort because his words had given her the glimmer of an idea. "We can send it back!" she whispered triumphantly. "Your father himself mentioned that his gift is rather improper, and we shall capitalize on that remark. We shall return the necklace with an indignant note from Mama. She will say that Lord Scarborough has demeaned her and she wishes never to see him again—"

"Would you be demeaned if Sir Neville presented you an expensive necklace?" Lord Fullerton interposed.

"Of course I wouldn't, but Neville and I are *engaged.*"

"It appears to me that Papa and Lady Ross are engaged as well," the viscount said coolly. "Or have, at least, reached some sort of understanding: he refers to their 'mutual home.' So it further appears that you are most eager to humiliate Papa. It has not escaped my attention that under your proposal, he alone would be jilted."

"He would *not!*" Gwen protested. It was entirely unlike him to be so obtuse, and she stamped her foot with impatience. "We need only put your letter in place of this one"—she waved Lord Scarborough's communication again—"and hide the necklace until I can compose a suitable note from Mama."

"But Mrs. Cunningham's butler took the box from Gibson," Lord Fullerton pointed out. "He—the butler, that is—will undoubtedly mention it to Lady Ross."

This was a distinct possibility, Gwen conceded, and she gnawed her lip a moment. "Then you must write another letter," she said at last. "You must say that the necklace is in the way of a farewell gift."

"In which event Lady Ross would not feel constrained to return it. A fortune hunter's dream come true."

"If you are concerned about the money," Gwen said furiously, "I shall find some means to repay you."

"I am concerned about Papa!" his lordship hissed. "He has poured his heart out upon that sheet of paper"—he

indicated the earl's letter, now shaking in Gwen's hand—
"and proved his sentiments with an expensive gift—"

"He has proved nothing!" Gwen stamped her foot once
more. "By your own admission, Lord Scarborough
scatters jewels about like so many drops of rain."

"And he is to be rewarded by a curt letter of dismissal."
The viscount went on as though he had not heard her.
"In theory, yes, the jilting would be simultaneous; in
execution, only Papa would be hurt. Lady Ross would
travel back to Kent and dangle her trophy about for a
time before she sold it. A fortune hunter's dream come
true," he repeated.

Gwen wanted nothing more than to lash out at him—
her free hand fairly itched to strike him—but she reminded herself that this might well be their last opportunity to separate Mama and the earl. She gulped down
rage and pride alike, fancying they left a bitter aftertaste
in her mouth.

"Let us not draw a hasty conclusion, Lord Fullerton,"
she pleaded. "Let us, for the present, hide both your
father's letter and the box; I shall make some excuse to
Crenshaw. We have several days yet to determine a
proper course of action—"

"Gwen?" Lady Ross was poised on the landing,
peering into the vestibule. "Whom are you talking to,
dear?"

It was clear she could not see the viscount from where
she stood, and Gwen shot him a desperate signal, darting
her eyes toward the library. But he stood his ground, and
as Mama began to descend the stairs, Gwen's eyes flew to
the side table. The box remained nearly invisible, still
balanced precariously against the wall, and Gwen
casually crossed her arms, thrusting Lord Scarborough's
letter behind her back.

"It is Lord Fullerton!" Mama trilled when she reached
the foyer. "But what brings you here so early in the day?
In other circumstances, I might conclude that you are
sparking my daughter."

To Gwen's vague astonishment, his lordship colored a bit, but he soon recovered himself and flashed one of his fetching smiles.

"Would that it were so"—he affected a great sigh—"but I fear I've come on a mundane errand, Lady Ross. Papa desired me to ensure that Gibson, his coachman, had delivered his letter. Papa's letter, that is."

He reached forward, deftly plucked the envelope from Gwen's fingers, and extended it to Lady Ross. She tore it eagerly open, pulled out the message, began to read; and her bright countenance swiftly collapsed.

"Seven days," she wailed softly. "Charles is to be gone for seven days." She read briefly on, then glanced up and about the entry hall. "He refers to a token," she said. "Where is the token, Lord Fullerton?"

"Token?" The viscount frowned and gazed around as well. "I'm afraid I couldn't say; where *is* the token, Mrs. Hathaway?"

"On . . . on the side table." Gwen's lips were almost paralyzed with fury.

Lady Ross rushed to the table, located and retrieved the box, and raced up the steps again, box and letter alike clutched to her bosom. When she had rounded the landing and disappeared, Gwen turned back to Lord Fullerton.

"I fancy it would be best if we were to abandon our project," she said coldly. "You are obviously determined to pursue your own course at any rate, with no consideration of our mutual interests—"

"*Our* interests or *your* interests, Mrs. Hathaway?" His voice was quite as frigid as hers. "If the latter, which I strongly suspect, I cannot perceive that any great harm has been done. To the contrary, I enticed Papa to quit town, thereby ensuring that he will not meet Lady Lynch. And that has been your true concern from the start, has it not? That Papa and Lady Ross would come between you and Sir Neville?"

"My true concern has always been for Mama's happiness," Gwen insisted. She wondered, even as she said it, whether this was entirely true.

"Lady Ross seemed happy enough to receive Papa's token. And if she is happy and he is happy, have we the right to interfere?"

"How you have changed your mind in ten short days!" The bitter taste was in her mouth once more, and she fairly spat the words out.

"Yes, perhaps I have changed my mind about a number of things," he said rather distantly. "Be that as it may, I agree with you that it would be best to abandon our project, and I see no point in further discussion. Therefore, if you will excuse me, I believe I shall go to White's."

He strode to the door without a bow, without so much as a nod, flung it open, stepped outside, crashed the door to behind him. Gwen continued to gaze in his wake long after the echo had died away, wondering why she did, in fact, feel most abjectly and utterly abandoned.

—9—

Eventually the clatter of Lord Fullerton's carriage died away as well, and Gwen gazed sightlessly across the vestibule, suddenly so tired she doubted she could climb the stairs to her bedchamber. However, as she trudged up the first flight, she was forced to own that the viscount had been right on at least one head: Lord Scarborough had been safely removed from London, and there was no longer any chance that he would encounter Lady Lynch. So was Lord Fullerton not also correct in saying that one of Gwen's primary objectives had been realized? Of course he was, she conceded: she had always been as much concerned for her own future as for Mama's. The viscount was a far nobler person than she, Gwen further admitted: he was willing to swallow his objections to Mama in order to ensure his father's happiness. On the other hand, it was easy enough for Lord Fullerton to be noble: he did not have a disapproving fiancé to contend with.

Gwen shook her head, rounded the landing, and was struck by a solution so simple that she wondered how she could possibly have failed to perceive it before. She had only to be honest with Mama, she thought with growing excitement. Yes, she need only explain Sir Neville's opposition to Lord Scarborough (perhaps confessing that she herself had been quite won over by the earl) and ask Mama to defer the announcement of their engagement till after Gwen and the baronet were married. At that juncture, Lady Ross could wed Napoleon himself, and there would be little Neville or his mother could do about the matter. Yes, honesty was certainly the best policy, particularly since her and the viscount's devious machinations had proved most dismally unsuccessful.

She would not speak to Mama until Sir Neville and Lady Lynch had left London, Gwen decided, passing the first-floor landing and speeding up the next flight of steps. The delay would give her nearly two more days in which to devise a proper approach, and there would be no danger that the baronet might get wind of her new plan. But as soon as the Lynches had quit town . . .

Gwen reached the second story, fairly flew along the corridor, and had nearly reached her bedchamber when she was caught up by a voice behind her.

"Gwen?" Lady Ross cried. "Come here, dear; you *must* see what Charles has given me."

Having determined to postpone their conversation, Gwen was in no frame of mind to admire and discuss the earl's present, but she glimpsed no suitable means of escape. She reluctantly retraced her steps to Mama's room and peered inside.

"Do you see?" Lady Ross demanded. "Is it not exquisite?"

In point of fact, Gwen did not see, for Mama was standing sidewise to the door, preening before the cheval glass. But at length she turned, and Gwen could not repress a gasp of astonishment. The necklace, for such, indeed, it had proved to be, was not merely "exquisite"; it was the most magnificent piece of jewely Gwen had ever beheld—a wide choker, fashioned mostly of diamonds, with perhaps half a dozen perfect roses spaced at even intervals about it. The roses were done in emeralds, and they made Mama's eyes look as brilliantly green as the stones themselves.

"Is it not exquisite?" Lady Ross said again.

"It . . . it's beautiful," Gwen stammered. "I fancy Lord Scarborough said the truth: you will hardly be able to forget him."

"Forget him?" Mama repeated sharply. "How did you know Charles said that?"

How indeed? "I . . . I merely guessed. It's precisely the sort of thing Lord Scarborough *would* say."

"It's precisely what he did say." Lady Ross turned back to the mirror, preened a moment more, frowned. "He also suggested that such a gift is a trifle improper. What do you think, Gwen?"

"Would you be demeaned if Sir Neville presented you an expensive necklace?" Lord Fullerton's voice echoed in her ears, and Gwen shook her head. "Not . . . not in the circumstances," she replied.

"You have altered your opinion of Charles then!" Mama clapped her hands with joy. "I am so delighted, dear." She unfastened the clasp, replaced the necklace in its box, gazed lovingly at the box. "Charles further proposed that I should wear the necklace in his absence so as not to forget him." She didn't seem to realize that she was repeating herself.

"And so you should, Mama," Gwen agreed, eager to terminate the discussion. "If you'll excuse me now . . ."

"However, I shall not wear it while he is away." Lady Ross went obliviously on. "I shall save it until his return. Until our ball."

"Very well, Mama." Gwen nodded absently and stepped into the hall, registered her mother's words and whirled back round. "Our ball?" she repeated.

"I conceived the idea just a few minutes ago." Mama clapped her hands again. "As it happens, the day of Charles's return—next Thursday—is his sixtieth birthday."

"Yes, I know," Gwen murmured.

"How do you know *that?*" Lady Ross asked.

"Lord Fullerton chanced to mention it."

"It strikes me that you have become exceedingly friendly with Viscount Fullerton," Mama said.

"Lord Fullerton and I are not friendly in the least!" Gwen protested. "Which is not to say that we are *un*-friendly . . ." Though she could not have explained why, her cheeks had grown decidedly warm, and her voice trailed off.

"Hmm." Lady Ross regarded her daughter with considerable suspicion, and Gwen hastily lowered her eyes. "In any event, as I stated, Charles's birthday is next Thursday, and I intend to hold a surprise ball in his honor."

"A surprise ball for Lord Scarborough?" Gwen's eyes flew up, but her nascent objection died on her tongue. By Thursday the Lynches would be long gone from London, and in their absence, the proposed assembly could cause no possible harm. "That is an excellent notion, Mama."

"An excellent notion?" Lady Ross's look of suspicion briefly deepened, but she soon shook her head with amazement. "You really have modified your view of Charles, haven't you? You will assist me with the assembly then?"

Gwen hesitated, realizing that she had not fully thought out her new plan. If she remained in London following Neville's departure, she would tacitly be deceiving the baronet, implying that she and Lord Fullerton were still plotting to separate their parents. But if she accompanied Sir Neville back to Kent without first speaking to Mama, Lady Ross and the earl might well seize upon the occasion of his birthday celebration to announce their engagement. The third, and surely the best, alternative was to speak with Mama at once, and, ill-prepared as she was, Gwen cleared her throat.

"Mama, there is a . . . a rather delicate matter we really must discuss—"

"There is no time for that now, dear," Lady Ross interposed crisply. "If we are to conduct a ball in a scant week's time, we must begin writing the invitations at once."

"I shall help you write the invitations very shortly," Gwen promised. "However, I cannot stay in town for the assembly—"

"What invitations?" Gwen spun around and watched, her mouth going dry, as Lady Lynch strode into the bed-

chamber. "What assembly?" Her ladyship's pale blue
eyes darted curiously from Gwen to Mama.

"Olivia!" Lady Ross's own eyes widened a bit. "I have
attempted repeatedly to see you, but Maggie invariably
informed me you were too ill to have guests. Am I to
collect that your condition has improved?"

"Somewhat." Lady Lynch drew a heavy sigh. "Of
course my health is never *good*," she elaborated quickly,
"but I daresay I feel as well as can be expected."

"Splendid," Mama said brightly. "Then perhaps you
will assist with the invitations too. I am planning a
surprise ball for—"

"Mama!" Gwen screeched. "The assembly can scarcely
be a *surprise* if the news gets about."

"I suppose not," Lady Ross agreed dubiously. "At any
rate, the ball is to take place next Thursday evening—"

"And unfortunately Lady Lynch and Neville will be
unable to attend," Gwen interrupted. "They are return-
ing to Kent on Saturday."

"Saturday?" Her ladyship frowned. "How did you
come by that idea?"

"Neville indicated you would quit town as soon as your
carriage was repaired, which, as I understood, will be no
later than tomorrow."

"Neville did *suggest* we quit town Saturday," Lady
Lynch said. "However, now there's to be an assembly, I
certainly shan't consent to leave. No, I am seldom well
enough to enjoy even the *slightest* amusement, and I
cannot afford to squander my rare moments of good
health. Of *relatively* good health. No, I shall definitely
stay for the ball, and I shall be pleased to help with the
invitations."

"But . . . but . . ." Gwen ground her fingernails into
her palms, frantically seeking deliverance from this
monumental new complication. "But we cannot have an
assembly," she blurted out at last. She was hard pressed
to determine whether Mama or Lady Lynch looked the
more puzzled. "It was silly of us not to remember,
Mama, that Aunt Constance has no ballroom."

"I *quite* remembered that Connie has no ballroom," Lady Ross snapped. "We shall use the saloon and the parlors; it is done all the time."

"It is done all the time by people with very large houses," Gwen said desperately. "Much, much larger than this one, and I am sure Aunt Constance would agree—"

"You are sure I shall agree to what?" For a big woman, Mrs. Cunningham was remarkably light on her feet; she had slipped into the room without a single rustle of her muslin skirt.

"Well, we shall soon see," Mama said. "The fact is, Connie, that I wish to have a surprise birthday ball for—"

"Mama!" Gwen warned.

"—for a *certain party*," Lady Ross finished, "whose identity I fancy you can guess."

Evidently Aunt Constance could indeed surmise the mysterious guest of honor, for she assumed a fierce glower of disapproval.

"Gwen thought it an excellent notion," Mama added.

"Guinevere thought it an excellent notion?" Mrs. Cunningham's scowl gave way to an expression of sheer astonishment, but apparently she decided that this was some new—albeit inexplicable—effort to dissolve her sister's liaison with Lord Scarborough. "Then we must certainly do so," she said firmly. "Conduct the assembly, that is."

"But Gwen now fears your facilities are inadequate," Lady Ross went on.

"Inadequate?" Aunt Constance pondered this latest contradiction at some length and eventually bobbed her head. "Then Guinevere must prefer to hold the ball elsewhere!" She flashed her niece a triumphant, conspiratorial smile.

"No," Gwen muttered. "No, I daresay we can have the assembly here after all."

Not surprisingly, Mrs. Cunningham's demeanor had deteriorated to one of utter bewilderment, but she had no opportunity to comment further, for Mama was once more clapping her hands.

"Oh, it will be such fun!" Lady Ross trilled. "I had hoped to start the invitations at once, but it has since occurred to me that I've no proper cards. If I may borrow the carriage, Connie, I shall hurry to the stationer and be back by one. With all of us working, I fancy we can complete the invitations within a few hours, and we shall then consider the food and the flowers and the orchestra . . ."

Mama chattered on awhile, but at last she dismissed them, and Gwen raced down the corridor without a word of farewell to anyone. Once inside her bedchamber, she collapsed against the door, her heart drumming in her ears, her palms soaked with perspiration. Never in her wildest nightmares had she envisioned an event so disastrous as the ball. It would have been sufficiently serious had Lady Lynch observed Mama and Lord Scarborough together in any circumstances, but a chance encounter might perhaps have been explained away. As it was, there would be no question that Lady Ross and the earl had formed an exceedingly strong attachment indeed, and it was entirely possible they *would* take advantage of the assembly to announce their engagement.

In short, the ball had to be prevented, and Gwen glanced nervously at the mantel clock. The hands were just approaching eleven, and they were to begin the invitations at one. Two hours remained, but it could as well have been two minutes, two seconds, for Gwen's mind was totally blank. If only Lord Fullerton were here to help her . . .

Lord Fullerton! Gwen rushed to the wardrobe, pulled her casquet bonnet from the shelf, and fairly jammed it on. She snatched up her gloves and reticule and literally ran out of the room, along the hall, and down the stairs. By some miracle, she met no one during her headlong flight, but she did not stop running till she had reached the intersection of Oxford Street.

Gwen paused to regain her breath and reflected that she could not possibly walk to White's; to be seen alone in St. James's Street would be scandalous in the extreme. Fortunately a hackney coach soon rolled toward her, and she hailed it and issued instructions to the driver.

"White's?" he echoed doubtfully. "That's a men's club, ma'am."

"I am quite aware of what it is," Gwen snapped. "Just drive me there as quickly as you can."

He nodded, though still rather dubiously, and Gwen entered the coach and sat wearily down. As the carriage clattered to a start, she realized she might well be at the point of making a dreadful cake of herself. Worse, she amended grimly: she might make an awful cake of herself and still accomplish nothing. The viscount had clearly stated that he would interfere no more between Mama and Lord Scarborough, but surely, when she explained how very essential it was to prevent the ball . . . For the first time, Gwen felt the swelling of a lump in her throat, and she closed her eyes and sniffed back an infuriating threat of tears.

"This is White's, ma'am," the driver announced.

The coach had stopped, and Gwen peered fearfully out at the new bow window of the club. It was reported that Beau Brummell often sat there for hours, passing acid judgment on the world beyond the glass. He was probably there now, Gwen thought darkly, wondering what member had fallen so low that he was compelled to rely on public transportation. Perhaps Lord Fullerton was with him, maliciously speculating as well—

"Ma'am?" the driver called sharply.

"Yes . . ." Gwen gulped. "Yes, I wish you to go inside and ask for Viscount Fullerton. Tell him Mrs. Hathaway must see him."

The driver sighed, as if to say that he had anticipated just this sort of foolishness, but he left his perch with only moderately poor grace and strode to the door. Gwen watched as the door opened, then closed again, and imagined all manner of horrid possibilities. The driver had no doubt stated her name in a great ringing voice clearly audible throughout the building, and dozens of members were crammed into the bow window, leering out at the carriage . . . After a seemingly interminable wait, the door opened once more, and, to Gwen's unutterable relief, Lord Fullerton preceded the driver through and hurried to the street.

"Mrs. Hathaway?" The viscount opened the coach door and studied her with alarm. "Whatever is the matter?"

"I . . . I . . ." But the tears were welling up again, and her voice expired in a strangled little cough.

"No, this is scarcely the place to talk, is it?" Evidently he had misinterpreted her abrupt pause, and he turned to the driver. "Please take us down to King Street," he said, "and on to St. James's Square, and then around the square."

"Yes, milord." The driver nodded. "And then where?"

"Just keep driving round the square till I tell you to stop," the viscount replied rather grimly.

"Yes, sir."

The driver smirked a bit, and Gwen shuddered to contemplate his assessment of the situation. He surely supposed her to be Lord Fullerton's mistress, probably fancied she had discovered herself in an embarrassing condition . . . But there was no time to dwell on it: the driver resumed his place on the box, the viscount climbed into the carriage, slammed the door, and the coach rattled to a start again.

"Now, Mrs. Hathaway." Lord Fullerton rotated toward her in the seat. "Now you must tell me what is wrong."

"I . . . Mama . . . You . . ."

To Gwen's unspeakable horror, the tears broke through at last, and she succumbed to a fit of uncontrollable sobbing. She was making a worse cake of herself than she could possibly have feared, and she tried to hide her face in her hands, tried to turn away. But suddenly— she was unsure precisely how it happened—she found herself in the viscount's arms, her face buried in his shoulder.

"Mrs. Hathaway," he murmured. "I do pray you'll forgive me; I didn't intend to overset you so."

Gwen recollected his view that women were inclined to fall apart in any crisis, and his gratuitous apology distressed her even further. She fairly burrowed into his shoulder, dismally aware that her bonnet had slipped half off and that she was no doubt ruining his splendid superfine coat.

"Mrs. Hathaway," he repeated. "Please, I beg you to stop crying."

Gwen was not entirely able to do so, but eventually her sobs subsided to sniffles, and she started to choke the story out. She had intended to speak frankly with Mama, she began, to ask her only to postpone her engagement to Lord Scarborough. And when Mama proposed a birthday ball for the earl, Gwen had seen no harm in it, not until Lady Lynch appeared and announced that she would stay in town for the assembly. "And then Aunt Constance came," she sniffed, "and as I had no chance to warn her, she agreed to the ball. And you must help me prevent it; you simply must. If the assembly goes on as planned, Lady Lynch will learn of Mama's attachment to your father, and she won't allow Neville to marry me . . ." She gulped back a threatened new freshet of tears and firmly bit her lip to stop its trembling.

Lord Fullerton said nothing, and perhaps it was the very silence that made Gwen abruptly, intensely aware of his nearness. She could feel the steady beat of his heart against her, the whisper of his breath on her temple; she fancied she could feel every muscle in the lean, strong arms around her. She waited, hardly daring to breathe herself, not knowing what it was she expected, wanted, feared. At length he released her, pushed her gently, slightly away, and she observed that his slate-colored eyes had darkened, had turned nearly black and entirely unreadable. She sensed that he was hesitating too, and she dimly realized that if he touched her again, if she permitted him to touch her again, she would cross some irrevocable line. She continued to wait, wondering—as though she were watching someone else—what she would do if he attempted to pull her back into his arms. But at last he shook his head and moved to the far side of the seat.

"I shall help you, Mrs. Hathaway," he said. His voice was a trifle hoarse and not altogether steady, and he cleared his throat.

"Thank . . . thank you," Gwen stammered. She could not quite define her emotion; maybe it was a peculiar blend of relief and disappointment. "I shouldn't have troubled you except that I could think of no way to prevent the ball without your assistance. It now seems to me that you need only tell Mama your father would object most strenuously to a celebration in his honor—"

"No." The viscount once more shook his head. "Lady Ross would perceive at once that you had sought me out, and I daresay she would judge such a circumstance exceedingly suspicious."

Yes, Gwen recalled, Mama already judged her "friendship" with Lord Fullerton suspicious. The recollection brought a blush to her cheeks, and she gazed studiedly at her hands.

"I can think of no credible way to prevent the ball either," his lordship went on. "My notion is to prevent Papa's *attendance* at the assembly."

"But how?" Gwen's eyes flew back to his face. "Lord Scarborough will not know the ball is in his honor, of course, but he will be excessively eager to see Mama after their separation. I very much doubt you can persuade him to decline the invitation—"

"Mrs. Hathaway." The viscount flashed his familiar wry grin, and the spell between them—whatever spell there might have been—was firmly, finally broken. "In the first place, Papa will not *receive* an invitation to your mother's ball; I shall destroy it as soon as it arrives. That clearly leaves the likelihood that Harold or Amanda will mention the assembly to him, and I shall try to avert that eventuality by delaying Papa en route. Papa is a creature of habit: during the course of his travels, he invariably stops for refreshment at certain inns along the road. Since he will be coming from the north, I fancy he will visit the Queen in Newham, and I shall await him there. I shall manufacture some errand that must be performed at once, and by the time we reach Berkeley Square, Harold and Amanda will have departed for the ball."

"Then . . . then you will not be at the assembly either," Gwen said.

"No, and I should think my absence all to the good. If I were at the ball, Lady Lynch might well remember me, inquire as to my identity, and begin to add two and two together. As it is, you have but to advise Sir Neville to keep a close eye upon his mother, to allow her no private conversation with any of the guests. Then you, of course, must ensure that *your* mother not reveal to Lady Lynch the name of the missing guest of honor."

It would work, Gwen decided; it had to work. "Yes, I shall," she said aloud. "And I should once more like to thank you for your help."

"I am delighted to be of service, Mrs. Hathaway."

Gwen fancied she detected a bitter undertone in his voice, but perhaps that was her imagination, for his expression was altogether blank. He instructed the driver to return them to White's and did not speak again until they had stopped in front of the club.

"I should offer to accompany you back to Orchard Street," he said, "but it would not do for Lady Ross to see us together."

"No," Gwen agreed. "No, it wouldn't."

"Will you be leaving for Kent immediately after the ball?"

Gwen had given the matter no thought, but, upon reflection, she could conceive no reason to remain in town beyond the assembly. "I suppose I shall," she said.

"Then in the event I do not see you again prior to your departure, permit me to say that I have quite enjoyed our . . . our acquaintance."

"Yes," Gwen murmured. "Yes, so have I."

"Good day then, Mrs. Hathaway."

He opened the carriage door, climbed out, and directed the driver to proceed to Orchard Street. As he strode away, Gwen recollected that it would not do for Mama to see her in a hackney coach either; and by the time she had requested the driver to deposit her at the intersection of Orchard and Oxford, Lord Fullerton had disappeared.

Not see him again, Gwen thought as the carriage once more rattled into motion. Indeed, it was possible she would never see him again; she certainly would not if Mama and Lord Scarborough ultimately parted after all. And even if Lady Ross did wed the earl, it was entirely likely that Neville would refuse to associate with the rakeshame Lovells.

Gwen drew a deep breath and recognized the same emotion she had experienced earlier: that odd mix of disappointment and relief. She could not define her feeling for the viscount, could not explain her reaction when he had held her in his arms; but she understood that he posed some sort of threat to the calm, secure life she had planned. On the other hand . . . But there was no "other hand," Gwen told herself sternly, and as soon as she and Neville were safely back in Kent, she would put Lord Fullerton altogether out of her mind.

The hackney driver discharged Gwen at the specified intersection, and as she hurried up Orchard Street, she calculated that it was not yet one o'clock. She slipped through the door of the house and sped toward the staircase; with any luck, Mama would not learn of her mysterious absence.

"Where the devil have you been?"

Gwen whirled around, and Neville stalked out of the library and across the vestibule to meet her.

"I . . . I had an errand to attend," she said.

"An errand?" he echoed incredulously. "At a time like this? Mama has lately informed me that we are to stay in London for the grand assembly Lady Ross is conducting on Thursday. An assembly in honor of *someone's* birthday, and I can well surmise who *someone* is." He lowered his voice. "Is it Scarborough?" he whispered fearfully.

"Yes." Gwen nodded.

"Good God! You assured me that you and Fullerton had the situation entirely in hand."

"And so we do," Gwen said soothingly. "Lord Fullerton has promised to prevent his father's attendance at the ball—"

"So that is where you were," the baronet interposed grimly. "Plotting with Fullerton again." His pale blue eyes narrowed. "You look excessively disheveled," he snapped. "Excessively flushed."

Gwen didn't know whether she had been "flushed" to begin with or not, but his accusation rendered her cheeks unquestionably warm, and she hastily straightened her hat. "I . . . I was in a monstrous hurry," she stammered. "As you yourself pointed out, time was of the essence." In fact, he had not pointed this out at all, and Gwen rushed on before he could issue a correction, briefly explaining the viscount's plan. "It will then be left to you," she concluded, "to make sure your mother doesn't hear about Mama and Lord Scarborough from anyone else. You must remain with her every moment, guide her every conversation into harmless channels."

"I daresay it will work," Neville conceded grudgingly. "Fortunately, Mama doesn't care to dance . . ." He stopped and squared his shoulders. "But let there be no mistake about it, Gwen: on the day following the assembly, we shall all depart for Kent. You and I and Mama. Fullerton will have to pursue his schemes without you; I shall tolerate no further delay."

"Yes, Neville," she said meekly.

"Very well. Then I fancy you should . . . should freshen up a bit before anyone else observes your lamentable appearance."

"Yes, Neville."

Gwen continued across the foyer and started up the steps, and she had reached the first landing before she recollected one of Lord Fullerton's remarks. The viscount had not exactly *promised* to prevent his father's attendance at the ball; he had said he would *try* to do so. But surely that was merely a figure of speech . . . Gwen shook her head and raced on up the staircase.

—10—

Along with the rest of Aunt Constance's household, Gwen was immediately and totally caught up in the preparations for Mama's ball. At one o'clock, as scheduled, she and Mama, Aunt Constance and Lady Lynch repaired to the breakfast parlor and began to write the cards of invitation. Lady Ross had already composed a guest list and divided it into four equal parts, and Gwen was careful to take the section that contained Lord Scarborough's name, lest Lady Lynch note the inclusion of the notorious earl. She then toyed with the notion of "overlooking" his lordship, but she feared Mama would discover her "mistake" and remark upon it in Lady Lynch's presence. So she penned the earl's name and direction on one of the envelopes after all, hoping Lord Fullerton would be sufficiently alert to destroy it before it could be observed by anyone else in Berkeley Square.

After the invitations were finished and entrusted to Tilson for delivery, Lady Ross elicited their opinions as to the flowers, the music, and the supper menu; and during the interminable debate that followed, Gwen recollected the sorry state of her wardrobe. However, she soon decided she couldn't possibly afford a new gown, and even if she could, the viscount would not be there to admire it. She further recollected that she had resolved to put *him* altogether out of her mind, and she hastily returned her attention to the discussion, which currently centered on Mama's preference for yellow roses versus Aunt Constance's keen partiality to red.

On Friday Gwen accompanied Lady Ross to the florist, where Mama ordered a combination of yellow *and* red roses, and the caterer; and on Saturday they interviewed some half-dozen orchestra leaders, Lady Ross wishing to be assured that the group selected was *quite* able to play a decent waltz. Aunt Constance wanted to start the cleaning of the house on Sunday, but —recalling Lady Lynch's intense opposition to Sunday labor—Gwen persuaded her to wait till Monday. The task proved to require nearly four full days, and Gwen soon found herself racing up and down the stairs again, helping to ensure that every chandelier was polished to a spotless sparkle, every floor waxed to a mirrorlike shine, every speck of dust removed from every piece of furniture.

By late Thursday afternoon, all appeared to be in readiness: the house fairly shone from cellar to roof, the roses had been tastefully arrayed about, and the caterer's staff were setting up supper tables in the library and the morning parlor. Lady Ross supervised the last preparations, critically surveyed the final results, and pronounced herself satisfied.

"Indeed," she declared, "if I do say it myself, I believe the assembly will be simply *splendid*. Oh, Charles will be so surprised. So *thrilled*."

She clapped her hands with joy, and, not for the first time, Gwen felt a twinge of conscience for her mother's bitter disappointment when Lord Scarborough failed to appear. But there was nothing to be done about it, and she merely nodded and retreated to her bedchamber to make her own preparations.

Gwen had decided to wear the yellow dress again: it was the least unsatisfactory of her limited choices, and the ever-vigilant Lady Jersey had not been invited to the ball. Maggie attempted to change her mind, pointing out that it was not the yellow gown's "turn" to be worn. But Gwen insisted, and eventually the abigail sighed, evidently resigned to Mrs. Hathaway's utterly inadequate wardrobe. She still looked like a milkmaid, Gwen thought, examining her reflection in the cheval glass, but there was nothing to be done about that either. Nor did it matter: tomorrow she would leave London, and it would be months, possibly years, before she once more mingled with the *ton*.

"And the white satin slippers, I suppose, ma'am?" Maggie was sighing again.

"Yes, please."

Gwen adjusted her bandeau while Maggie went to the wardrobe and withdrew the shoes, and, in the mirror, she saw the maid frown.

"I do believe there is something *in* the slippers, ma'am." She reached inside one of the toes and pulled out a handful of scraps. "Some . . . some paper, it appears."

"The paper!" Gwen whirled around and managed a bright smile. "Yes, I . . . I often put paper in my shoes so they will hold their shape."

"But wouldn't it be easier to use whole pieces?" The abigail's frown deepened. "Instead of tearing it into little bits?"

"I daresay it would!" Gwen eagerly bobbed her head. "That is an excellent suggestion, Maggie."

The maid shook her own head—no doubt adding "stupidity" to her mental catalog of Mrs. Hathaway's deficiencies—but she brought the slippers across the room and emptied out the scraps. She then helped Gwen into the shoes, into her jewelry, into her gloves; and Gwen hurried out of the bedchamber and along the corridor.

The assembly was to begin at nine, and as it was already five minutes before the hour, Gwen fancied that Mama had long since gone down to the saloon. However, as she passed her door, she observed it ajar, and Lady Ross cried out to her to come inside.

"I cannot decide what to wear," Mama lamented when Gwen stepped into the room. "To best set off the necklace."

It did apear that she had been pondering the matter at some length: she was clad in only her underthings and Lord Scarborough's glittering choker, and every gown she owned was strewn on the bed.

"I have a white dress trimmed in green," Lady Ross went on, "and a green one, but neither of those is the *right* green. So perhaps I should wear the white one with *no* trim. Or should I wear the white satin with the *rose* trim? Rose goes with green, does it not?"

Gwen quickly inspected the indicated gowns and counseled Mama to select the plain white.

"Very well," Lady Ross agreed. "I shall at least try it on again."

"Try it on!" Gwen protested. "It lacks but three minutes to nine, Mama."

"Is it that late?" Lady Ross gasped. "Well, it doesn't signify; I shan't announce the surprise till midnight. Till we start supper. But I daresay you should rush on down, dear, and greet the guests as they arrive. When Charles comes, assure him that I shall be there very shortly."

She smiled and fondled the necklace a moment, and Gwen sped back into the hall and down the staircase. She once more regretted Mama's imminent disappointment, but, perversely, she was relying on this very factor to keep Lord Scarborough's identity a secret. Lady Ross might well conclude that the earl *had* jilted her; in any event, she was unlikely to advise Lady Lynch that her intended guest of honor had spurned his invitation to the ball. Poor Mama. But his lordship would call tomorrow, of course, and explain that his invitation had been lost, that he had been unavoidably detained en route to London . . .

Aunt Constance, Lady Lynch, and Sir Neville were milling about the drawing-room entry, the latter gazing fretfully at the long-case clock, which was just chiming the hour. The baronet was clad in the same ensemble he had worn to Lady Bascomb's rout, and Gwen calculated that he had gained another half-stone in the intervening weeks. Indeed, he was coming more and more to resemble his mother, who—her perennial "ill health" notwithstanding—was far too plump and threatened fairly to burst the seams of her simple muslin dress. Aunt Constance, for her part, was attired in an elegant, perfectly fitting gown of midnight blue net over satin; and despite her great, raw bones, her rather horsish face, she looked almost pretty.

"It is nine o'clock," Neville announced gratuitously. "Where is Lady Ross?"

"She has been delayed a moment," Gwen replied, "but I fancy she'll be down soon."

The baronet pursed his lips with disapproval: he would never be late to a ball and certainly not his *own*.

"Do not tease yourself about it, Neville," Gwen snapped.

Now that the fateful hour had struck, she was exceedingly nervous, and she peered fearfully over her shoulder, expecting to find Lord Scarborough bounding up the stairs. But he was not, and she realized it was scarcely fair to punish Sir Neville for her own poor humor.

"Do not tease yourself about it," she repeated in a more moderate tone. "Mama desired me to greet the guests in her stead." They had previously agreed that as the group was to be relatively small, there would be no receiving line.

"You?" Aunt Constance protested. "I fancy I am the logical substitute; it is my house."

"It may be your house," Lady Lynch said, "but I did at least as much to prepare for the assembly as you did. Furthermore, I am Fanny's dearest friend."

This was so far from being the truth that Gwen's mouth briefly fell open, but there was no time to continue the argument; the doorbell pealed, signaling the arrival of the first guest. Apparently they must have a receiving line after all, and Gwen determinedly stationed herself at the head: if Lord Scarborough did come, perhaps she could somehow forestall his introduction to Lady Lynch. Tilson ushered Lady Bascomb up the staircase, Crenshaw announced her, and behind Gwen the

rest of the reception committee jostled for position. Gwen
thought Lady Bascomb eyed her yellow gown with some
disdain, but she was far beyond caring for anything so
trivial. She murmured a polite welcome and passed her
ladyship on to Aunt Constance, who had evidently
defeated Lady Lynch in the battle for second place.

By half-past nine the saloon was excessively crowded,
many of the guests already dancing, and Gwen permitted
herself a sigh of relief. If Lord Fullerton's plan had
failed, she reasoned, the earl would have reached the
assembly promptly at nine, eager to see his beloved. As it
was—she glanced around and performed a rapid mental
count—it appeared that virtually all the invited guests
had arrived. She waited five minutes more, but Tilson
escorted no one else up the steps, and she suggested to
Aunt Constance and the Lynches that they disband the
line. They nodded and wandered away, and Gwen
prayed that Sir Neville would keep his wits about him.

She glanced around again, glimpsed Lord and Lady
Blake, and suffered a sudden jolt. If Neville engaged the
Blakes in conversation, Lord Scarborough's name would
inevitably come up; indeed, the viscount might well
mention their potential connection to Lady Lynch.
Gwen's stomach fluttered with panic, and her eyes raked
the crowd for Neville. But he and his mother had disappeared, and Gwen hurried toward the Blakes, intending, if necessary, to guard them throughout the evening.

"Mrs. Hathaway." The viscount frowned down at her,
and Gwen entertained a horrid notion that he was
reading her mind. "Where is your charming mother? I
should hate to learn that she was taken ill at the last
instant and compelled to miss her own ball."

"No, no, nothing like that," Gwen said rather too
brightly. "No, Mama is still dressing; I fear she tends to
be a bit skitter-brained in matters of time."

"I am delighted to hear it. That Lady Ross is not ill, I
mean. I shall look forward to greeting her soon."

There was a silence, and Gwen perceived that she
should inquire after Lord Scarborough; it would look

extremely odd if she did not. "But where is your father?"
she asked in the same overbright voice. "I have observed
that *he* is normally very punctual."

"I was wondering the same thing," Lord Blake replied.
"As you are no doubt aware, he has been out of town
above a week, but we expected him back by today. It is
his birthday, you know."

"N-no, I didn't know," Gwen stammered. "I . . . I do
hope he has come to no harm."

"I fancy not," his lordship said. "Papa is quite in-
destructible, and I daresay he has merely been delayed."

Another silence. Gwen was not certain that normal
courtesy dictated an inquiry after Lord Fullerton, but she
was overcome with curiosity.

"And your brother?" she asked casually. "Where is
Viscount Fullerton?"

"I'm afraid I couldn't say. He drove out in his curricle
early this afternoon, but I've no idea where he was going.
Nor when he planned to return."

"I see."

Gwen repressed another sigh of relief, for it was clear
that Lord Fullerton's plan had worked, that he had
successfully intercepted the earl. The orchestra ended the
current quadrille, and Lord Blake's eyes darted about
with unmistakable impatience. Gwen looked round as
well, searching for Neville, but there was no sign of him.
She *must* keep the Blakes talking, and as she groped for
some fascinating topic of conversation, there was a great
gasp in the drawing room, followed by a hush, followed,
in turn, by an eerie hiss as everyone began to whisper at
once.

Gwen spun toward the entry, anticipating the worst,
but it was only Mama who stood there, smiling at her
guests. And though Lady Ross did look stunning in her
white gown, her swaying ostrich plumes, Lord Scarborough's necklace, Gwen hardly judged her beauty sufficient to generate such excitement.

"Good God!" Lord Blake choked. "That . . . that necklace!"

"Is it not lovely?" Gwen said. "Your father gave it to her."

"Good God," the viscount repeated. "It is a duplicate of the one he gave the Golden Vixen. Her roses are of rubies rather than emeralds, but . . . Good God; what could Papa have been thinking?"

His question was obviously rhetorical, but Gwen pondered it nevertheless, her mind whirling with confusion. The earl's letter had persuaded her that he sincerely loved Mama, so Gwen could only assume he had made an appalling error of judgment. Perhaps he didn't realize the choker was so distinctive, didn't perceive that it would be universally recognized. And the terrible irony of it—that the necklace he had given Mama chanced to be like that of the Golden Vixen. His lordship could not have known that that particular bird of paradise had a special, awful significance for Lady Ross and her daughter; his judgment, however poor, could not have been clouded to that extent . . .

The whispering intensified, became a murmur, a buzz, and Gwen ceased her speculation and rushed toward the entry. Mama must be told before the situation grew any worse—although, Gwen thought grimly, there seemed no way it *could* grow worse.

"Gwen!" Mama trilled. "Evidently you recommended the right dress, dear, for it seems I have made a great hit."

"Lady Ross!" Lord Blake panted up beside Gwen, jerking Lady Blake behind him. "My dear Lady Ross, I can only apologize, apologize most abjectly, for my father's reprehensible conduct. I cannot imagine what he was at—"

"Fanny!"

Lord Scarborough loomed up over Mama's shoulder, and the buzz in the saloon became a roar. The situation had grown worse after all—infinitely worse—and Gwen's knees weakened most alarmingly. She feared, then *prayed*, she was at the point of an apoplectic seizure, preferably fatal. But Lord Blake solicitously

took her arm, and Lord Scarborough chattered on.
"My dear Fanny." He seemed entirely oblivious to the
furor in the drawing room. "I am deeply sorry to be late,
but I daresay I should count myself lucky to be here at
all. Mr. Fowler fell ill, and we were unable to conclude
our negotiations till late this morning. We drove back
like the devil, but I nearly missed your assembly nevertheless, for it appears my invitation was mislaid. I should
not have known of the ball except for Culver, my butler;
he mentioned that Harold and Amanda had gone to Lady
Ross's assembly. But it doesn't signify, does it? I *am* here
and happy indeed to see you."

He gave Mama a fond smile, his eyes swept eagerly
over her, and the smile abruptly faded.

"Good God!" He blanched. "Where the *deuce* did you
get that necklace?"

"Oh, come now, Charles," Mama said coquettishly.
"We are amongst family; you can admit to your magnificent, generous gift."

"*My* gift? My dear Fanny . . ."

His voice sputtered off, and Gwen feared *he* was at the
verge of a seizure. But eventually he lowered his head
and began to whisper in Mama's ear, and she soon turned
as pale as he. At length the earl straightened and stepped
behind Mama, unfastened the necklace, removed it,
dropped it in his pocket; and the crowd in the saloon
emitted another incredulous gasp.

"I have explained the . . . the character of the necklace
to Fanny," his lordship said tightly, "and assured her it
was not a gift from me."

"Not from you?" Lord Blake echoed. "Who could have
sent it then?"

Who indeed? Gwen felt the stirring of a terrible
suspicion, and her knees grew weak again.

"That is precisely what I intend to discover," the earl
replied grimly. "I suspect this necklace"—he slapped his
pocket—"is merely a paste imitation; I shall have it
checked at the earliest opportunity."

"An imitation?" Lord Blake said. "Then perhaps Chad

was right. You no doubt recollect, Papa, that he fancied one of your former . . . ah . . . friends was responsible for the letter. It must have been the Golden Vixen, and when that maneuver failed, she had her necklace copied, hoping to embarrass Lady Ross."

"That is possible," the earl agreed. "However, as it happens, I do chance to possess a necklace identical to this one." He colored a bit. "At least I did a week since; we shall soon see if it has disappeared. In the interim, I judge it best to proceed with the ball as though nothing were amiss. I shall put the word about that someone has perpetrated a nasty prank—"

"Fanny!"

Lady Lynch stormed past Gwen and Lord Blake, elbowing the latter in the ribs, and he grunted with pain and dropped Gwen's arm. Evidently her ladyship *had* suffered a seizure, Gwen noted distantly; at any rate, her face was altogether purple. She planted herself in front of Mama, trembling from head to toe with indignation, and Sir Neville rushed up beside her.

"Fanny!" Lady Lynch repeated. "I have never been so shocked, so horrified, so mortified, so . . . so . . ." But apparently she could conjure up no further adjectives. " . . . in all my life. Mr. Lovell indeed!" She cast Lord Scarborough a baleful glance. "Though I suppose I shouldn't wonder that you elected to hide the identity of your . . . your paramour."

"Paramour!" Mama screeched.

"Who is this person?" Lord Scarborough demanded.

"Lady Lynch," Gwen begged, "please listen a moment—"

"Lady Lynch," the earl interposed smoothly. "I am delighted to make your acquaintance at last."

He reached for her hand, and she snatched it away, stumbling several steps backward in the process.

"Do not touch me!" she shrieked. "I am well aware of your reputation, and you must not think to seduce me as you did Fanny."

Lord Scarborough's mouth quivered. "I shall not attempt to seduce you, Lady Lynch," he said solemnly. "Nor have I seduced Fanny. You, all of you"—he tossed his gray head toward the throng in the drawing room— "have quite misconstrued the events of the evening. In point of fact, I did not give Fanny the necklace which has created such a stir; it was someone's notion of a trick. My intentions toward Fanny are honorable in the extreme; indeed, I hope to make her my wife—"

"Your wife!" Lady Lynch yelped. "That is even worse. Well, it is not *worse,*" she amended, "but it is certainly no *better.* No, I will have nothing to do with you, Lord Scarborough; not in any circumstances. And if Fanny is to be connected with you, I will have nothing to do with her either."

"*Please,* Lady Lynch," Gwen pleaded. "Please be reasonable—"

"Or with you either," her ladyship snapped. "You deceived me as well, with your 'Mr. Lovells' and the squirrel in the tree when Fanny was riding by in that curricle, *his* curricle, I fancy . . ." She ran out of breath and stamped her foot. "No, I will not associate with any of you again. I only regret that I must spend another night in this house, but I fear it's a trifle late to set out on the road. However, you may be assured that I shall leave at *dawn* tomorrow."

She started to stalk away, then spun back round. "If I *survive* until tomorrow," she added dramatically, "for I have also never been so *ill* in my life. Come, Neville; see me to my room. Perhaps, with rest, I may recover."

Lady Lynch sagged against the baronet, and as he assisted her through the entry, Lord Scarborough took Mama's arm and escorted her on into the saloon. The earl spoke briefly with Lady Bascomb, and when he turned to Lady Heathcote, Lady Bascomb turned to Lady Sefton. Yes, Gwen thought, word of the "prank" would soon be all about; Lord Fullerton's plan had failed—

"Are you all right, Mrs. Hathaway?" Viscount Blake

asked anxiously. "I do believe Papa will soon set matters aright."

"Yes, I daresay he will," Gwen murmured. "And I am fine; I only need to rest a moment."

Lord Blake nodded, guided her to a nearby chair, bowed, led Lady Blake away; and Gwen ground her fingernails into her palms. Lord Fullerton was excessively clever, she conceded: after sending the necklace to Mama, he had come ahead to Orchard Street, pretending that their plot was to proceed. He had manufactured all manner of reasons not to hide "Papa's" gift, and Gwen now owned that her suspicions should have been aroused. But she had fancied him "nobler" than she, willing to swallow his objections to Mama.

Naturally the viscount had intended for Mama to wear the necklace while Lord Scarborough was away; he had carefully suggested as much in his letter. With the earl out of town, unable to explain the truth, Lady Ross would not have been merely "embarrassed"; she would have been utterly humiliated, forced to slink back to Kent on the first mail. So Lord Fullerton must have been most distressed to learn that Mama planned to save the necklace for her projected birthday ball, but he had recovered very nicely. He had, of course, insisted that the assembly could not be prevented, meanwhile scheming to ensure his father's absence. He had probably been honest about his machinations on that head: he had no doubt destroyed the invitation and driven out from London to intercept Lord Scarborough on the road. Except that he couldn't know precisely when the earl would return from the north; he would have been compelled to travel to Newham for several days together. Had he encountered Lord Scarborough yesterday or the day before, he would have fabricated some "errand" that required another lengthy trip.

But the viscount's devious, treacherous plan had failed: his father had been delayed and had raced back to town "like the devil," not pausing for refreshment at his usual haunts. Gwen wondered if Lord Fullerton was still at the inn in Newham. She hoped so; indeed, she sincerely hoped he would remain there till his miserable flesh rotted from his wretched bones.

Gwen felt a prickle of tears behind her eyelids and tried to persuade herself that her reaction was one of pure, white anger. But she soon recognized that it was more than that, worse than that: she had believed the viscount to be her friend, and he had betrayed her. Betrayed her coldly and carelessly, with no thought as to how his plot might affect her future with Neville . . .

Neville! Good God. Gwen blinked her tears away and peered around the drawing room. But the baronet was not in sight, and upon reflection, Gwen judged that he would be obliged to spend the rest of the evening with his mother. She wondered whether she should join them, apologize to Lady Lynch, beg her forgiveness; but she decided it would be best to wait till her ladyship's anger had cooled a bit. If, she thought grimly, ever it did.

Gwen stood wearily up, assumed her very brightest smile, and marched into the crowd.

—11—

Gwen had not expected to sleep at all, but apparently she did, for at some juncture she opened her eyes and found a bright ribbon of sunlight splashing through the draperies. She lay still a moment, staring sightlessly at the canopy above her head, and reviewed the final hours of the assembly. By midnight, when supper was served, everyone in attendance was quite persuaded that Lady Ross had been wickedly tricked by the Golden Vixen; but as this was nearly as delicious an *on-dit* as their original supposition, no one was disappointed. After the party were seated at the supper tables, Mama announced that the ball was in celebration of Lord Scarborough's birthday, and the earl blushed with embarrassed pleasure as the group sang several boisterous songs in his honor. His lordship then rose, and Gwen fully expected him to make an announcement of his own—that of his engagement to Lady Ross. But he did not; he merely thanked Mama and all assembled for his wonderful birthday surprise. Not that it signified, he had already declared his intentions to Lady Lynch . . .

Lady Lynch! Gwen bolted upright, peered at the mantel clock, and discovered it was approaching ten; if her ladyship had departed at dawn, as threatened, she had been gone for many hours. Gwen suddenly recollected Sir Neville's earlier insistence that they were *all* to depart for Kent today—he and his mother and Gwen as well—and she judged it an exceedingly ominous sign that he had neglected to have her wakened. Evidently he had left for Kent without her, and she thought it entirely possible that *she* would soon receive a letter of dismissal.

Gwen continued to sit in the bed, wondering what best to do. If she packed at once and borrowed sufficient funds from Aunt Constance to hire a chaise, she herself could be in Kent by early evening. The baronet might have composed his letter by then, but he would not have had an opportunity to post it, and perhaps Gwen could set matters aright with him and Lady Lynch. But if she quit town now, Gwen reflected, Lord Fullerton would never know that she had discerned his plan; he would assume that she, like everyone else, believed the Golden Vixen responsible for the necklace. And Gwen could not permit him that satisfaction, could not allow him to suppose he had successfully deceived her. No, she would go to Berkeley Square and exact her vengeance, however hollow: she would take keen delight in mocking the failure of his treacherous plot.

Gwen was dressed within half an hour, and though she had eaten almost nothing at supper, she was so impatient to confront Lord Fullerton that she decided to forgo breakfast. She hurried out of the house and down to Oxford Street, thinking to hail another hackney coach. But it was not a great walk to Berkeley Square, and— her blood fairly boiling now—Gwen doubted she could bear to be confined in a carriage. She strode briskly along Oxford Street to Davies and then down Davies, growing angrier and angrier as she walked; and by the time she reached Lord Scarborough's home, she was almost shaking with rage. No, she amended, when she raised her hand to ring the doorbell, she *was* shaking with rage, and she drew a deep breath in hopes of regaining some measure of composure.

"Good morning, ma'am." Gwen presumed it was Culver, the butler, who gazed at her from across the threshold.

"I wish to see Lord Fullerton," she snapped.

"Very good, ma'am." The butler stepped aside and

beckoned her through the door. "Who shall I say is calling?"

"Tell him it is a surprise," Gwen replied sweetly. "And say that I must see him without delay."

Culver frowned a bit at these rather unseemly requests but eventually nodded his agreement. "Yes, ma'am. May I ask you to wait in the library?"

He ushered her into the room on the left side of the foyer, bowed, retreated up the stairs, and Gwen's eyes darted briefly about. The furniture was very tasteful, obviously expensive, and in other cirumstances, she would have been eager to explore the contents of the towering shelves. As it was, however, she could only pace the Brussels carpet, desperately attempting to keep her fury under some semblance of control. At length she heard the tap of footfalls in the vestibule, and she whirled toward the door just as the viscount stepped through.

"Mrs. Hathaway! I must own that your visit *is* a surprise; I was in the process of dressing so as to come to you in Orchard Street."

Gwen did not suppose for an instant that he had intended to call on her, but he *was* clearly in the process of dressing: he was wearing only his pantaloons and shirt, the latter still open at the neck, the collar down. For some reason, his dishabille rendered him even more attractive than normal, and she willed herself not to succumb to his undeniable magnetism.

"Were you indeed?" she said coldly. "I daresay you planned to apologize for the failure of your efforts."

"Apologize?"

His slate-colored eyes flickered with puzzlement, and Gwen was again compelled to concede his enormous cleverness. He moved on into the library, moved unnervingly close, and Gwen backed well away.

"Apologize?" he repeated. "To the contrary, I count it most fortunate that I *did* fail to intercept Papa. Had he not arrived when he did, I collect—from Harold and Amanda's reports—that Lady Ross would have been hideously embarrassed."

"Oh, she would have," Gwen said bitterly.

"The necklace is a copy, by the by," he went on. "That is one of the things I wished to tell you: the original was still in Papa's box. And the copy is paste; Papa took it to his jeweler early this morning."

"Paste." Gwen shook her head. "How very niggardly of you, Lord Fullerton. I had hoped you would give Mama a small . . . small *token* to ease the pain of her humiliation. An expensive necklace might have provided some slight comfort. But, no, you must give her paste."

He was silent so long that Gwen fancied he hadn't heard her, but at last his eyes widened, and he assumed a perfectly splendid look of astonishment. "*I?*" he gasped. "You believe *I* sent the necklace to Lady Ross?"

"Do not waste your thespian talents on me," Gwen hissed. Had she tried to speak in a normal tone, she was sure it would have emerged a shout. "Extensive though they are—your dramatic abilities, that is—they may not be inexhaustible, and you can ill afford to expend them in a hopeless cause. I know very well what you were at, Lord Fullerton; I puzzled it all out last night. Puzzled it out without much difficulty, I might add, so perhaps you are not as clever as I thought. As clever as *you* no doubt fancy yourself to be. You had the necklace copied, had it delivered to Orchard Street . . ."

She continued to relate his scheme, immensely gratified to note that his eyes narrowed, and his jaws hardened, and his cheeks flushed with color as she spoke. "But you failed," she concluded triumphantly. "That is what I wished to tell *you*, Lord Fullerton: that I unraveled your plot and I am monstrous glad it failed."

There was another long silence as he stared down at her, his eyes narrowed to the merest charcoal slits. His expression was so forbidding that Gwen grew frightened, physically frightened, but eventually he expelled a great breath, and his eyes turned to shards of gray ice.

"I shall, for the moment, put aside the question that is uppermost in my mind, Mrs. Hathaway." Gwen had never heard a voice so frigid, had never imagined there could be one. "The question of how you could possibly believe me so dishonorable as to perform the actions you have described. I am almost as offended by the realization that you judge me sufficiently stupid to have conceived such a plan. To begin with, it would be entirely unworkable. Suppose Lady Ross *had* worn the necklace in Papa's absence—the very night of his departure, let us say. She would, indeed, have been wretchedly humiliated; it is quite likely she would have fled town. But as soon as Papa returned, he would have heard the story and rushed after her, and what would have been accomplished?"

"I daresay you had concocted some means to prevent Lord Scarborough from *rushing* after her," Gwen said. "You are a veritable storehouse of devious ideas."

"Very well." He nodded. "For the sake of argument, I shall grant that possibility and direct your attention to a second problem: your alleged plot is absurdly complex. The person who wrote the letter did not, in fact, know that Papa would return to London yesterday; he or she included the remarks about his birthday merely to persuade Lady Ross that the letter was genuine."

"Yes, I puzzled that out as well," Gwen said. "How good of you to admit it."

"I admit nothing, Mrs. Hathaway!" His hand flew up, and Gwen briefly thought he would seize her, shake her, but he shook his head and ran his fingers through his hair. "Good God, you try my patience," he muttered. "My point is that whoever wrote the letter did not know *when* Papa might come back. Do you fancy me an utter sapskull? If I had intended to breach our agreement, to humiliate Lady Ross, could I not have figured an easier way to do so? Why should I devise a complicated scheme that required her to wear a necklace within a few days of receiving it?"

"It wasn't complicated in the least," Gwen said. "Not in your view, at any rate, because you think Mama a fortune hunter. You no doubt believed she *would* wear the necklace the very night of Lord Scarborough's departure."

"I do admit to that, Mrs. Hathaway; I am frankly astonished that she did not. But I have always found women highly unpredictable, and I should never have *relied* on such a factor."

His tone had moderated considerably—indeed, he sounded almost mild—and Gwen felt a twinge of doubt. But he was excessively clever, she reminded herself; her snide remarks had been but a childish effort to set him down. He was infinitely clever and prodigious glib, and she shook her own head.

"As I indicated before, Lord Fullerton, you are quite wasting your talents. I do not credit a single word you have said, and I shall not believe anything else you might tell me."

"Then it appears I am wasting my time as well as my *talents*." His voice had gone frigid again. "I must consequently beg you to excuse me, Mrs. Hathaway; as you yourself pointed out, I should not squander my limited resources in a hopeless cause."

He gave her a nod so brusque as to be effectively non-existent, turned away, strode to the door; but Gwen caught him up.

"There is one more thing, Lord Fullerton." He turned back round. "You once mentioned that your father keeps a *supply* of necklaces on hand. Was it only by chance you elected to copy the one like the Golden Vixen's? No, I fancy not; I daresay that was a cruel little embellishment of your plot."

"There was no plot, Mrs. Hathaway," he said wearily.

"Why didn't you *tell* me?" Gwen's anger had not abated, but another emotion had crept beneath it—the abject sense of betrayal she had experienced at the assembly. "We talked about her the day we drove to the park; why did you not tell me the Golden Vixen was one of Lord Scarborough's women? Had you conceived your plan even then?"

Evidently her voice had risen; at any rate, the viscount glanced over his shoulder and crossed to her side again.

"I shall not continue to bore you with my insistence that there was no plan," he said. "I did not tell you of Papa's liaison with the Golden Vixen because I didn't want to prejudice you unreasonably against him."

"*Unreasonably!*"

"Your reaction merely proves the wisdom of my course. The Golden Vixen has no particular significance to anyone but you; one cyprian is precisely like another."

"I shall defer to your opinion in that regard," Gwen said frostily, "for I am sure you are an expert judge of cyprians. Indeed, now I think on it, I can only own *myself* a sapskull ever to have trusted you. I knew your reputation before we met—"

"Ah, my reputation." His voice was very soft, but there was a bright, dangerous glitter in his charcoal eyes. "I am glad you brought that up, Mrs. Hathaway; I had nearly forgotten my foremost question. Which was, you may recall, the question of my honor. I now collect that your view of my character is based entirely on my past. My presumed past, I should have said; I have ever been haunted by my boyhood indiscretion. I count it most unfair, and I sometimes regret I am *not* the magnificent rake I've been rumored. Be that as it may, I do feel you could have granted me some small credit for my conduct with you."

"Your conduct with *me?* You deceived me, betrayed me—"

"I had you in my evil clutches, Mrs. Hathaway, and I let you go. Surely you remember our hackney ride." He closed the space between them, and Gwen tried once more to back away, but his long, lean fingers clamped upon her shoulders. "I let you go," he repeated, "and as I received no credit, I should like to rectify my error."

His mouth smashed down on hers, hard, punishing, but he lifted his head almost at once and gazed down at her. Gwen distantly thought he had scored his point, exacted his own vengeance; that if she tried to back away

again, he would again let her go. But the brief touch of
his lips had unleashed a strange, wild excitement, a
raging curiosity; and she hesitated and was lost. His arms
slipped round her, and when he took her mouth again,
his was gentle, almost lazy, and Gwen parted her lips as
though she could somehow drink him in. His mouth
moved to her throat, and she strained against him and
found her fingers in his hair; she had always wanted to
touch his hair. His lips returned to hers, hungry now, and
his hands on her body were urgent, but Gwen was
powerless to resist him. Whatever he was, whatever he
had done, he had stirred something deep within her,
something she had never known was there. She wanted
this, wanted more, and the world beyond Lord Fullerton's arms had altogether ceased to exist.

But exist it did, for there was a sudden furor in the
street outside: the clatter of a carriage, the snort of a
winded horse, an incomprehensible shout. The viscount
released her, stood her away, and Gwen could only stare
at him, stunned by the intensity of her response. His eyes
seemed black, but perhaps that was merely in contrast to
his skin; she had never seen him so pale.

"Gwen," he whispered. "Gwen, please listen to me—"

The front door crashed open, and Gwen heard the
drum of rapid footfalls in the vestibule.

"Lord Fullerton!" A frantic bellow. "Lord Blake! Lord
Fullerton! Lord Blake!"

The viscount rushed to the library door and into the
foyer, Gwen hard on his heels. "Stop your yelling,
Gibson!" he yelled. "Here I am; what is it?"

"It is Lord Scarborough, sir," the coachman panted.
"He has had an accident, a dreadful accident—"

He was interrupted by the arrival of two grooms, or so
Gwen assumed, and she gasped when she saw the form
they bore between them. The earl was utterly limp, there
was an enormous gash on his forehead, and rivulets of
blood ran down his face and spilled onto his neckcloth.

"Good God!" Lord Fullerton said. "What the deuce
happened?"

"Oh, it was terrible, sir; simply terrible—"

"Never mind," the viscount snapped. "We must get him to his bedchamber and fetch the doctor."

"I took the liberty of attending to that, sir. Lady Bascomb chanced to be driving by when the accident occurred, and I asked her to fetch Dr. Saunders, and she very kindly consented—"

"Never *mind!* We must take him to his room."

They started up the stairs, Lord Fullerton helping to support his father, Gibson trailing behind and whimpering under his breath. Gwen would not have followed without being asked except that she was most awfully dismayed by the sight of Lord Scarborough's blood. She dashed back into the library, opened her reticule and snatched out her handkerchief, pounded up the staircase, and began mopping the dreadful cut on his lordship's brow. Blood continued to seep from the wound, rendering her handkerchief quite soaked, but Gwen judged this a good sign: she was under the impression that corpses did not bleed.

At length they reached the second story, reached the chamber at the end of the corridor, and the grooms deposited the earl in a great four-poster bed. Lord Fullerton dismissed them and busied himself with his father's clothes—removing the neckcloth and shoes, unbuttoning the waistcoat and shirt.

"You must help me with his pantaloons," he snapped to Gibson, who was hovering just beside him, still whimpering and now wringing his hands.

The viscount seemed entirely oblivious of Gwen's presence, but modesty clearly dictated an immediate exit. She slipped into the corridor, closed the door, and sagged against the nearest wall. The earl's accident had briefly driven the scene in the library from her mind, but her cheeks now blazed in recollection of her shameless behavior. She did not want to face Lord Fullerton again —today or ever—and her inclination was to flee back to Orchard Street at once. But she realized that she would be compelled to inform Mama of Lord Scarborough's mishap, and it would surely be best to know the physician's prognosis when she did. She gazed impatiently toward the stairs, and as if in answer to her unspoken summons, a black-clad figure hove into view and hurried down the hall.

"Lady Blake," he panted as he arrived at her side. "I am sorry to encounter you again in such unfortunate circumstances."

Since Gwen did not resemble Lady Blake in the least, she could only hope the doctor's vision would improve when he examined Lord Scarborough. But she elected not to issue a correction; she merely nodded and opened the earl's bedchamber door. Dr. Saunders bounded into the room, leaving the door ajar, and Gwen heard a short, indecipherable murmur of conversation. Then the door creaked fully open, and Lord Fullerton emerged and pulled it to.

"I am excessively eager to finish our discussion," he said. He gazed down at her, his eyes turning black again, and Gwen felt another rush of color into her face. "However, as I am sure you understand, I must first look to Papa—"

The door once more opened, and Gibson stepped into the corridor. "Dead," he muttered as the door clicked shut behind him.

"*Dead!*" the viscount barked. "Papa is *dead?*"

"No, sir; at least I pray not." He wrung his hands again. "No, I was just remarking to myself that one of the *rabbits* is dead. The others got away."

"Rabbits?" Lord Fullerton echoed. "What the devil are you talking about?"

"That is how the accident happened, sir: his lordship was driving in Hyde Park when a herd of rabbits hopped out of the bushes and in front of his curricle."

Gwen did not believe rabbits traveled in "herds," but she chose not to correct this either.

"Some half-dozen, I'd guess," the coachman went on. "That's very odd, isn't it, sir? I've never seen so many rabbits together and certainly not in Hyde Park."

"Yes, that is very odd." The viscount looked at Gwen, his eyes narrowing a bit, but she could neither agree nor disagree, for she knew nothing about rabbits. "And I daresay the rabbits quite terrified Papa's horses."

"Well, of course they did, sir; you know how skittish his horses are. The worst part of it is that he was on his very way to Tattersall's to trade them for another team. Well, not his *very* way; we were actually driving to Lady Ross's."

"We?" Lord Fullerton repeated. "You were in the curricle with Papa?"

"No, sir; I was just behind in the barouche. Lord Scarborough had arranged everything with Lady Ross, you see. Her ladyship had been begging him to trade the bays, he told me; she thought they were much too wild. So last night he finally agreed, and he was to take Lady Ross to Tattersall's to help him pick another team. He promised her ladyship he'd drive the bays just once more through the park and on to Tattersall's, but she wouldn't ride with him even *that* far. So I was driving behind him so as to fetch Lady Ross . . . I did, by the by, sir, also take the liberty of asking Lady Bascomb to notify Lady Ross of the accident. After Lady Bascomb had spoken to the doctor."

"Very good, Gibson. To return to the *accident*"—the viscount seemed to stress the word a bit—"I collect that when the rabbits appeared, Papa's horses bolted."

"That they did, sir; I'll warrant they could have outrun any entry at Newmarket. They trampled one of the rabbits—I believe I mentioned that—and raced on down the road. His lordship got them round the first curve, but when they came to the second, they ran off into the grass. It was monstrous bumpy, as you can imagine, and Lord Scarborough was jolted out of the seat and struck his head against a tree. One of the grooms was with me in the barouche, and after we'd put his lordship in the carriage, I instructed him to drive the curricle back. I do hope *he* will come to no harm."

"Oh, I judge that very unlikely," Lord Fullerton said grimly. "Do you not concur, Mrs. Hathaway?"

"I . . ." Why was he asking her? He knew her irrational fear of horses. "I'm afraid I couldn't say," she murmured.

"No? How unfortunate; I'm sure your opinion would be most instructive. Indeed, I suggest you consider the matter while I confer with Dr. Saunders—"

"Gwen! Lord Fullerton!" They all whirled toward the stairs and watched as Mama streaked down the corridor, her bonnet ribbons untied and flapping round her shoulders. "Oh, my poor dear Charles," she wailed, panting to a stop beside them. "Is he . . . is he . . ." She observed Gwen's bloody handkerchief, and her wail became a shriek.

"Please!" Lady Ross's scream had masked the creak of the bedchamber door, and they all spun round again at the sound of Dr. Saunders' voice. "Please," he repeated. "I have just explained to Lord Scarborough that he must have rest. Rest and *quiet.*" He cast Mama a look of keen vexation.

"But he will survive . . ." " . . . be all right . . ." " . . . recover . . ." " . . . mend . . ."

They all posed the question in one form or another, and the physician nodded.

"Yes, I am confident his lordship will enjoy a full recovery. However, I suspect he has been concussed, and I have consequently insisted he remain in bed till I advise him to the contrary. I shall, of course, return each day until he is *quite* well." He smiled for the first time, perhaps calculating the magnitude of his fee. "In the interim, he wishes to see 'Fanny.' "

"Oh, my poor darling!"

Mama rushed past the doctor, rushed into the room, and he winced as she slammed the door behind her.

"I do pray . . . er . . . Fanny will remember that his lordship requires *rest,*" he muttered.

Gwen started to inform the physician that "Fanny"

was not at all the sort of woman he supposed, but, on second thought, it didn't seem to signify.

"Thank you, Dr. Saunders." Lord Fullerton's voice was ragged with relief. "Please show the doctor out, Gibson, and check to see that the curricle is safely back."

"Yes, sir."

The coachman walked toward the staircase, beckoning Dr. Saunders in his wake, and Gwen glanced nervously at the viscount.

"I . . . I fancy I should go too," she stammered. "I was only waiting to learn your father's condition—"

"Yes, I daresay you were." Lord Fullerton gazed down at her, his eyes narrowed to the merest slits, and eventually shook his head. "I shall freely confess, Mrs. Hathaway, that you have quite amazed me. As you know, I began some days since to regret our treatment of Papa and Lady Ross, and I somehow collected that you were a trifle remorseful as well. Be that as it may, I should never have judged you capable of murder."

His words were so shocking that Gwen momentarily thought she had misunderstood. But he was still staring at her, his eyes now pale as frost, and she frantically shook her own head.

"*Murder?*" she gasped. "You can't possibly believe that I attempted to kill Lord Scarborough."

"No, I shall give you the benefit of doubt, Mrs. Hathaway. I shall assume you set out merely to injure Papa, to injure him so severely that a wedding would be out of the question for some time to come. But you were surely aware that the 'accident' could prove fatal, and you proceeded nevertheless. You knew the nature of Papa's horses, and when you heard him and Lady Ross making their plans at the assembly last evening—"

"I heard nothing! I had no notion what they were at—"

"You decided to seize your final opportunity." He went heedlessly, relentlessly on. "I now perceive why you imagined—or affected to imagine—that I should concoct an absurdly complex scheme, for yours was ludicrous in the extreme. Rabbits, for God's sake! Wherever did you get them? You must have been compelled to drive into the country and purchase them from a breeder. From someone who raises rabbits for food. Could you conceive no easier way to frighten Papa's horses?"

Gwen wanted nothing more than to stalk away from him, to leave him babbling of rabbits for the rest of his days, but she realized she could ill afford to do so. If he truly believed she had caused the earl's mishap, he might well notify the police.

"Be reasonable, Lord Fullerton," she said as levelly as she could. "I was here when the accident occurred, here with you—"

"And wasn't that convenient?" he drawled. "No, Mrs. Hathaway, I did not suppose that you personally loosed the rabbits; you clearly had a confederate. Sir Neville, I should guess; apparently I misjudged the depth of his affection for you."

"Neville has quit town," Gwen protested desperately. "He left hours ago—"

"You hired someone, then—a street urchin, I daresay. Yes, for a penny or two, any little beggar boy would open a box of rabbits."

"Please, Lord Fullerton—"

"I've only one question. Did you come here, fabricate your wild accusations, merely to create an alibi? Or did you honestly think I had sent Lady Ross the necklace? Never mind; I don't expect an answer. You are fortunate in one regard, Mrs. Hathaway. Your plot was so very ridiculous that I dare not bring you up on charges; I fear I'd be viewed as a raving lunatic. However, a second *accident* would lend my story considerable credibility, would it not? I trust you are sufficiently clever not to take that risk."

"Lord Fullerton—"

"I wish no further conversation with you, Mrs. Hathaway. Not now and not in future. I therefore suggest you take yourself downstairs and summon your carriage."

"I . . . I have no carriage," Gwen said inanely. "I walked."

"Then you can damned well walk *back!*" the viscount hissed.

He turned on his heel, strode away, disappeared into the shadows at the far end of the corridor; and Gwen squeezed her blood-soaked handkerchief till her palm had grown quite red.

—12—

In the event, Gwen did not walk back to Orchard Street, for she discovered her knees almost too weak to bear her down the stairs and out of Lord Scarborough's house. Fortunately a hackney coach appeared just as she reached the footpath, and she raised her bloody handkerchief and flagged it down. The driver studied the gory cloth with considerable apprehension but eventually accepted her instructions and nodded her into the carriage. However, he must have judged himself at some risk, for they fairly raced back to Aunt Constance's, and when they arrived, he demanded two full shillings as his fare.

"Two shillings!" Gwen protested. "That is . . ." Her voice trailed off as she recollected that she had left her reticule in the earl's library. "That is more than I have," she muttered. "I shall have to go inside."

The driver refused to permit such a dubious character out of his sight: he trailed her up the front stairs and held the door ajar as Gwen stepped into the vestibule. Sir Neville bounded forward to meet her, and Gwen was reminded of Gibson because the baronet was also wringing his hands.

"Thank God you are back," he said breathlessly. "What is the news of—"

The hackney driver cleared his throat.

"I . . . I seem to have misplaced my reticule," Gwen

161

said. "Could you give the man two shillings for my fare, Neville?"

"Two shillings!" he barked. "For a trip from Berkeley Square?"

"Was it Berkeley Square?" the driver gasped. "I somehow had it in my mind that I picked the lady up in *Leicester* Square. It will be only one shilling, of course, sir."

Gwen thought even this rather too much, and evidently Sir Neville agreed: he grumbled aloud as he extracted a coin from his purse and added no tip. The driver snatched the proffered coin from the baronet's hand and rushed away, slamming the door behind him, and Gwen turned back to Neville.

"How did you know I was in Berkeley Square?" she asked.

"When I returned from my morning walk, Mrs. Cunningham advised me of Scarborough's accident, and I assumed you had accompanied Lady Ross to see him." Gwen elected not to correct this assumption. "Needless to say, I have been most eager to learn his lordship's condition."

"He has a dreadful cut on his head," Gwen said, "and the doctor believes he was concussed. But he was conscious when I left, and Dr. Saunders predicts a full recovery."

"Hmm." The baronet could not repress a small moue of disappointment. "We shall have to think of something else then."

"Think of something else?" Gwen echoed. "Surely *you* don't believe . . ." She suddenly remembered that he was not supposed to be here, that she had fancied him well on the way to Kent. "Why are you still in London?" she inquired. "Did Lady Lynch stay as well?"

"Oh, indeed not." He shuddered a bit. "No, Mama quit town at dawn, but I felt compelled to remain. It has become quite clear to me that you and Fullerton require my assistance." He frowned with annoyance. "I trust while you were in Berkeley Square you availed yourself of the opportunity to rip him up for his failure last evening."

"Yes, I ripped him up," Gwen said grimly.

"I must own that your *notion* was very clever," Neville said. "It was most ingenious of you to send Lady Ross that odious necklace. Had Fullerton succeeded in keeping Scarborough from the ball, I daresay *your* mother would have quit town at dawn this morning. But he did not, and, as I stated, it is now clear that I must help you."

"You think that I . . . that I . . ."

She stopped, for it was a gratuitous question: he obviously believed that she and the viscount had conspired to give Mama the "odious" necklace. Gwen briefly wondered how he could fancy her so cruel, briefly thought to set him straight. But she was not prepared to reveal Lord Fullerton's treachery; the wound was still too fresh.

"Never mind," she mumbled. "As I am sure you can imagine, Lord Fullerton was monstrous overset by the failure of the plan. Indeed, he and I have reached a . . . a parting of ways; we have decided not to plot against Mama and Lord Scarborough any longer." Gwen distantly congratulated herself for uttering not a single falsehood.

"I fear you will have to reverse your decision." The baronet heaved a great sigh. "The fact is—much as it pains me to tell you—Mama has forbidden me to marry you."

The worst had happened at last, and Gwen found herself remarkably calm. "Has she?" she said coolly. "And what was your response?"

"I . . . I offered none." He had the grace to blush. "I am in hopes Mama can be persuaded to forgive you— you and your mother as well. I have already convinced Mama that Lady Ross is not Scarborough's concubine," he added proudly.

"How splendid," Gwen snapped.

"Oh, it wasn't that difficult." He had clearly failed to

register her tone. "Mama is really very charitable by nature. Which is why, if we succeed in separating your mother from Scarborough, I am confident Mama will overlook their previous attachment."

"We cannot separate them, Neville," Gwen said wearily. "They are so suspicious by now that they would not be deceived by any scheme, however brilliant it might be. I had thought at one point to ask Mama to postpone the announcement of their engagement till after you and I are married. But I daresay it is too late even for that: Lord Scarborough informed your mother of his 'honorable intentions.' "

Sir Neville gnawed his lip a moment. "Perhaps it is not too late," he said at length. "If there is no public announcement of an engagement, you could tell Mama that Lady Ross's affection has cooled—"

"*I* could tell her?" Gwen interposed.

"*I* certainly won't lie to her," the baronet said indignantly. "At any rate, if Mama was under the impression that Lady Ross and Scarborough had dissolved their liaison, I believe she would withdraw her objection to our marriage."

"And if she did not?"

He flushed again. "I shall cross that bridge when I must."

"I see." She was so tired, so numb, that she could generate no anger. "Let me think on it, Neville. We have some days: they are unlikely to proclaim their engagement while Lord Scarborough is languishing in bed. Furthermore, I judge it unwise to speak to Mama until he has recovered; I doubt she would be in a receptive humor. Let me think on it," she repeated. "For the present, I am quite exhausted, and I must beg you to excuse me."

Gwen tottered toward the stairs, but she had not yet mounted the first riser when Sir Neville caught her up.

"It occurs to me that Fullerton might still prove useful," he said. "You could ask him to discuss the situation with his father, persuade *Scarborough* to defer the engagement."

Gwen spun around. "I do not intend ever to see Lord Fullerton again," she hissed; and before the baronet could respond, she whirled back round and raced on up the steps.

Gwen had said the truth about her exhaustion as well, and when she reached her room, she tumbled, fully dressed, into the bed. She fell asleep at once and did not wake until the mantel clock was chiming four, the hour at which Aunt Constance served dinner *en famille*. Much as Gwen dreaded the prospect of idle conversation, she had eaten scarcely anything for four-and-twenty hours, and she was nearly ill with hunger. She leapt out of bed, dashed to the cheval glass, and beheld a most wretched sight indeed: her dress was a hopeless mass of wrinkles, her eyes were puffy, and her hair was in total disarray. But there was no time for a proper toilette, and she straightened her hair as best she could and hurried to the dining room.

The rest of the party were already seated, already eating, already talking, but the conversation ceased as Gwen slipped into her chair. She gazed sheepishly around, intending to apologize for her tardiness, and observed Lady Ross in her customary place.

"Mama!" she said. "I fancied you would dine with Lord Scarborough."

"And so I should have except that poor Charles is resting. You no doubt recall that Dr. Saunders counseled a great deal of rest."

She sounded rather chilly, but Gwen counted that a symptom of her distress.

"Yes, I do recall," she murmured.

"I was telling the others about the accident," Lady Ross went on. "But I believe you know the story, do you not, Gwen? About the rabbits?"

Her eyes seemed a trifle hard, and Gwen entertained a sudden awful notion that she and the earl had overheard

Lord Fullerton's accusation. Had the viscount raised his voice as he spat out his terrible suspicions? Gwen reconstructed the scene in the corridor, decided he had not, and merely nodded.

"Yes, I know about the rabbits."

"Then I shall continue," Mama said frostily. "The rabbits, as I was saying, jumped out of the bushes . . ."

She proceeded to relate his lordship's mishap in excruciating detail, Neville and Aunt Constance hanging on her every word, Gwen paying scant attention and fairly wolfing down her food. Lady Ross conveniently ended her tale just as they finished the blancmange, and the baronet and Mrs. Cunningham sighed in appreciation of her narrative skills.

"And how long will Lord Scarborough be indisposed?" Gwen asked politely.

"A week or more, I should guess," Mama snapped.

Yes, Gwen thought, the strain of the earl's injury had definitely rendered Lady Ross cross as crabs.

Aunt Constance proposed a rubber of casino after dinner, but to Gwen's relief, Mama pronounced herself too tired and overwrought to play at cards. Sir Neville then invited Gwen to join him for a postdinner walk, but she declined, and he marched somewhat huffily out the front door. Gwen selected a new novel from Aunt Constance's library, returned to her room, and, early as it was, dressed for bed. She sprawled atop the counterpane and opened the book, but her visit to the library had inevitably reminded her of the library in Berkeley Square.

How could she have behaved so shamelessly? Her face flamed with the memory of her conduct, and though there was no one to see, she flung the book aside and buried her head in her hands. How could she have reacted so, and to Lord Fullerton of all people? To a man who had deceived her, betrayed her, a man who judged her capable of a heinous crime? It had been purely a physical response, of course, a perverse trick of nature, but why must she respond to *him?* She had found Peter's lovemaking distasteful at best, painful and degrading at worst; and Neville's chaste kisses had never aroused her in the slightest.

Gwen shook her head, retrieved the book, and tried to put the incident out of her mind. But she could not, and at length she closed her eyes and pondered the viscount's motives. His first brutal kiss had clearly been designed to punish her, but after that? After that, had he seen her as just another woman to seduce, merely another conquest? Somehow Gwen thought not; he had been so very pale . . .

Pale! Gwen's eyes flew open, and she sucked in her breath. She had seen Lord Fullerton almost as pale once before, when he had read the letter that accompanied the infamous necklace. And devious as the viscount was, Gwen did not suppose him able to regulate his blood supply. Which meant that he had *not* written the message, *not* sent the necklace; he had not betrayed her after all.

Gwen was briefly inclined to jump up, dress, order out Aunt Constance's carriage, race to Berkeley Square, beg Lord Fullerton's forgiveness; but she swiftly reconsidered. Though she had recognized her error, the viscount had not perceived his, and he might well refuse to see her. No, she amended, he *would* refuse to see her; he had unequivocally stated that he did not wish to speak to her again. She must write a letter then; curiosity alone would impel him to read it.

Gwen hurried to the writing table, but as she fumbled in the drawer for a sheet of paper, she realized that elation had temporarily clouded her mind. If Lord Fullerton was not to blame, someone *else* had sent the necklace to Mama. Furthermore, it now appeared certain that the same person had loosed the rabbits in Hyde Park. That was why Mama had been so overset at dinner: she and the earl were persuaded that his mishap had not been an accident. And as Lord Fullerton had pointed out, the "mishap" could easily have proved fatal.

Good God! The person, whoever he was, had to be

stopped before he could strike again, and Gwen
abandoned any notion of a letter. She must go personally
to Berkeley Square, convince the viscount of her
innocence, explain that his father's life was in danger
from another quarter. She slammed the drawer shut and
gazed at the wardrobe, wondering if she should go at
once. No, she decided; Lord Scarborough was safe in
bed, and Lord Fullerton was probably out for the
evening. She would go tomorrow, see the viscount tomorrow; and the prospect set her heart to drumming quite
madly against her ribs.

Gwen debated her choice of attire at considerable
length, eventually selecting an apple-green walking dress
with a high frilled collar and an emerald-green spencer which (or so she liked to believe) precisely matched
her eyes. Nevertheless it was only half-past seven when
Maggie straightened the last of the flounces round
Gwen's skirt, adjusted the last of her brown curls; and
Gwen judged this far too early to pay a call in Berkeley
Square. Consequently, though nerves had quite
destroyed her appetite, she went to the breakfast parlor
and managed to choke down half a slice of toast and one
cup of coffee. She then returned to her bedchamber,
donned her green French bonnet, and fussed a full ten
minutes with the ostrich plume adorning the crown.

Gwen descended the stairs as slowly as she could, but
her dawdling proved insufficient, for it was not yet half-
past eight when she reached the vestibule again. Still too
early to leave, she decided, so she began to pace the
foyer, attempting to rehearse her conversation with Lord
Fullerton. However, her thoughts grew ever more
muddled as she walked toward the stairs, toward the
door, toward the dining room, toward the library; and
when the clock in the latter struck a quarter to nine, she
could bear to tarry no longer. If she strolled very leisurely
to Berkeley Square, she would not arrive before nine, she
calculated; and she put on her gloves and proceeded to
the front door. Her hand was already on the knob when

the bell pealed, and she absently pulled the door open.

"Good morning, Mrs. Hathaway," the viscount said.

Gwen could not have been more startled to find the Prince Regent himself on the doorstep, and she felt her mouth drop indelicately open with astonishment.

"I trust you will forgive the earliness of the hour?" Lord Fullerton said politely. "I . . . I wished to return your reticule."

He extended it, his eyes never leaving her face, and Gwen took it, continuing to gaze at him as well.

"Thank . . . thank you," she stammered. "As it happens, I was just on my way to retrieve it."

"Yes, I observed that you are dressed to go out. You . . . you look quite handsome," he added gruffly.

"Thank . . . thank you."

They went on staring at each other, his eyes darkening to coals, Gwen's heart pounding so that she was certain he could hear it. All her rehearsing had gone for naught; her mind was whirling, utterly blank . . .

"I must talk to you!"

They spoke in unison, smiled simultaneously, rather shakily; and the viscount recovered first.

"My curricle is just outside." He affected a dramatic whisper. "Dare we risk another drive in Hyde Park? As I recall, that was how this bumblebath began."

"So it was," Gwen agreed, her voice not altogether steady. "But, yes, I fancy it would be best to speak in private."

To Gwen's relief, Lord Fullerton's curricle was not so high-sprung as the earl's, and his horses—a splendid pair of grays—were immeasurably better behaved. They clattered along in silence, Gwen reflecting that their previous excursion had created a bumblebath indeed. If only she could travel back to that day, decline his lordship's proposal . . . But would she? she wondered. Had she refused to assist him, she would not have seen him again, and that circumstance seemed somehow worse than her present coil.

The viscount drove well inside the park and, as he had

before, pulled off the road and stopped beneath a copper beech. Gwen thought he toyed rather too long with the reins, but at last he turned in the seat to face her.

"I shall permit you to speak first, Mrs. Hathaway."

Gwen did not *want* to speak first, but she doubted it would be any easier to delay, and she cleared her throat. "I . . . I want to apologize for the statements I made yesterday. I have since come to realize that you did not send Mama the necklace."

"Have you indeed? And what, may I ask, prompted you to that conclusion?"

"I . . ." But she couldn't tell him, could not confess that she had recollected his pallor after he kissed her, and she groped for a plausible alternative. "As you pointed out, I had no reason to suppose you so dishonorable."

"Not then, at any rate." He smiled, but his mouth wavered a bit at the edges.

"My only excuse"—Gwen rushed on—"is that you wouldn't allow me to hide the necklace from Mama and send it back."

"But my objections on that head were quite sincere. I had not recognized the depth of Papa's sentiments for Lady Ross, and I found myself . . ." He stopped, and his eyes briefly clouded. "The ironic aspect is, of course, that they were *not* Papa's sentiments."

"Whose then?" Gwen demanded rhetorically. "We have to discover that because the person who sent the necklace was surely responsible for Lord Scarborough's accident as well. You must believe me when I say that I had nothing to do with it—"

"I do believe you," Lord Fullerton interposed. "I didn't care a damn about your reticule; I also wished to apologize. *My* only excuse is that I was monstrous overset. When Gibson described Papa's mishap, I knew at once it was not an accident, and there you stood, waving your bloody handkerchief about . . ."

Gwen did not believe she had waved her handkerchief at all, but it didn't signify. She and the viscount were friends again, and despite the gravity of the situation, she was wildly, irrationally happy.. "Yes," she murmured. "Yes, I understand."

"There . . . there is one other matter, Mrs. Hathaway." He coughed, and a slight flush rose to his cheeks. "The incident that occurred in the library just prior to Papa's arrival. You are no doubt aware that I was exceedingly vexed with you, but I shall not claim that as an excuse. Indeed, there *is* no conceivable excuse, and I must simply beg you to overlook my odious conduct."

Odious conduct; he viewed the moment as nothing more than odious conduct. Gwen's joy evaporated, and she clenched her hands. "Yes," she said tightly. "Yes, I shall overlook it."

"Very well." He drew a rather ragged breath. "It occurs to me that amidst yesterday's tribulations, I neglected to inquire about Lady Lynch. Harold mentioned that she flew quite into the boughs at your mother's assembly."

"Yes, and she subsequently forbade Neville to marry me."

"Did she?" His tone was wonderfully casual, as though it didn't matter a deuce. "And what was Sir Neville's response?"

"He hopes to convince Lady Lynch that Mama and your father have parted. He wants me to persuade Mama to defer their engagement till after he and I are married."

"I daresay you agreed? As I remember, you once had a similar notion."

"Yes, I had a similar notion, but, no, I did not agree. I told Neville I would think on it."

"Really? And why is that?"

"This is hardly the time to discuss Mama and Lord Scarborough's engagement," Gwen snapped. "If we do not discover who is plotting against them, there may *never* be an engagement. Your father is temporarily safe in his bed, but as soon as he's up and about again, his life might well be in danger."

"Papa's life? Have you not perceived, Mrs. Hathaway, that Lady Ross is equally at risk?"

In point of fact, Gwen had not considered this, and her eyes widened with horror.

"Do not tease yourself about it," Lord Fullerton said soothingly. "I doubt the culprit would perpetrate another attack so hard on the heels of the last, so I fancy our parents are secure for the moment. However, you are quite right: we must unmask the plotter as quickly as we can."

He lapsed into silence, his brow furrowed in thought, and Gwen set her mind to work as well. She had been too shocked the night before to deliberate the plotter's identity, but she now reviewed every detail of his activities.

"It has to be someone in your household," she said at last.

"Why do you assume that?"

"Because the letter and the necklace were delivered by a man driving one of Lord Scarborough's carriages, and the letter was fastened with his seal."

"You saw them?" the viscount asked. "The carriage and the seal?"

"I saw the seal, and Aunt Constance's butler told me it was the same as the crest on the carriage door. He recognized it—"

"He *claimed* to have recognized it," Lord Fullerton interjected. "I believe you know my opinion of butlers: they are ever wont to project an air of omniscience. Furthermore, it is entirely possible that he was lying."

"Lying?" Gwen echoed. "Why should Crenshaw lie?"

"Because the plotter might reside in *your* household. Papa once mentioned that Mrs. Cunningham is violently opposed to him, and I'm sure I needn't remind you of Sir Neville's attitude. Though I daresay we can discount him since he quit London early yesterday morning."

"But he didn't," Gwen said slowly. "He didn't quit town after all, and he suddenly offered to assist us with *our* plotting."

"Did he?" The viscount's tone was excessively cool, and his jaws briefly hardened. "It could have been either of them then—Sir Neville or Mrs. Cunningham. He or she could have instructed Crenshaw to say that the letter and the package came in Lord Scarborough's carriage. Butlers also tend to be remarkably loyal; they well know on what side their bread is buttered."

"But you are forgetting the necklace itself," Gwen protested. "The original from which the copy was made is in *your* house, in Lord Scarborough's own jewel box."

"That means absolutely nothing." Lord Fullerton shook his gray head. "As you have undoubtedly surmised, the Golden Vixen's necklace is familiar throughout London, and I fancy any jeweler in the city could have duplicated it in paste. And it would have been quite logical for the plotter to specify emeralds rather than rubies; anyone acquainted with Lady Ross would have observed that her eyes are green."

"It appears to me," Gwen said stiffly, "that you are prodigious eager to shift the blame from your household. What of Lord Blake? Should he not be considered?"

"Harold?" The viscount laughed. "Harold possesses both the imagination and the courage of the rabbits that ran in front of Papa's horses. But, yes, I fancy he should be considered. Indeed, Mrs. Hathaway, we can ill afford to dismiss *anyone*. Crenshaw might well have said the truth: it would be an easy matter to paint a crest on a carriage door and paint it out again within the hour. In short, it is useless to speculate as to who the plotter is. Though . . . Though . . ."

"Though what?" Gwen prodded.

"Though I seem to have a vague recollection of rabbits." He frowned a moment, once more shook his head. "Never mind. I can't remember, and it is, as I stated, useless to speculate. I believe our only course is to *trap* the culprit, and in order to do that, we must force his hand."

"But how?" Gwen demanded.

"Use your pretty head, Mrs. Hathaway. The plotter is

obviously determined to prevent a marriage between our parents, so in what circumstances would he be compelled to act? Compelled to act _immediately?_"

"He would be compelled to act immediately if he thought they planned to wed immediately."

"Precisely. He would have to attempt to stop them if he believed they were eloping."

"_Eloping?_" Gwen gasped. "You intend to persuade Mama and Lord Scarborough to elope?"

"Mrs. Hathaway." He heaved an exasperated sigh. "I fear you have no natural talent for conspiracy, and evidently I have proved a lamentable teacher. No, of course we shall not persuade them to elope; we shall make it _appear_ that they've eloped."

"They can hardly elope while your father is confined to his bed," Gwen said testily.

"Indeed they cannot, so we shall have to await a suitable opportunity. I fancy it will come very shortly after Papa's recovery, for he does not take kindly to inactivity. In fact, we shall _create_ an opportunity: I shall put it in Papa's mind that he and Lady Ross should celebrate his return to health with a long drive in the country."

"And then?" Gwen asked.

"As soon as they are gone, we shall leave notes in both households declaring their intention and their destination. As these notes will no doubt be passed widely round, we must take great care with the handwriting . . ." He stopped and wrinkled his forehead again.

"What is it?"

"I was remarking to myself how very closely the letter —the letter that accompanied the necklace—resembled Papa's script. But I daresay anyone could have secured a piece of his correspondence. In any event, we must be equally accurate, so I propose we begin the notes at once. To allow ourselves time to perfect them."

"But the plotter could be _anyone,_" Gwen objected. "If he is not in either of our households, the notes will serve no purpose."

"Yes, they will, Mrs. Hathaway, because the plotter unquestionably has *contact* with someone in one of our households. Consider how quickly he learned of Papa's journey to Essex."

"No one at Aunt Constance's knew of Lord Scarborough's journey before his departure. No one but me."

"You did not mention it to Sir Neville?"

"I . . . I did tell him that I expected your father to quit town shortly, but I suggested no date."

"That doesn't signify. Sir Neville could have ascertained the time of Papa's departure by watching the house. Or he could have informed Mrs. Cunningham of the impending journey, and she could have dispatched one of her servants to watch the house. Or one of her servants might have overheard your conversation and repeated it. Or one of *our* servants might have overheard *my* conversation with Papa. The possibilities are endless, Mrs. Hathaway; we must simply trust that the plotter will learn of the elopement the same way he learned of Papa's trip."

"Very well." Gwen nodded. "And then?"

"And then we shall take our parents' places."

"*Take our parents' places!*" Gwen screeched.

"It shouldn't be too difficult," Lord Fullerton said airily. "Papa and I are approximately the same size and much alike in coloring, and you bear a keen similarity to Lady Ross as well. When we are dressed in their clothes and viewed from a distance—"

"Dressed in their clothes!" Gwen protested. "I cannot walk blithely out of Aunt Constance's house clad in one of Mama's gowns."

"Nor can I parade about in Papa's things, and I shall consequently arrange a place for us to change. Indeed, some delay is necessary; we must grant the plotter time to learn of the elopement and move to intercept us. Let me calculate. After Papa has gone, I shall require five minutes to purloin his clothes and another five to drive to Orchard Street. Except that I shall not drive to Orchard Street, of course; I shall pick you up in Oxford Street, at the intersection. I daresay I shall have to wait for you as it will take *Papa* five minutes to come for Lady Ross and five after that for you to assemble *her* clothes."

Gwen's head was spinning with confusion, and the viscount flashed her a soothing smile.

"Never mind; do not tease yourself about the schedule. As soon as your mother has left, gather up her clothes and meet me in Oxford Street. We shall then need perhaps half an hour to change our attire, and it is a drive of about an hour to the destination I have in mind. An hour and three-quarters altogether, let us say, and I fancy that is *perfect.*"

"Lord Fullerton!" Gwen wailed.

"Do you wish not to do it, Mrs. Hathaway? I shan't pretend that my plan is without hazard. As I indicated yesterday, when I thought *you* responsible for Papa's accident, I do not believe the plotter set out to kill him. However, it is clear that he does not scruple to employ the most severe measures in pursuit of his objective."

"It isn't the hazard," Gwen said, not certain this was entirely true. "It is just so . . . so complicated."

"But it isn't complicated in the least," the viscount said cheerfully. "As it happens, I am well acquainted with the vicar of St. John's Church in Greenwich; he was a schoolmate of mine at Oxford. Remember that name, Mrs. Hathaway; you must state in your note that you are to be wed at St. John's in Greenwich. At any rate, I shall drive out there this afternoon and alert Andrew to what we are at. I shall request him not to interfere no matter what occurs."

Gwen could not repress a shudder, and his expression softened.

"Do you wish not to do it, Mrs. Hathaway?" he repeated.

"Yes, I wish very much not to do it," she moaned, "but I daresay we must."

"Spoken like the splendid little confederate you are." He started to pat her shoulder, then hastily withdrew his hand and plucked up the reins instead. They left the grass and sped along the park road, Gwen half-expecting an army of rabbits to assault them from the bushes.

—13—

Lord Fullerton deposited Gwen at the northwest corner of Oxford and Orchard streets, reminding her that this was *precisely* where he would pick her up on the day of their "elopement."

"Do not forget," he went on as he handed her out of the curricle, "that as soon as your mother has departed, you are to gather up her clothes, leave your note in a prominent place, and come at once to meet me. And the church is St. John's in—"

"For God's sake," Gwen interrupted irritably. "I may have no 'natural talent' for conspiracy, but I am not a child, Lord Fullerton."

"No," the viscount said rather distantly, "no, you are assuredly not a child."

His eyes briefly darkened—with the memory of his "odious conduct" no doubt—and Gwen felt her cheeks warm.

"Good day then, Mrs. Hathaway. I shall see you at the appointed time."

Gwen nodded and watched as he climbed back into his carriage and clattered east on Oxford. He did not turn at Davies, she noted, and she collected that he was, indeed, en route to Greenwich to speak with the vicar of St. John's. She shuddered again, but as she hurried up Orchard Street, she found her step astonishingly light. Hazard or no, she could no longer deny that she quite enjoyed scheming with Lord Fullerton, and by the time she reached Aunt Constance's, she was fairly tingling with excitement.

Evidently Sir Neville had been once more lurking in the library, for he materialized in the vestibule even as Gwen closed the front door.

"Where have you been *now?*" he demanded querulously. "I wished you to join me for my morning walk, but no one could locate you."

Gwen hesitated a moment. She viewed Neville much as the viscount viewed Lord Blake: she thought he lacked the imagination to devise, the courage to execute, the actions against Mama and Lord Scarborough. But, as she and Lord Fullerton had agreed, they could ill afford to discount anyone, and she dared not reveal the truth.

"I . . . I went shopping," she said. The baronet frowned at her empty hands. "But I did not find what I was seeking," she added quickly.

"Umm." His frown deepened. "I was in hopes you had gone to Scarborough's to speak with him and Lady Ross. To persuade them to delay their engagement."

It suddenly occurred to Gwen that her and Lord Fullerton's plan was most advantageous in this respect. Their unmasking of the plotter would be an enormous relief to Mama and the earl, and they, in their gratitude, would surely consent to a brief postponement of their betrothal.

"I shall speak to them soon after Lord Scarborough has recovered," she said aloud. "I have reason to believe they will then be highly receptive to such a suggestion." Sir Neville narrowed his pale blue eyes, and Gwen had the glimmer of a further idea. "Indeed, I am quite confident I can convince them to defer their engagement, so I perceive no reason for you to stay in town. Perhaps you should travel back to Kent immediately; I fancy I shall be able to join you in under a week's time."

"No." Neville shook his head. "No, you might require my assistance after all. And I judge it best not to see Mama until I have . . . ah . . . good news to relate."

Gwen studied his plumpish face, but it told her

nothing. He might, in fact, merely fear to confront his mother; he might be concocting another attack on Lady Ross or the earl.

"As you will," she said. "For the present, I must ask you to excuse me; I have an urgent matter to attend."

He nodded—somewhat huffily, Gwen thought—and she hastened across the foyer and up the staircase. As the viscount had pointed out, they must take excessive care with their notes, and Gwen's first requirement was to obtain a sample of Mama's handwriting. She paused outside Aunt Constance's bedchamber door, thinking to request one of Lady Ross's old letters, but, upon consideration, she realized she could not confide in Mrs. Cunningham either. She proceeded to Mama's room, intending to search for some memorandum or shopping list; but as she lifted her hand to knock, she remembered that she had chanced to save her portion of the invitation list for the ball. She sped on down the corridor and into her own bedchamber, removed her bonnet and gloves, and hurried to the writing table. The list was in the center drawer, atop the remaining stationery, and Gwen sat down, arrayed list and paper alike before her, and seized a pen.

Gwen's script was naturally quite similar to her mother's, and fortunately the invitation list contained nearly every letter in the alphabet. Nevertheless she found it exceedingly difficult to duplicate Mama's writing *exactly*, and after several hours of effort she decided to make the note as short as she credibly could. Even so, it was almost dinnertime when—fingers throbbing and stained with ink—she completed the task and reviewed the final message.

> To whom it may concern,
>   In order to avert any additional difficulties, Charles and I have elected to be privately wed at St. John's Church in Greenwich. As you read this, we shall be on our way there.
>
>   F.R.

Gwen doubted that Lady Ross would ever compose a communication so brief, but it would have to do. She folded the paper, slipped it in an envelope, and carefully penned "To Whom It May Concern" on the front of the envelope as well. She rose and went to the bed, withdrew her valise from beneath it, placed the envelope in the valise, slid it back under the bed. The mantel clock was chiming four, and Gwen stepped to the washstand, scrubbed the ink from her fingers, and rushed down to the dining room.

The note finished and hidden, there was nothing more to do until the day of the "elopement," and time passed with excruciating slowness. As long as there existed the possibility, however slight, that Sir Neville or Aunt Constance was the culprit, Gwen counted it wisest to avoid them; she feared she might somehow drop a hint of her and the viscount's trap. Consequently, though she had never fancied shopping, she left the house just after breakfast every morning and wandered about the streets of London, peering into the shop windows and buying nothing. Much as she attempted to resist the temptation, her daily excursion invariably took her to St. James's Street, where—her hat carefully adjusted to hide her face—she strolled along the footpath across from White's and furtively watched the entrance of the club. She fairly ached for a glimpse of Lord Fullerton—a longing she attributed to the fact that he had become the only person she could trust. But while she spotted Beau Brummell on two occasions and Lord Blake once, the viscount did not appear; and at half-past three each afternoon, Gwen trudged back toward Orchard Street for dinner.

Gwen soon observed that Mama had adopted a predictable schedule as well. One of Lord Scarborough's carriages called for her every morning promptly at ten, bore her to Berkeley Square, and returned her at six, after she had dined with the earl and he had retired for the night. Gwen noticed that Lady Ross carried great loads of boxes and packages back and forth, a circumstance from which she inferred that Mama, too, spent part of each day shopping. But Gwen declined to question her on this head, for Lady Ross was sufficiently peevish when she inquired after the earl.

"And how is Lord Scarborough today?" Gwen would ask casually. She always managed to be in the vicinity of the entry hall as the hour of six approached.

"Improving," Mama would snap. Or, "Slightly better." Or, "As well as can be expected."

Gwen fervently wished she could advise her mother what she and Lord Fullerton were at, put Lady Ross's mind at ease. But that wouldn't do, of course; Mama might inadvertently betray the plan to the plotter. There would be time enough to explain, time enough for Mama's relief and gratitude when the guilty party was exposed.

Be that as it might, the days crept by so very slowly that Gwen began to entertain a notion that time had altogether stopped, and she was caught unawares when the waiting ended. It was Friday evening, a week after the earl's accident, and when Lady Ross stepped into the vestibule, Gwen absently noted that she had no parcels.

"And how is Lord Scarborough today?" she said. She had posed the question so often that it sprang to her lips quite by rote.

"He is entirely recovered," Mama replied coolly. "Dr. Saunders has discharged him."

"How nice," Gwen murmured. She started to turn away, then belatedly registered her mother's words. "Recovered?" she gasped. "How wonderful, Mama. I . . . I daresay you have devised something in the way of celebration."

"In point of fact, we have." Lady Ross's tone remained monstrous chilly. "We intend to drive into Surrey tomorrow and have a picnic in the country."

"How wonderful," Gwen repeated. "What . . . what time do you plan to leave?"

"Charles will come by for me at two. Then, as I indicated, we shall drive directly to Surrey."

Two. If all proceeded according to plan, the situation

would be resolved in under four-and-twenty hours.
Gwen repressed a shiver. "I . . . I hope you will have a
splendid time," she stammered.

"Oh, I fancy we shall." Lady Ross hesitated, her eyes
flickering with an emotion Gwen couldn't read, but
eventually, almost invisibly, she shook her head. "If you
will pardon me now, I wish to be thoroughly rested for
our adventure."

She granted Gwen a curt nod, ascended the staircase,
disappeared round the landing; and Gwen sagged against
the newel post. Tomorrow would see the success or
failure of her and the viscount's last, most desperate
scheme, and the consequences of failure could literally
prove fatal.

Gwen's bedchamber was at the rear of the house, per-
mitting no view of the street, so at a quarter before two,
she slipped across the corridor and into the guest room
Lady Lynch had occupied. Impatient as she had been
during the preceding six days, she now discovered her
knees nearly knocking with fright, and as she peered between the draperies, she uncharitably prayed that Lord
Scarborough had suffered a relapse. But it was not to be:
at two o'clock precisely, the earl's landau clattered to a
stop in front of the house. It appeared, Gwen noted idly,
that Mama and his lordship had planned a splendid
outing indeed, for some half-dozen pieces of luggage
were lashed to the carriage roof. Gibson—who looked to
be fully recovered himself from his master's harrowing
experience—left the box and disappeared from Gwen's
sight, and she soon heard the distant peal of the doorbell.
She then began to pray that *Mama* had been taken ill, but
her hopes were once more dashed: when Gibson
reappeared, Lady Ross was at his side. The coachman
assisted her into the landau, remounted the box, and the
carriage rolled away.

Gwen whirled around, her legs so unsteady she almost
stumbled, and raced out of the guest bedchamber and
down the hall to her mother's room. She had previously

decided to wear Mama's infamous hat—the leghorn Lady
Lynch had observed in Hyde Park—and when she
opened the wardrobe, she snatched it immediately from
the shelf. She then glanced down, thinking to select a
dress that reasonably matched, and frowned with puzzlement. Except for Lady Ross's ancient black bombazine
carriage dress, the wardrobe was empty; evidently
Mama, for some reason, had moved her clothes to
another room. But there was no time to search for them;
Gwen jerked the dress off its hanger and rushed back to
her own bedchamber.

Gwen's hands had begun to tremble rather more than
her legs, and after pulling her valise from beneath the
bed and laying it on the counterpane, she was compelled
to fumble at maddening length with the clasps.
Eventually, however, she succeeded in wresting the case
open, and she plucked out the note and placed the dress
and hat inside. If anyone questioned her departure from
the house with baggage in hand, she intended to say that
she was taking several gowns to a mantua-maker for
alterations. She fervently hoped this fabrication would
not prove necessary because—intentions notwithstanding
—she was quite persuaded that any challenge would send
her into a swoon of sheer terror. She closed the valise, tip-
toed to the door, checked the corridor, and found it
deserted. Apparently there was to be no escape, and
Gwen drew a great breath and dashed down the hall and
down the stairs to the foyer.

Lord Fullerton had instructed her to leave the note in a
prominent place, and Gwen fancied that the side table in
the vestibule best fit this description. She had planned
merely to leave the envelope on top of the table, but,
upon reflection, she feared it might become mixed with
Aunt Constance's mail. She therefore positioned the
envelope upright, propping it against the wall, and as she
opened the front door, she turned back to evaluate her
effort. The envelope could not be missed, she judged; the
next person who passed through the entry hall would spot
it at once. She stepped out of the house, slamming the

door much too forcefully, and—lest she be seen at the last instant—fairly galloped down Orchard Street to Oxford.

No carriage waited at the northwest corner of the intersection, and Gwen's eyes darted frantically amongst the other three, in the event she had misunderstood the viscount's directive after all. But there was no sign of Lord Fullerton, and she stepped off the footpath and anxiously watched the steady stream of traffic. The viscount had clearly indicated that he expected to precede her to their rendezvous, and when, by Gwen's reckoning, some ten minutes had elapsed, she could only collect that he had somehow been forced to abort the plan. She experienced a familiar emotion—that peculiar blend of relief and disappointment—but as she started to turn and make her way back up Orchard, she glimpsed his lordship's gray horses emerging from Park Street. A few moments later he reined in beside her and leapt out of his father's curricle.

"Pray forgive my tardiness, Mrs. Hathaway." He seized her valise and secured it in the luggage compartment atop his own. "I encountered an obstacle which I shall explain as we drive."

Lord Fullerton assisted Gwen into the passenger seat, resumed the place beside her, and eased the carriage back into the flow of traffic. Whatever dangers they might shortly encounter, Gwen was prodigious glad to see him, and she could not keep her eyes from his gray hair, his lean dark face, now slightly flushed, the firm curve of his jaw. When the carriage was smoothly under way, the viscount looked toward her, and Gwen hastily averted her gaze.

"The obstacle was one I neglected to consider when we devised our plan," he said. "I knew I must use one of Papa's carriages, of course, but it occurred to me just last night that I must first ascertain which carriage he would use. Then there was the matter of the grooms: I could not allow the same one to hitch two vehicles for Lord Scarborough within the space of half an hour. I was consequently compelled to send the groom who had hitched the landau on a mythical errand, and I advised a second groom that Papa had changed his mind and desired to drive his curricle instead. I am in hopes I created sufficient confusion that, should the plotter talk to the grooms, he will be unsure which carriage Papa actually took."

"And the horses?" Gwen asked. "This is your team, not Lord Scarborough's."

"That presents no problem. The entire household is aware that Lady Ross will have nothing more to do with the bays, so Papa would have borrowed another team had he elected to drive his curricle. No, Mrs. Hathaway, I believe our ruse has thus far proceeded very nicely. And I am delighted that Papa and Lady Ross will spend the day in Hertfordshire, well out of harm's way."

"Hertfordshire?" Gwen echoed sharply. "Mama told me they were going to Surrey."

"Surrey? You are certain?"

"Quite certain. She said it twice and made rather a point of it the second time."

"Well, perhaps the two of them were in disagreement as to where they should conduct their picnic. It really doesn't signify; neither Hertford nor Surrey is in the direction of Greenwich. I did, by the way, speak with Andrew last week, and he consented not to interfere in our charade."

Gwen's hands began to shake again, but before she could altogether succumb to panic, Lord Fullerton pulled to the side of the road and stopped the carriage.

"Fladong's Hotel." He answered Gwen's unspoken question. "It caters primarily for naval personnel, but as it is convenient, I booked a room."

"In the name of Captain Lovell, no doubt," Gwen said dryly.

"Captain Chadwick, actually."

He flashed his mischievous grin, and Gwen felt immeasurably better. Rake or no—and she supposed she would never be sure on that head—he projected an unmistakable aura of strength; and as he helped her down from the seat, she managed, though somewhat tremulously, to return his smile.

The viscount left Gwen just inside the hotel entrance, their cases at her feet, while he stepped across the lobby to talk to the reception clerk. The latter glanced up from his books and favored Gwen with a knowing smirk, and she was reminded of the hackney driver who had taken her to White's. At this juncture, it doubtless appeared that "Captain Chadwick" had engaged a room for a few hours of romantic entertainment . . . Gwen shook her head, wondering for perhaps the thousandth time how she had got herself into such a hobble.

Their room was clearly not the best Fladong's had to offer: it was on the first story and—or so Gwen surmised from the noises and odors wafting through the floor— situated directly above the kitchen. Lord Fullerton had decided he need only wear his father's coat and hat, he said, and he opened his valise and withdrew them. Evidently he had given no thought to coordinating his ensemble, for Lord Scarborough's plum-colored coat fairly did battle with the viscount's rust pantaloons. Furthermore, the coat was a trifle too long and a bit too full in the midsection and noticeably tight across Lord Fullerton's broad shoulders. The hat was hopeless, sliding nearly to the bridge of the viscount's nose, and eventually, rather irritably, he declared he would wear his own hat as no one would be able to detect the difference.

"Now I shall leave you to change, Mrs. Hathaway." With a final frown at his hideous color scheme, Lord Fullerton turned away from the mirror. "I shall be just outside in the corridor."

Gwen nodded and, when the door had closed, opened her own case, removed her gown, and pulled on Mama's carriage dress. She reached behind to fasten it and discovered, to her dismay, that it was secured with hooks and eyes rather than buttons. She succeeded in closing the top two and the bottom three, but—her fingers unsteady, keenly aware of the passing time—she could manage no more. She could scarcely stroll out of the hotel with the better part of her dimity corset exposed to the world, and she went to the door and cracked it.

"I . . . I shall need your assistance, Lord Fullerton."

He stepped into the room and shut the door again, and Gwen turned her back and lowered her head. Nothing happened for a moment, and she entertained an odd notion that he was inexplicably reluctant to touch her. She was hardly *indecent*, she assured herself, and at length she felt his fingers against her spine. Maybe he wasn't a rake after all, she thought distantly, because his hands were unsteady as well. Unsteady and excessively, fearfully warm, and she drew a ragged breath of relief when he had finished. But he did not move away, and when Gwen raised her head, she met his eyes in the mirror. Eyes gone black, as they had in Lord Scarborough's library, and she wondered what would happen if she simply stood there, so close that she could feel his breath in her hair. Would he turn her around, take her in his arms again? She realized, was horrified to realize, that that was what she wanted. But this time there would be no conceivable excuse for her conduct, no rescue, no retreat; and she bounded forward like a terrified animal released from a trap.

"And now for your hat, Mrs. Hathaway."

His voice was hoarse, and he cleared his throat, but when Gwen looked back into the mirror, fumbling with Mama's bonnet strings, his eyes had reverted to slate, and his face was altogether blank.

She looked little better than the viscount, Gwen judged, when the hat ribbons were secured and she examined her reflection. Since Mama was slightly shorter than she, the dress awkwardly ended just below Gwen's calves; and as Lady Ross was some inches thicker through the middle, the gown gapped grotesquely around Gwen's rib cage, lending her a distinctly rectangular aspect. Furthermore, the leghorn could not have matched the black of the dress more poorly: it was a rich chocolate brown in color, trimmed with rouleaux of almond satin and a deep peach cord. Gwen's eyes met Lord Fullerton's again, and he shook his head and grinned.

"I fear," he said solemnly, "that we shall simply have to pray that the plotter will be too preoccupied to remark our dreadful taste in attire."

Gwen nodded, and they left the room and crept down the stairs and into the hotel lobby. The reception clerk was gazing proprietarily about, and Gwen could scarcely bear to contemplate his opinion of their extremely brief stay. But, to her gratification, he did not appear to recognize them; after a moue of disdain for their apparel, he shifted his scrutiny to a group of uniformed officers.

Gwen did not expect the culprit to act in the busy streets of London, and she remained relatively relaxed until they had crossed the Thames and turned southeast toward Greenwich. The buildings soon grew farther apart, the road increasingly deserted, and she began to glance nervously from side to side.

"I do not believe he will attack until we reach St. John's."

Evidently the viscount had noted her distress, and Gwen could not but wish he had employed a word more comforting than "attack."

"If he knows Greenwich at all," his lordship continued, "he will be aware that the church itself is the ideal place to accost us. It is situated well off the main road, and except for the vicarage, there are no dwellings nearby."

This intelligence was hardly comforting either, and Gwen clenched her hands and peered studiedly down at them.

"You no doubt perceive, Mrs. Hathaway, that we shall have to react very quickly to . . . to whatever occurs. Quickly and in concert so as to project a credible impression. One of us must take the lead, and at the risk of sounding immodest, I daresay it should be I. As you yourself have owned, you have no great talent for conspiracy."

Gwen did not recollect having owned to this at all, but

she fancied their mutual fate would be far safer in his hands than in hers. "Very well," she said. Her voice was shrill with fright. "I shall follow your instructions."

"Excellent. Perhaps I should mention that I am quite familiar with Greenwich. I grew up near there, you know."

Gwen hadn't known, of course, and she suspected he was speaking merely to distract her, but she was content to follow his lead in this regard as well. "In . . . indeed?" she stammered.

"Yes, on the other side from London. Between Greenwich and Croydon."

"Lord Scarborough has a home there?"

"No, my grandparents had a home there. Lord and Lady Lydney." He paused and sighed. "I'm afraid Papa was no better a father than he was a husband. I daresay he married my mother principally to serve as Harold's *step*mother, and when she died, he could not abide the prospect of rearing two small sons alone. So he sent Harold to his maternal grandparents, me to mine, and we were together only a few weeks in the year. At Christmas and during our summer holidays. Normally we visited Papa in London or at one of his estates, but one summer he was abroad. I'm sorry to say that Harold and I didn't much like one another, but Papa was determined we *should*, and he insisted we hold our summer reunion without him. Harold was compelled to spend two weeks at Lydfields, after which I went to *his* grandparents' . . ." He stopped, and his eyes narrowed.

"What is it?" Gwen looked fearfully about.

"A memory, Mrs. Hathaway—a nagging memory that won't quite come." He shook his head. "Well, in any event, when Harold and I were grown, Papa found us tolerable after all, and we've been great friends from then."

"And you don't resent it?" Gwen asked. "Resent that Lord Scarborough neglected you?"

"I did when I was younger, but I've since come to understand Papa. He could not have lived quietly in the country with two little boys tugging at his breeches. No, I no longer resent him, but *my* life will be quite different. I shall spend every moment with my children that I can."

His children; Gwen could not conceive why the notion overset her so. He would marry and produce slate-eyed sons and daughters she would never see—

"But what of your childhood?" he said. "Was it a happy one?"

Gwen told him about Mama and Papa and Portia and the numerous dogs and cats that had populated Rosswood over the years and the terrible crisis occasioned by Aunt Constance's decision to wed Sylvester Cunningham, at which he laughed. "Yes, I was happy," she concluded. "Though we were not well-fixed, and after Papa's debts were settled, we became positively poor." She belatedly recalled his view of Lady Ross's financial circumstances. "But Mama is *not* a fortune hunter," she added hastily.

"You needn't have said that, Mrs. Hathaway." His voice was low, almost gentle. "We've come too far for you to have to say that."

Too far, too far. How peculiar their relationship had been, Gwen reflected. How . . . how backward. Despite the brevity of their acquaintance, she thought she knew Lord Fullerton, knew his *character*, better than Peter or Neville or any other man she could cite. And she suspected he might claim the same of her. Yet here they were, at the end rather than the beginning, exchanging the trivial details of their pasts.

"We are here," the viscount said.

Gwen momentarily fancied he had read her mind, but she soon glimpsed a structure she recognized from pictures as the Royal Greenwich Observatory.

"We are still some distance from St. John's," Lord Fullerton went on, "but we may be watched as we approach. Pull your bonnet down as far as you can." He tilted his own hat well over his forehead. "And lower your head; I shall warn you if I sense that action is near."

Gwen obediently adjusted her bonnet and dropped her head to stare again at her hands. She discovered them

tightly clasped together and wryly realized that she had
assumed a posture of prayer—not inappropriate in the
circumstances. They clattered on in silence, rounding
several corners, and when the curricle at last came to a
halt, Gwen ventured an upward peep.

They were obviously in the church coach yard, the
simple steeple of St. John's rising directly in front of
them, the small vicarage off to the right, and—though
Gwen tried not to see it—the cemetery to the left. As
nearly as she could determine, the coach yard was empty,
but she had not supposed the plotter would leave his
carriage in the open.

"Now," the viscount whispered, "we shall get out and
walk to the door. Fairly rapidly, as if we were impatient.
Keep your head down but inclined toward me; it should
appear that we are talking."

Gwen nodded, and Lord Fullerton climbed down from
his seat, walked around the curricle, and assisted her out.
He took her arm and ushered her quickly forward, and
Gwen discovered it impossible to *appear* to be talking
without actually doing so.

"I am terrified," she moaned under her breath. "I am
utterly terrified, and I cannot bear this another
second—"

"You are doing very well." He squeezed her arm. "You
are doing exceedingly well indeed; just keep walking."

They reached the shallow steps of the church, started
to ascend them; and Gwen began to fear, to *pray*, that
their plan had gone awry, that the culprit had failed to
learn of the "elopement." They mounted the last riser
and proceeded toward the portal, and they were perhaps
a yard away when a shot rang out. A shot—there was no
mistaking the sound; Gwen had once gone hunting with
Papa.

"Scream!" the viscount hissed. "Scream and fall to the
ground."

In point of fact, Gwen needed little encouragement to
scream, and she emitted a piercing shriek, went to her

knees, then sprawled as painlessly as she could on the stone platform.

"Fanny!" Lord Fullerton bellowed. He fell to his knees beside her. "Fanny! Fanny!"

He clutched his chest, as though he were suffering a coronary arrest, and Gwen quelled an insane urge to laugh. Then the viscount collapsed atop her, pinning her beneath him, and in the sudden awful silence, there was nothing to do but wait.

"Try to hide your breathing," Lord Fullerton whispered.

Gwen found this directive quite easy to follow as well because, in truth, she *could* scarcely breathe. The viscount, lean as he was, was all muscle, astonishingly heavy; and she began to fear she had escaped the plotter's ball only to be suffocated by her confederate. She lay motionless, drawing an occasional shallow breath as best she could; and after an eternity, it seemed, she heard the approach of cautious footsteps.

"They are dead." The voice was a strangled whimper, but Gwen recognized it nevertheless as that of Lord Blake. "You promised we shouldn't have to hurt them, Amanda."

"I did not fire the gun," Lady Blake snapped. "You were supposed to fire above their heads, and if you were so clumsy as to miss, it is hardly my fault."

Amanda Lovell, Gwen marveled. Mousy little Amanda Lovell, who never uttered a word . . .

"Besides," Lady Blake went on, "we can't be sure they *are* dead. Go and see, Harold."

There was another tap of reluctant footsteps, and Gwen could not resist the temptation to crack one eye. Lord Blake's Hessians appeared in her limited circle of vision, stopped mere inches from her face, and one boot moved tentatively forward to prod Lord Fullerton's shoulder. The viscount's hands snaked round his brother's ankle, jerked it, and with a howl of pain, Lord Blake

thudded to the ground. Lord Fullerton leapt to his feet
and pulled Gwen up beside him.

"Are you all right, Mrs. Hathaway?" he asked.

"Yes," Gwen wheezed, "yes, I am fine."

"Mrs. Hathaway!" Lady Blake screeched. She rushed
forward for a better view. "Chad!" she gasped.

"Yes, it is I. What a pleasure to see you, Amanda. And
Harold, too, of course."

He gazed with loathing at his brother, who—though
with considerable difficulty—was in the process of
heaving himself erect. In the course of his fall, Viscount
Blake had dropped his pistol, and Lord Fullerton bent,
plucked it up, and shoved it in his pocket.

"Empty, I expect," he said, "but I shall take no
chances. I must own myself amazed, Harold." He shook
his gray head. "I should have wagered my last groat
against the possibility that *you* were plotting against
Papa and Lady Ross."

"It was Amanda's idea," Lord Blake whined.

"Was it indeed?" The viscount shifted his gaze to his
sister-in-law. "And what was *your* objection to the
marriage?"

"I shouldn't expect you to understand." Her tone was
bitter as gall, and her blue eyes fairly blazed with hatred.
"You needn't care a deuce for your father's estate. How
much did Lord Lydney leave you? Close to a quarter-
million pounds, I'll warrant, to say nothing of the
property and the jewels. Whereas Harold and I must live
from hand to mouth, waiting for Scarborough to die.
And if he had married his darling Fanny, who knows
how much he would have willed to *her?* She has quite
bewitched him; he might have left her everything that is
not entailed."

"So you set out to part them." Lord Fullerton frowned
a moment. "As I recollect the course of events, you did
not learn of Papa's departure for Essex until a few hours
before the event. How did you have the necklace copied
so speedily?"

"The copy had been made long since," Lady Blake

replied. "I thought it was the perfect means of driving Lady Ross away; I knew the Golden Vixen's connection to Mrs. Hathaway." She shot Gwen a superior smirk. "I consequently had the necklace copied as soon as it became clear that Scarborough had conceived a *tendre* for Lady Ross. I then began to ponder a way to entice your dear father to quit town, but he spared me the trouble."

Actually, Gwen thought, Lord Fullerton had spared Lady Blake the trouble, but she doubted he would wish this circumstance brought to her ladyship's attention.

"And you wrote a note to accompany the necklace." Lord Fullerton looked back at his brother. "Yes, I now remember that your handwriting is very similar to Papa's —a trifle larger but otherwise identical. You then posed as Gibson and delivered the message and the package to Mrs. Cunningham's butler—"

"No," Lord Blake interposed. "Papa also aided us in that respect. *He* had written Lady Ross a letter to explain his abrupt departure. He was in a monstrous hurry that morning, and he desired me to give Gibson the letter and dispatch him to Orchard Street. It was an easy matter to substitute the necklace and my own note."

"I see." Lord Fullerton nodded. "Naturally you expected Lady Ross to wear the necklace in Papa's absence, be abysmally humiliated, and flee back to Kent. But how did you plan to prevent Papa from going after her after he had returned to London and heard the story?"

"He would have heard another story as well," Lady Blake said. "The exceedingly interesting story that Lady Ross had commissioned the copy of the necklace. I posed as darling Fanny, my face heavily veiled, of course, and went to the jeweler. I did not take the necklace itself, for the *real* Lady Ross could not have procured it. Instead I made a drawing, and as I had anticipated, the jeweler recognized it at once. Scarborough's necklaces are famous amongst the city's jewelers. At any rate, when he delicately pointed out the impropriety of 'Lady Ross' wearing such a piece, I confidentially told him what I was at. What Lady Ross was at, that is. I told him Lord Scarborough would presume the Golden Vixen had tricked me and be so remorseful that he would feel compelled to wed me."

"And Harold was to ferret out this information prior to Papa's return, no doubt," the viscount said. "Harold was to be persuaded that *Papa* could not possibly have sent a gift so tasteless and rush about town like a dutiful son to discover who had. And regretfully advise Papa that 'darling Fanny' had deceived him. Do you think he would have believed it?"

"My performance was quite flawless," Lady Blake said, "but we shall never know, shall we? No, Lady Ross decided to save the necklace for her ball, and Scarborough came back at precisely the wrong moment."

"And why did you not attempt to prevent *that?*" Lord Fullerton inquired.

"Oh, I did," Lady Blake said. "I was convinced Lady Ross would wear the necklace at the ball, and when Scarborough hadn't returned by Wednesday, I glimpsed a ray of hope. I recalled that he normally stops at the Queen in Newham, and I engaged a man to go out there and await him."

"Await him and do what?" the viscount asked grimly.

"He was to immobilize Scarborough's carriage. If that proved insufficient, if it appeared Scarborough could hire a chaise and still reach London in time for the ball, my man was to use his own judgment."

"You didn't tell me that, Amanda." Lord Blake was whining again. "You assured me Papa would be safe—"

"As safe as he was when you loosed the rabbits?" Lord Fullerton snapped. "The memory has eluded me for days, Harold, but I now recollect your rabbits. The summer I visited you at Lord and Lady Porters', you kept a great hutch of them as pets. You still do, I surmise, and you live in the present Lord Porter's dower house, not twenty miles from London. It was another easy matter to race out there, arm yourself with half a dozen rabbits, race back to town, release them in Hyde Park—"

"I didn't!" Lord Blake's voice was nearly as shrill as a woman's. "Amanda let the rabbits go."

"You sniveling little coward." The viscount shook his head with disgust. "I'm surprised you didn't have Amanda fire the gun as well; I daresay you would have, given the time to teach her how. Just what was your intention, by the by?"

"Only to frighten you—to frighten Papa and Lady Ross, that is. They would scarcely have proceeded with their elopement if they believed someone was trying to kill them."

"And what of tomorrow?" Lord Fullerton said. "Next week? Next month? How did you plan to prevent their marriage *permanently?*"

"We . . . we had not decided," Lord Blake mumbled.

Gwen glanced at Lady Blake and beheld eyes as cold as ice, as hard as steel. She *would* have killed, Gwen thought with an inward tremor. If necessary, she would have arranged a final, fatal accident, and her spineless husband would have been powerless to stop her.

"Well, you needn't tease yourselves about it any longer," Lord Fullerton said frigidly. "I shan't relate our conversation to Papa; I don't wish him to know how very eager you are for him to be called to his final reward. No, I shall merely inform Papa that you have elected, quite precipitately, to immigrate to North America."

"North America!" Lady Blake screeched.

"That is but a suggestion, Amanda. I fear you would find the Continent a bit unsettled just now, but you might prefer India or Australia or some other outpost of the empire. I only insist you depart England at once. I shall grant you four-and-twenty hours to go to Porter Manor and pack your things; twenty-four hours and no more."

"But our good clothes are in London," Lady Blake wailed.

"I shall have them sent to you when you've advised me of your direction. But you are not to go to London; I won't permit you near Papa again. And if you return to England while he is yet alive, I shall do everything in my power to have you imprisoned."

"But how are we to *live?*" Lady Blake had begun to whine as well. "We shall have to provide our own lodging, our own food—"

"Yes, it will be a new and interesting experience, will it not? I should propose you have your own jewels copied in paste and sell the originals, but I suspect you've already done so." She flushed. "So perhaps you and Harold will be compelled to *earn* your way, either that or starve. I frankly favor the latter alternative, but I shall leave the choice to you. For the present, I strongly recommend you get out of my sight before I borrow a leaf from your book and resort to violence."

Lady Blake's flush deepened, but further argument was clearly useless: Lord Fullerton's eyes had turned to gray stone, and his jaw was implacably set. She took her husband's arm and led him round the side of the building, much as he had always tugged her about in public. How deceptive appearances could be, Gwen marveled again. At length she heard the sounds of a carriage—evidently they had concealed their conveyance behind the church—and it soon rolled into view and through the coach yard and disappeared.

"My curricle," the viscount said dryly, "and two of Papa's aged horses. I daresay they'll sell the lot before they go, but it's a small price to be rid of them. We have accomplished our objective, Mrs. Hathaway; let us return to town."

He sounded rather bleak, and Gwen discovered herself oddly out of spirits as well. They drove back to London in uninterrupted silence, Gwen pondering the immediate future. There was no longer any reason to delay her discussion with Mama, and she thought—in the circumstances—Lady Ross would agree to postpone the announcement of her engagement to the earl. Although, Gwen suddenly recollected, Lord Fullerton had determined not to disclose the Blakes' conspiracy to his father. She wondered what the viscount *did* plan to say to Lord Scarborough, but when she glanced at him from the corner of her eye, she found his jaw once more set; and she judged it not the time to ask. He would devise something; he invariably devised something. In any event, with Mama's cooperation secured, Gwen and Neville would travel back to Kent, tomorrow probably, and confront Lady Lynch. Perhaps it would not be necessary actually to *lie* to her ladyship; perhaps they could merely dissemble a bit. But even that prospect rendered Gwen enormously tired, and she closed her eyes and laid her head against the seat. She did not sit up again until the curricle had halted, and when she opened her eyes, she saw the familiar facade of Aunt Constance's house.

"We are here, Mrs. Hathaway," Lord Fullerton said gratuitously.

It seemed to Gwen that a prodigious long time had passed since she left, years maybe. But in fact, she calculated, it could not be much beyond six, and Orchard Street was still bathed in sunlight.

"So we are," she murmured.

"I doubt Papa and Lady Ross are back, and as they will stop here first, I shall come inside and wait with you. I fancy it would be best if we spoke to them together."

"But what do you intend to tell them?" Gwen said. "You indicated to Lord Blake that you wanted to spare your father's feelings."

"I shall tell them we unmasked the persons responsible for their recent misfortunes, but honor precludes a revelation of their identities. You are aware how exceedingly honorable I am, Mrs. Hathaway." He flashed a wry smile, but Gwen thought it was a trifle bitter at the edges. "And I shall then help you persuade them not to proclaim their betrothal till you and Sir Neville are wed."

"How . . . how did you know?" Gwen stammered. "How did you know I'd decided to do that? Decided to do it this evening?"

"Because I know how your keen little mind operates."

His voice was so low she could hardly hear him. "I know perhaps better than you do yourself."

It was an echo of the notion she'd entertained on the road to Greenwich, and she could only stare at him, watching his eyes go dark.

"As I stated, I shall come inside with you," he went on. "However, as we shan't be alone again, I should like to take this opportunity . . . In view of the fact . . ." She had never seen him so uncertain. "I should like to say good-bye, Mrs. Hathaway."

They had said it twice before, in one form or another, and Gwen remembered that the third time for anything was believed to work a charm.

"But it isn't good-bye!" she burst out desperately. "We shall surely see one another after Mama and Lord Scarborough are married. They will live in one of his houses, no doubt, and Neville and I shall come to visit, and you will be there—"

"I think not, Mrs. Hathaway," he interposed firmly. "Are you ready then?"

No! she wanted to cry. No, I am not ready to leave you like this, without another private word, with no hope we'll ever meet again . . . But he had already climbed out of the carriage, already walked round to help her down. His hands were a trifle unsteady, Gwen noted distantly, and he did not touch her again once her feet were safely on the ground. They proceeded across the footpath and up the steps as though a great chasm yawned between them, and Gwen—her own hands trembling—opened the front door.

"Gwen!" "Lord Fullerton!" "Mrs. Hathaway!" "Fullerton!" "Guinevere!"

Gwen had never before witnessed a scene of such consternation: Sir Neville, Aunt Constance, and—or so it appeared—all the latter's servants were milling about the vestibule. The baronet had evidently been rending his clothes—at any rate, his neckcloth spilled untidily down his waistcoat—and the rest were shuffling their feet, wringing their hands, and exhibiting various other symptoms of distress.

"Thank God you have arrived!" Aunt Constance was the first to utter a complete and comprehensible sentence. "Fanny has *eloped!* Eloped with . . . with *him!*"

Gwen had neglected to consider the havoc their ruse would wreak amongst the innocent, but, upon reflection, she perceived no way it could have been avoided. "Mama has not eloped," she said soothingly. "She and Lord Scarborough have merely driven to the country for a picnic. I shall explain in due course why I left a note purporting to be from Mama, but I assure you the message you found was from me." She gestured toward the side table, looked toward the side table, and, to her horror, glimpsed a familiar envelope on the floor beneath it. "My note!" she gasped. Apparently it had fallen from the table when she slammed the front door. "But then what . . . where—"

"The note *I* found was in my bedchamber," Aunt Constance said. "Lying on my dressing table when I returned from Mrs. Weaver's. I had gone there to see her new grandson, but I must say I judge him a rather inferior infant—"

"For God's sake, Aunt Constance! Let me see the note!"

Mrs. Cunningham extended a sheet of Mama's cream-colored stationery, and Gwen snatched it out of her hand.

"To whom it may concern," she read. At least, she thought dryly, she had employed the proper form of address.

> As it has become clear that there are those who seek to prevent Charles's and my marriage, we have elected to wait no longer. We have gone to be wed and are in hopes the ceremony can be conducted yet today.
>
> Yours truly,
> Frances Ross

"They *have* eloped," Gwen said to Lord Fullerton.

She passed him the note and, as he began to read, recollected Mama's empty wardrobe, the parcels she had carried between Orchard Street and Berkeley Square, the luggage heaped on the roof of Lord Scarborough's carriage. Lady Ross had not been shopping after all; she had smuggled her clothes out of the house a few items at a time . . .

"Yes, they have eloped," Sir Neville said, "and it is imperative that we stop them. I'm sure I needn't remind you, Gwen, of the consequences if Mama learned that they were *married.*" He visibly shuddered.

"Perhaps there is a solution," the viscount said sardonically, glancing up. "Perhaps you could tell Lady Lynch that Lady Ross married Papa but they were immediately divorced."

"*Divorced?*" The baronet had obviously failed to register Lord Fullerton's sarcasm. "Mama would *never* permit me to marry into a family in which there'd been a divorce." He stopped, and his eyes narrowed. "Why, by the by, are you here, Fullerton? Gwen recently advised me that she did not intend to see you again."

"My . . . my plans changed," Gwen said.

"Umm." He glowered at her and the viscount in turn. "Be that as it may, we must stop Scarborough and Lady Ross; we can only pray it is not too late. You will recall that Lady Ross said they were *in hopes* of marrying today. We must pray they were unable to do so and set out at once to intercept them." He strode purposefully toward the door, then spun back round. "Er . . . have we any notion where they might have gone?"

"Mama said they were going to Surrey," Gwen replied.

"Surrey." Sir Neville nodded and took another forward step.

"And *Papa* stated they were going to Hertfordshire," the viscount said.

"Hertfordshire." Neville frowned. "We shall have to divide our efforts then—"

"So I believe it can safely be assumed," Gwen interjected, "that they did *not* travel in the direction of Surrey or Hertford either one."

"An excellent conclusion, Mrs. Hathaway." Lord Fullerton bobbed his head approvingly. "Perhaps my instruction in conspiracy *has* borne fruit. Yes, it seems certain they did not proceed north or south out of London."

"That leaves east or west," the baronet said helpfully.

"Thank you, Sir Neville." The viscount's mouth quivered a bit. "Now if you would be silent a moment and let me think . . ." He narrowed his own charcoal eyes, and at length he snapped his fingers. "I fancy I have it. You no doubt recollect, Mrs. Hathaway, that I selected St. John's in Greenwich because—"

"Selected St. John's in Greenwich for what?" Neville demanded suspiciously.

"Do you wish to stop the elopement or not?" Lord Fullerton snapped. "If so, please allow me to speak without interruption." He returned his attention to Gwen. "I selected St. John's because I am well acquainted with the vicar there. It now occurs to me that Papa also has a former schoolmate in the church—the Bishop of Chelmsford."

"And if anyone could arrange a marriage on exceedingly short notice . . ." Gwen nodded. "Yes, they surely went to Chelmsford."

"However," the viscount added, "I don't believe they would dine or stay the night there. You remember, Mrs. Hathaway, that I once mentioned Papa's habit of patronizing certain inns—"

"It appears to me," the baronet interposed stiffly, "that you and Gwen have spent an excessive amount of time in one another's company."

"Oh, I should hardly term it 'excessive,' Sir Neville. I daresay Mrs. Hathaway will agree that we merely utilized our time together to the fullest."

Lord Fullerton's lips quivered again, and lest Neville observe her furious blush, Gwen peered hastily down at the viscount's boots.

"In any event," Lord Fullerton went on, "I fancy the White Rose in Basildon is Papa's favorite establishment in all of England, and Basildon is but a few miles from Chelmsford. I could be entirely wrong, of course, but if I were to go after them, I should go there."

"If?" Gwen's eyes flew back to his face. He could not abandon her now; he simply could not.

"Very well, Mrs. Hathaway." The viscount sighed. "I shall drive you to Basildon. Fortunately, my curricle team is strong, and I daresay they can manage another twenty miles or so."

"No," Sir Neville said firmly. "You have been alone with Gwen far too much as it is, Fullerton. Alone to no avail, I might add; had any of your schemes succeeded, we should not be in the present hobble. No, I shall go with you; we cannot afford another mistake. So if Mrs. Cunningham will lend us her carriage . . ."

Aunt Constance readily consented and desired two grooms and Jenkins, the coachman—all of whom were still wringing their hands—to see to the preparation of the landau. However, this was insufficient for Neville: he insisted the three of them go to the coach house as well so as to provide any assistance they could and be ready to depart the *instant* the carriage was hitched. Gwen suspected their presence proved a hindrance rather than an aid—the baronet narrowly missed being stepped on by one of the horses—but at last the task was completed. Lord Fullerton handed Gwen into the forward-facing seat and appropriated the place beside her, leaving Sir Neville to occupy the opposite seat; and Jenkins whipped the horses to a start.

Impossible though it seemed, it was still daylight, not yet seven, Gwen calculated; and as the landau turned into Oxford Street, Neville scowled across at his companions.

"Why the devil are you dressed in those outlandish costumes?" he growled. "I hadn't noticed before, but . . . Good God, Gwen, your legs are scarcely covered."

Gwen was growing tired again; in truth, she could not

conceive how she was to survive nearly three more hours on the road. But the baronet, now their co-conspirator, was entitled to some sort of explanation, and she recounted a considerably abbreviated version of her and Lord Fullerton's own "elopement."

"And you left Mrs. Cunningham's and traipsed about town in *that?*" Sir Neville said when she had finished.

"No," Gwen murmured, "no, we changed clothes at Fladong's Hotel."

"You went to a *hotel?*" Neville drew himself indignantly up. "I am indeed glad that this whole sordid episode is drawing to a close, Fullerton." He shot the viscount a glare. "It appears, given further opportunity, you might well have compromised Gwen beyond redemption."

Gwen distantly wondered just what his notion of "beyond redemption" was. But she was far too tired to inquire, even had she dared, and she once more closed her eyes and laid her head against the seat.

—15—

When Gwen opened her eyes again, it was dark—moonlight bathing the road and splashing through the windows of the carriage. She was astonishingly comfortable, and at length she realized that her head had come to rest on Lord Fullerton's shoulder. She grimly wondered Neville's reaction to this latest breach of propriety, but she soon heard the sound of snoring from the facing seat and cautiously raised her head. The viscount was gazing down at her, his eyes seeming pale as silver in the moonlight, but when he detected her own eyes upon him, he looked abruptly away.

"I was just at the point of waking you, Mrs. Hathaway," he said. "We are nearly there."

Evidently this information penetrated the baronet's unconscious, for he hastily heaved himself upright and vainly attempted to stifle a yawn. "Nearly there, are we?" He spoke as if he had been quite alert throughout their journey. "What is the time, Fullerton?"

The viscount withdrew a watch from his waistcoat pocket and tilted it toward the window. "Almost half-past ten."

It was later than Gwen would have reckoned; she had forgotten how excessively slow Aunt Constance's horses were.

"You were right on one head, Sir Neville," his lordship went on. "We must indeed pray that Papa and Lady Ross were thwarted in their attempt to marry today, for they have certainly had the *time* to do so. Well, we shall shortly know; the White Rose is immediately ahead."

Gwen peered apprehensively out the window, watching as the lights of Basildon flickered into view, and within a few moments they reached a commodious inn. Jenkins, as previously instructed, turned into the yard and slowed the horses fairly to a crawl, and they were halfway to the entry when Lord Fullerton gripped Gwen's arm.

"There it is!" he hissed. "Papa's landau. They are here."

He rapped on the front window and, scarcely waiting for Jenkins to stop the carriage, threw his door open and leapt to the ground. He tugged Gwen down beside him, Sir Neville clambered out the other door, and the three of them raced into the inn and panted to a halt in front of the desk.

"Yes?" The landlord glanced up with no hint of welcome, and Gwen surmised that his establishment was fully booked.

"We wish to see Lord Scarborough," the viscount said.

"Do you indeed?" the innkeeper retorted frostily. "Have you any reason to suppose that his lordship wishes to see *you?*"

"I am his son," Lord Fullerton snapped. "Viscount Fullerton."

The landlord stared suspiciously at Lord Fullerton's ill-matched ensemble, at Gwen's wretched attire, but apparently decided it would not do to irritate a viscount, however peculiar his tastes might be. "Very well," he said grudgingly. He made a great show of examining his register. "Ah, yes, here it is," he continued at last. "Lord and Lady Scarborough are presently dining in their private room."

"Lady Scarborough," Gwen moaned. "We are too late then."

"Perhaps not," Neville said optimistically. "Perhaps they are merely *posing* as man and wife. So as to . . . to . . ." But he could evidently perceive only one reason for such an imposture, and he flushed and bit his lip.

"Perhaps they are," the viscount agreed. "They would assume that anyone seeking to stop the elopement would think himself too late. But we shan't know until we see them, shall we? Where is their dining room?" he asked the innkeeper.

"On the . . . the . . ." He had been following their conversation with keen, incredulous attention, and it seemed to have rendered him temporarily speechless. "On the first story," he eventually choked. "Just to the right of the stairs."

The baronet bounded toward the staircase, and Gwen hurried to catch him up.

"I really do believe, Neville, that Lord Fullerton and I should speak to them alone. They are *our* parents, after all, and they might resent your interference."

"Mrs. Hathaway is correct." The viscount had moved to their side. "Indeed, they might feel we are attempting to overwhelm them by sheer force of numbers."

"Umm." Sir Neville frowned. "Very well; I shall await you in the taproom. However, you must *promise* that if they do not agree to postpone their marriage, you will come for me at once."

Gwen and Lord Fullerton solemnly promised, and as Neville proceeded toward the taproom, the viscount ushered Gwen up the steps to the first floor. They paused outside the door immediately to the right of the landing, gazed at one another, drew deep, simultaneous breaths; and Lord Fullerton knocked on the door.

"Come in."

It was Lord Scarborough's voice, and with another deep breath the viscount twisted the knob, pushed the door open, and nodded Gwen into the room ahead of him. Mama and the earl were seated at a small table, and it appeared they were nearly finished with their meal: nothing remained on the linen cloth but two bowls of blancmange, two glasses of champagne, and perhaps an additional half-bottle of the latter.

"Chad." Lord Scarborough sounded remarkably

unsurprised. "And the lovely Mrs. Hathaway." He studied them a moment. "I observe that you are wearing one of my coats, Chad, and I fancy I recognize Fanny's carriage dress on Mrs. Hathaway. I shan't even ask what you've been at *now.*" He peered over their shoulders. "Where is Harold?" he demanded.

"Harold?" Lord Fullerton was clearly unprepared for the question.

"Your brother," the earl prompted dryly.

"Ah, yes, Harold. The fact is, Papa, that he and Amanda have decided to emigrate. To North America, I believe. They reached their decision quite . . . quite suddenly, and they were in a monstrous hurry to be gone—"

"Never mind," Lord Scarborough interrupted testily. "You needn't make excuses for Harold; he never was a towering pillar of strength. I shall at least grant you credit for confronting me to my head." He stopped and sipped his champagne. "I should invite you to join us in a toast, but I fear we've only two glasses. And I doubt you'd have the heart for it. You are too late, you see; Winslow married Fanny and me some three hours since."

Too late, Gwen silently repeated; too late. She should have been prodigious overset, but, instead, she was oddly relieved.

"Then I am sure I speak for Mrs. Hathaway as well as myself when I tender sincere best wishes," the viscount said. "And I am certain she will concur that we should not intrude any further. If you will excuse us—"

"No, I will not excuse you!" the earl roared. "I fancy Fanny and I have deduced the greater part of your machinations, but now you've slunk into the open, I should like to have our conclusions confirmed. Let us begin with the first incident—the letter purporting to be from Lady Lynch. I should have suspected something afoot when I found you at Mrs. Cunningham's so very early in the morning"—he glared at his son—"but I regret to own that I did not. In any event, it later became clear that Mrs. Hathaway had written the letter."

Gwen did not perceive *how* this could have become clear, but Mama was now scowling at her, and she judged it best not to inquire.

"Obviously the letter was designed to drive Fanny back to Kent," Lord Scarborough went on. "And you must have concocted some means by which to keep us permanently apart. Since you have shown yourselves inordinately fond of forgery, I should guess that you planned to write each of us a letter of dismissal—both messages appearing to come from the other party. Mrs. Hathaway was to write the letter from Fanny, no doubt, and Harold the one from me."

"Harold?" Lord Fullerton echoed sharply.

"Your second scheme was considerably more imaginative." The earl continued as though he had not heard the interjection. "The business with the necklace was, conceptually, quite clever. You seized upon the one sure method to entice me from town, Harold's note requested Fanny to wear the necklace at once—"

"Harold?" the viscount said again. "You believe I— we—were in league with *Harold?*"

"You did not expect me to see the note, of course." Lord Scarborough flew heedlessly on. "No, you expected poor Fanny—miserably humiliated—to tear the letter to shreds before she fled London forever. But your plot did not unfold as you'd anticipated, and when Fanny showed me the note, I readily recognized Harold's handwriting. I then questioned Gibson, and he revealed that Harold had given him a package as well as an envelope to deliver to Orchard Street."

"We *are* somewhat puzzled as to how you thought to prevent Charles from coming after me." Mama took up the story. "You had written a letter of farewell in my behalf, Gwen; I discovered the scraps of it in your bedchamber. That was when I realized you had also forged the letter from Olivia." Her eyes briefly flickered with pain. "But did you really suppose that Charles, once he perceived I'd been tricked, would fail to follow me to Kent?"

Gwen and Lord Fullerton exchanged glances, said nothing.

"It doesn't signify," the earl said. "Your scheme did not work, and you were compelled to employ far more drastic measures. At Fanny's assembly, Harold or Amanda or Mrs. Hathaway—perhaps all three—overheard our plans in regard to the curricle team, and Harold raced out to Porter Manor for his rabbits. Yes, as soon as my head had cleared, I remembered Harold's rabbits; always despised the filthy little things."

He paused a moment, and his gray eyes clouded. "Would you have suffered the slightest twinge of remorse had I been killed? I fancy not; I fancy you would have settled happily down to live off the fruits of my estate. The fruits you have sought so desperately to protect. Your payment to Mrs. Hathaway—and I imagine she was to be rewarded very handsomely for her participation—would have made but a tiny dent in the proceeds. There would have been ample funds left to see the rest of you quite comfortably through the remainder of your days."

"Papa . . ."

The viscount's voice was strangled, his own eyes imploring, but he shook his head and compressed his lips. Gwen suddenly recollected that *she* hadn't promised not to disclose Lord and Lady Blake's activities, and she drew herself up.

"You have altogether misconstrued the situation," she said firmly, looking at the earl and Mama in turn. "Lord Fullerton and I did set out to part you—I shan't deny that —but money had nothing to do with it. We believed . . ."

She related the entire tale, from her initial conversation with the viscount, through their entrapment of the Blakes, to this—their final effort to abort the elopement. When she had finished, there was an interval of silence.

"It is fortunate you weren't motivated by visions of my wealth," Lord Scarborough said at last, "because I shan't leave you sixpence to scratch with. I summoned my solicitor yesterday and revised my will: Fanny is to inherit everything that is not entailed. And I shall now attempt most vigorously to deny Harold the entailed property and my title as well. I daresay that if I catch his highness over a heavy wet one night—and he does adore his cherry brandy, you know—he might well permit me to designate another heir."

The earl lapsed again into silence, and Gwen fancied there was nothing more to say. She stole a sideward peep at Lord Fullerton, found him similarly glancing at her; and by mutual, unspoken consent they started to back out of the room.

"You should be particularly ashamed, Mrs. Hathaway," Lord Scarborough said sternly. "After I had blurted my intentions to Lady Lynch, the night of Fanny's ball, I wished to announce our engagement, but Fanny wouldn't allow it. No, she said, it was clear that Lady Lynch was most bitterly opposed to the infamous Earl of Scarborough"—he flashed a wry smile —"and we must wait till you and Lynch were safely married. Fanny was even prepared to deceive Lady Lynch, to persuade her that we had dissolved our liaison."

"I came to tell you so the morning following the assembly," Mama put in. "That was when I discovered the scraps of paper in your bedchamber."

"In short," the earl said, "Fanny's primary concern was always for your happiness, Mrs. Hathaway. And how did you repay her devotion?"

His question was clearly rhetorical, and Gwen gazed sheepishly down at her shoes.

"Well, I want nothing more to do with you," Lord Scarborough snapped. "Not with either of you." He hesitated, and when Gwen looked up, she saw that his expression had softened a bit. "However, before you go, permit me to suggest that you look very carefully to *your* lives. For a change." Another sardonic smile. "If you wed Lynch, Mrs. Hathaway, if Chad allows you to do so, you will both be committing a fearful error, for I've never encountered two people more besotted with one another."

"Charles!" Mama said reprovingly.

"Except for us, my dear," his lordship hastily amended.

But Gwen scarcely registered their interchange, for her eyes had flown to the viscount's face. He was pale, as pale as he had been in his father's library, and she could only stare at him, her heart beginning to crash against her ribs.

"Chad has been wandering about the house with eyes any sheep would envy."

The earl's voice seemed to come from far away, but evidently Lord Fullerton had heard, for his cheeks flushed a deep brick red.

"When, that is, he was not with you, Mrs. Hathaway, which—I am given to understand—was at every conceivable opportunity. And Fanny has advised me that the mere mention of his name sets you to blushing like a schoolroom miss."

Gwen's own cheeks flamed, and she feared she was blushing quite as furiously as Lord Scarborough had described.

"Get yourselves married, for God's sake!" the earl bellowed. "And don't delay about it," he added in a somewhat more moderate tone. "Don't afford anyone the opportunity to strew obstacles in *your* path. No, do it now; do it tonight. Return to your friend in Greenwich—Andrew, is it?—and do it tonight. And now, if you will pardon us, we should prefer to spend the remainder of our honeymoon alone."

Gwen and the viscount backed on to the door, stepped into the corridor; and Lord Scarborough drew them up.

"We may eventually forgive you," he growled. "Come to us in a month or two, when we've assumed possession of our seaside estate, and we shall see."

Gwen and Lord Fullerton fled wordlessly down the stairs, across the lobby of the inn, and into the moonlit yard. They were nearly to the carriage when the viscount stopped and seized Gwen's arm and spun her round to face him.

"Well, what is it to be?" he said levelly. "Will you heed Papa's advice? Will you marry me tonight?"

"I . . . I . . ." It had all occurred so quickly that her head was whirling with confusion. "I have never thought of you in that way, Lord Fullerton."

"The deuce you haven't. What did you suppose was happening that day in Papa's library? He is quite right, you know: I'm mad for you. And you . . ." His voice trailed off. "You've time to consider it," he finished. "I shall instruct Jenkins to drive us to Greenwich, but Greenwich is in the direction of London as well. You can always change your mind."

"But I . . ."

Gwen had a nagging notion that she was overlooking something, but the viscount was already tugging her ahead. Jenkins was seated on one step of the landau, and he jumped to his feet as they approached.

"There has been a slight change of plans, Jenkins," Lord Fullerton said briskly. "Mrs. Hathaway and I have decided to go to Greenwich."

"You and Mrs. Hathaway? But we cannot—"

"I am sure you hesitate to risk Mrs. Cunningham's displeasure," the viscount interrupted. "I shall write her a note of explanation."

"But, sir—"

"I will brook no further argument, Jenkins! We wish to depart at once."

"Very well, sir."

The coachman sighed, handed Gwen into the landau, resumed his place on the box; and Lord Fullerton climbed in beside her and closed the door behind them.

"I lied," the viscount hissed as the carriage clattered to a start.

Gwen spun toward him in shock and found his eyes once more pale and bright as silver.

"I lied," he repeated, "for I shan't permit you to change your mind. I have let you go time and time again, and I won't do so now. I shall abduct you if I must, but I won't let you go."

He pulled her into his arms, turned her about, cradled her against his chest as though she were, indeed, a child.

"Dear God, how I've longed to hold you," he whispered. "From the very instant we met, I believe; I've often suspected that was what prompted my insane proposition. I had no other excuse to see you, and I was prepared to do anything merely to see you."

He lowered his mouth to hers, gently at first, but they had been denied too long. Gwen had not answered him in words, but her body knew its destiny, had always known perhaps; and all restraint was gone. She opened her lips and wound her arms around his neck, twined her fingers in his hair. She felt his mouth on her throat, his teeth on her throat; and she moaned and writhed against him. His lips returned to hers, and his hands explored her body, touching soft flesh here, bones there, devouring her mouth all the while. At length he raised his head and gazed down at her, both of them gasping with desire.

"Get thee away from me, my darling Gwen," he paraphrased with a shaky laugh. "If we proceed in this fashion, I fear my conduct could become extremely odious indeed."

He released her, maneuvered her upright in the seat, clasped her hand in his. Gwen sat a moment, dazed and trembling, and suddenly everything grew clear.

"I understand now!" she cried. She looked at him in wonder. "I understand why I feel this way, why I felt this way in your father's library. I love you, Chad. I love you!"

"Well, I should certainly hope so." He affected great indignation.

"But I never thought I could; I once told Mama I doubted love existed. I chided her for claiming that she and Lord Scarborough had loved from the first moment they saw one another. Chided her, and then it must have happened to me." She shook her head, astonished all over again. "I love you."

"I knew that," he said softly. "I told you this afternoon

that I knew your mind better than you did yourself. You loved me, but you judged it safer to marry Lynch."

"Sir Neville," had become "Lynch," Gwen noted dryly; the long weeks of gratuitous courtesy were gone as well.

"Do you recollect what I said to you at Lady Heathcote's ball?" Chad asked. "That if I were to fall in love, I should not allow anything to come between me and the object of my affection?" Gwen nodded. "I discovered that to be untrue: *you* stood between us. As long as I thought you might be happier with Lynch than with me, I could not bring myself to attempt to part you. To the contrary, I felt constrained to *abet* your marriage. As late as this afternoon—after I'd seen Lynch for what he is, tried to make *you* see it—I felt I had to help you prevent Papa and Lady Ross's elopement."

He paused and ran the fingers of his free hand through his hair. "My position was devilish difficult at times," he continued. "The night at Almack's comes especially to mind. I *was* exceedingly happy to find you there; I wanted nothing more than to sweep you into my arms. But Lynch was there, figuratively at least, hovering in the background. That is why I refused to hide the necklace. Papa's note—which turned out to be Harold's note, of course—convinced me that he loved Lady Ross as deeply as I loved you. And in view of my own suffering, I was determined not to destroy *his* chance for happiness."

He hesitated again, lightly stroked Gwen's hand, and she shivered.

"My excessive nobility notwithstanding, I did succumb to a moment of weakness in Papa's library." He flashed a crooked grin. "And after I'd apologized, I entertained hopes that you were wavering: Lynch had asked you to persuade your mother to postpone her engagement, and you hadn't yet consented. But today, in the hotel, when I helped you with your dress, you had to perceive how desperately I wanted you. Had to perceive it, but you walked away, and I fancied you'd decided, once and

forever, to marry Lynch. And I should never have seen
you again, Gwen, not in those circumstances; I couldn't
have borne it."

There was another interval of silence, and then he took
her hand in both of his. "Perhaps I'm *not* as safe as
Lynch," he said. "I don't believe I was ever a *bona fide*
rake, but neither am I a saint. I can't promise I'll never
hurt you, promise we'll never quarrel. But I daresay I
love you as much as a man can love a woman, and by
God, I'll make you happy. But why am I pleading for
your hand?" He grinned again. "You are honor-bound to
wed me."

"Honor-bound?" Gwen echoed through the swelling
lump in her throat. "And why is that?"

"Because you failed to return my neckcloth, my *favorite* neckcloth, and you owe me something for my depriva-
tion. Forty or fifty years, let us say." He sobered. "Ah,
Gwen, those children I mentioned today; I wanted them,
want them, to be *our* children. Though I wish them to
look precisely like you."

"But I should prefer them to look like *you*," she
protested.

"Umm." He frowned. "Perhaps we can agree on only
one point then: none of them is to be named 'Chadwick'
or 'Guinevere.' "

"Yes, I shall agree to that."

"Aha!" he said triumphantly. "I have tricked you: you
have consented to marry me. Now must we really go all
the way to Greenwich and knock Andrew up in the dead
of night? There is an alternative as I recall: we still have a
room at Fladong's Hotel."

"Chad!"

But he was jesting; she had known that he was jesting,
and she smiled and laid her head against the seat. Poor
Aunt Constance, she thought; could she possibly bear the
indignity of being *twice* related to the rackety Lovells?
And poor Neville. Gwen could not quell a tiny tremor of
guilt for her abrupt abandonment of her erstwhile fiancé,
but, upon reflection, she suspected he would have

terminated their engagement once he'd learned of Mama's marriage. The baronet would no doubt find a tractable young woman with connections entirely to Lady Lynch's liking and be altogether content. There remained only to inform him of the night's events . . .

"Neville!" Gwen bolted upright. "That is what Jenkins was trying to tell us: we left Neville at the inn."

"Did we indeed?" Chad drawled. "My, what a lamentable oversight."

"You remembered," Gwen said accusingly. "You remembered, and you deliberately set off without him . . ." But she could not repress a laugh, and, still laughing, she moved closer to him and coiled her arms once more round his neck. "Wicked," she whispered. "You are quite, quite wicked."

"And likely to become considerably more so if you persist in assaulting me." His mouth brushed hers. "I warned you of the potential for excessively shocking conduct."

"I fancy I shall simply have to take my chances," Gwen murmured.

But there was no chance to take; she was, at last, truly safe. She nestled against him, and the carriage rolled on toward Greenwich, rolled into tomorrow.

About the Author

Though her college majors were history and
French, Diana Campbell worked in the com-
puter industry for a number of years and has
written extensively about various aspects of data
processing. She had published eighteen short
stories and two mystery novels before undertak-
ing her first Regency romance.

Her previous Regencies—THE RELUCTANT
CYPRIAN, A MARRIAGE OF INCONVEN-
IENCE, LORD MARGRAVE'S DECEPTION,
and THE COUNTERFEIT COUNTESS—are
also available in Signet editions.

RAPTURE ROMANCE
BOOK CLUB

*Bringing You The World of
Love and Romance With
Three Exclusive Book Lines*

RAPTURE ROMANCE • SIGNET REGENCY ROMANCE • SCARLET RIBBONS

**Subscribe to Rapture Romance
and have your choice of two
Rapture Romance Book Club Packages.**

- **PLAN A:** Four Rapture Romances plus two Signet Regency Romances for just $9.75!

- **PLAN B:** Four Rapture Romances, one Signet Regency Romance and one Scarlet Ribbons Romance for just $10.45!

Whichever package you choose, you save 60 cents off the combined cover prices plus you get a FREE Rapture Romance.

"THAT'S A SAVINGS OF $2.55 OFF THE COMBINED COVER PRICES"

We're so sure you'll love them, we'll give you 10 days to look over the set you choose at home. Then you can keep the set or return the books and owe nothing.

To start you off, we'll send you four books absolutely **FREE.** Our two latest Rapture Romances plus our latest Signet Regency and our latest Scarlet Ribbons. The total value of all four books is $9.10, but they're yours **FREE** even if you never buy another book.

To get your books, use the convenient coupon on the following page.

YOUR FIRST FOUR BOOKS
ARE FREE

Mail the Coupon below

Please send me the Four Books described **FREE** and without obligation.
Unless you hear from me after I receive them, please send me 6 New
Books to review each month. I have indicated below which plan I
would like to be sent. I understand that you will bill me for only 5
books as I always get a Rapture Romance Novel **FREE** plus an
additional 60¢ off, making a total savings of $2.55 each month. I will
be billed no shipping, handling or other charges. There is no minimum
number of books I must buy, and I can cancel at any time. The first 4
FREE books are mine to keep even if I never buy another book.

Check the Plan you would like.

☐ **PLAN A:** Four Rapture Romances plus two Signet Regency
Romances for just $9.75 each month.

☐ **PLAN B:** Four Rapture Romances plus one Signet Regency
Romance and one Scarlet Ribbons for just $10.45
each month.

NAME _____
(please print)

ADDRESS _____ CITY _____

STATE _____ ZIP _____ SIGNATURE _____
(if under 18, parent or guardian must sign)

RAPTURE ROMANCE

This offer, limited to one per household and not valid to present
subscribers, expires June 30, 1984. Prices subject to change. Specific
titles subject to availability. Allow a minimum of 4 weeks for delivery.

JOIN THE REGENCY READERS' PANEL

Help us bring you more of the books you like by filling out this survey and mailing it in today.

1. Book title:_____

   Book #:_____

2. Using the scale below how would you rate this book on the following features.

Poor		Not so Good			O.K.			Good		Excellent
0	1	2	3	4	5	6	7	8	9	10

Rating

Overall opinion of book.................... _____
Plot/Story .... _____
Setting/Location .... _____
Writing Style .... _____
Character Development .... _____
Conclusion/Ending .... _____
Scene on Front Cover .... _____

3. On average about how many romance books do you buy for yourself each month?_____

4. How would you classify yourself as a reader of Regency romances?
   I am a ( ) light ( ) medium ( ) heavy reader.

5. What is your education?
   ( ) High School (or less)   ( ) 4 yrs. college
   ( ) 2 yrs. college   ( ) Post Graduate

6. Age_____   7. Sex: ( ) Male ( ) Female

Please Print Name_____

Address_____

City_____State_____Zip_____

Phone # (   )_____

Thank you. Please send to New American Library, Research Dept, 1633 Broadway, New York, NY 10019.